THE CONFIDENCE OF WILDFLOWERS

THE CONFIDENCE OF WILDFLOWERS

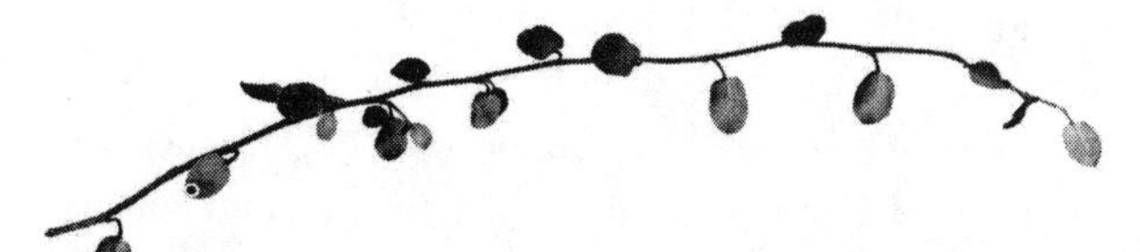

MICALEA SMELTZER

Page & Vine
An Imprint of Meredith Wild LLC

Cover Design by Emily Wittig Designs

Paperback ISBN: 979-8-9871901-0-4

For everyone who's had to fight for something they love.
Whatever that might be.

Trigger Warning:

This book is intended for readers 18+ and deals with mature themes. There are mentions of sexual abuse, cancer, and death.

"Love is like wildflowers;
It's often found in the most unlikely places."

—Ralph Waldo Emerson

PROLOGUE

Five Years Ago

I didn't cry when my dad died.

As the cancer consumed his body, eating away at his muscle, tissue, every little bit of him—I didn't cry.

When his body was hauled out of the house in a black bag on a stretcher, I didn't cry.

Staring at his once emaciated form in the casket puffed up with fillers and whatever magic the mortician worked, I didn't cry.

On the drive to the cemetery, I didn't cry.

I didn't cry as the preacher spoke of life and death, the inevitability of it all despite a life well lived.

I didn't cry.

My sister didn't cry either.

Neither did my mother.

Abusers don't deserve tears.

When the last flower was placed on the casket, and it was all over, I didn't cry.

I smiled.

CHAPTER ONE

You're supposed to have your whole life figured out at eighteen.

No one says that, not explicitly, but it's implied in the way you're expected to have a college picked out, an entire career path already in mind. A plan on where you want to be and who you want to be.

My older sister knew she wanted to go to college to be a nurse. From there she wanted to move to a big city and do big things and be this big person.

But now she's back home in our small town of Hawthorne Mills, Massachusetts.

Plans don't always work, but people push them on others anyway, like if you have the path set before you everything will be okay.

What a fucking lie.

I don't have a plan and I don't want one.

Two weeks ago, I crossed the stage and became a high school graduate with no plans to go to college. My boyfriend is going, and he still doesn't understand why I don't want to follow him to his school.

I'm not a dog on a leash.

Following someone else's desires sounds like a one-way ticket to my version of hell—I've already been there and I'm not going back.

A light wind ruffles the hair around my shoulders, and I pull it back, securing it with an elastic. Drawing my knees up to my chest, I wrap my arms around my legs. There's a bruise on my knee that I have no idea how I got.

My mom's car turns onto the street, and I scurry back through my window before she can spot me on the eave of the roof outside my bedroom. She hates it when I sit out there, convinced I'm going to fall off, despite the fact I've never even slipped. I've explained numerous times that roof tiles are textured, but she doesn't listen. But I guess she's just doing her motherly duty looking out for me.

Closing the window shut behind me, I let out a sigh and smile at my black cat with glowing green eyes curled up on my bed. He peeks at me with a look that says, *"You're going to be in trouble if she spotted you."*

I nod back. I know.

I found Binx, named after the cat in my favorite movie, as a kitten—he was dumped in the alley behind the antique shop my mom owns. I couldn't leave him there. At the time, I only had a learner's permit and was riding my bike. I wrapped him up in my jacket and took him home, begging and pleading with my mom to let me keep him. I didn't think she would say yes, but by some miracle she did. I think he stole her heart too.

The front door opens, and a moment later my mom calls out, "Salem?"

Yep, I'm named after a fictional cat too.

Actually, I'm named after the city I was conceived in—or so I've been told. Talk about gross.

"Yeah?" I venture out of my room and stand at the top of the steps.

The Victorian home my mom has slowly been remodeling boasts a grand sweeping staircase, the kind you see in old movies where the debutant comes gliding down with her hand elegantly perched upon the railing.

Unfortunately, I'm no debutant and there's nothing elegant about me.

Not if my ripped jean shorts, dirty sneakers, and tank top have anything to say about it.

"Do you have plans this afternoon?" She blows her bangs out of her eyes, her hands full of paper grocery bags. I head down the stairs, taking some from her.

"Not at the moment."

"After I put these away," she heads toward the kitchen and I follow her, "I thought maybe you might want to help me bake some cupcakes. Thelma is going to host a bake sale and I want to try out some different recipes."

Thelma Parkington, otherwise known as the town busybody. She's well into her seventies, always wears oversized glasses and colorful, weirdly patterned dresses. She's a big gossip and knows everything there is to know about everyone in this small town.

I shrug, pulling out a box of cereal from one of the bags and setting it on the counter. "Sounds fun."

"Good." She smiles, a box of crackers clasped in her hands. "I love it when you help me in the kitchen."

I smile back. Things weren't always this simple and easy, not while my dad was alive. He was an abusive, controlling asshole behind closed doors, while in public he portrayed something entirely different. Life was hell. My mom, sister, and I lived in a constant state of holding our breath, waiting to see what would upset him next. It could be something as small as a light left on or not cleaning up the kitchen as fast as he thought we should.

Now, we can make cupcakes together and leave the kitchen

a mess for days if we want.

We won't, but it's the fact that we can.

We get all the groceries put away before my mom pulls out one of her many aprons, this one brightly colored with pie slices on it, and passes me one of her others with a floral design.

"What flavors do you want to try out?" I tie the apron around my waist, securing it tightly so I won't dirty my clothes. Knowing me, it won't matter, and I'll get flour or frosting somewhere on my body.

"I was thinking my honey and lavender recipe, chocolate since it's tried and true, maybe lemon and mint." She bites her lip. "It was too minty last time, so I'll have to tweak the recipe."

"What about your cookie dough cupcake? That's always a crowd pleaser."

She chuckles, her eyes following me as I reach for her personal recipe book in case she makes adjustments to anything.

"You only want that one because it's your favorite."

I turn to her, laying the book on the island. "Guilty."

She shakes her head, her lips twisted with amusement, but she doesn't deny my request, so I smile with glee. We work companionably, pulling out ingredients, mixing bowls, and everything else we'll need.

I'm not as good of a baker as my mom, but I'm decent and it's something I enjoy doing with her.

It's already a bit hot in the house—the joys of living in an old house and not having central air—so I turn on the ceiling fan as well as the floor fan to help keep the kitchen cool. Once the oven starts preheating it'll get miserable.

My mom puts some music on while we work, both of us singing and dancing along. Our laughter fills the space and I remember a time when that sound was entirely absent in our old home.

I try not to think too often about *before*—our life when my dad was still alive—but some days it's hard to ignore those thoughts.

Taking the batter, I put even amounts into the lined pans while my mom starts making the three different frostings. The kitchen is the most updated part of the house, and my mom insisted on having double ovens since she loves baking so much. At times like this with multiple batches of cupcakes, it certainly comes in handy.

Popping them in, I set the timer—even though it's useless.

My mom always has this sixth sense about these types of things. It's strange how she can tell when things are ready, but the skill has never failed her yet.

She glances at her phone, wrinkling her nose. "What is it?" I wash my hands free of batter that splattered on me.

"Your sister."

I roll my eyes. I have a decent relationship with my older sister, but it doesn't mean I'm blind to her faults—of which there are many.

"What did she do now?" Drying my hands on a dish rag, I start gathering up dirty bowls and spatulas.

"She won't be home for dinner. She's going out with Michael."

I try to hide my reaction. Michael has been Georgia's on-again off-again boyfriend for years now. He's not the worst person, but the two of them together are a lethal combination. Wild, spontaneous, an absolute disaster waiting to happen.

Georgia swore when they ended things the last time that she'd never see him again.

What a little liar.

Don't get me wrong, it's her life to do what she pleases with, but I want to see her find someone who treats her like a queen and not a second thought, who, despite years spent together, runs at the mention of marriage. I might only be eighteen, but I'm not stupid. A couple should be on the same page about things they want, and those two are all over the place.

"I thought they were done?" I scrub at the stainless-steel mixing bowl harder than necessary.

"You know Georgia. She loves him and thinks things will be different every time."

"Maybe they will this time." I try to instill some false hope into my voice, but we both laugh, knowing that's not likely to happen.

I finish washing everything up and help her finish up the frostings.

"The cupcakes are done." Her head jerks up quickly and she rushes to the oven, slipping a mitt onto her hand. She sets the trays out to let them cool. "Would you mind seeing if the mail has been delivered?"

"No problem."

Opening the side door, I take two steps down and my feet land on the driveway. It's recently paved—my grandparents paid for it to be done—and I miss being able to kick at the gravel.

I glance at the house next door. It sold a while ago. No one's moved in yet, but today a truck is parked outside. I squint my eyes as I walk further toward the street, trying to make out the writing on the truck.

Holmes Landscaping.

Huh. Maybe whoever bought it hired a landscaper to come in and clear out all the overgrowth. It certainly needs some TLC, the yard and the house, but like ours it's beautiful with so much potential. When my mom purchased this house, at first, I thought she was crazy for not getting a new build, but then I understood. There's so much more character in an older home. All you have to do is show it a little love.

Opening the mailbox, I grab the letters and turn to head back inside when I hear a grunt of pain come from over the side of the fence separating our yard from the one beside it.

"Hello?" I call out.

There's no response, but it sounds like someone's struggling.

Hesitantly, I step into the yard and find the gate open to the backyard. I glance back at the truck parked on the street.

Salem, this is how people get murdered.

But that thought doesn't stop me from going into the backyard.

"Hello?" My voice rings out in the afternoon heat. "Is someone there?"

Huffing and puffing, like someone is about to blow a house down, is the only response I get.

I round the side of the house and find a man furiously weeding overgrown flowers and brush. On his hands and knees, it's impossible not to notice how muscular his arms and legs are. Not to mention his ass.

Stop staring at the stranger's ass!

He's deeply tanned, the kind of tan you only get with hours spent in the sun.

Which, I guess, makes sense if the landscaping truck belongs to him. His hair is a chocolate brown, with natural streaks of blond in it.

He throws everything behind him, a lot of it landing in the dirty pool that's sat unused for way too long.

"Hey. Can I help you?"

He freezes at my voice and turns around. Chestnut brown eyes narrow upon me. He looks me up and down. Dirty shoes, the mail clasped in my hands, up my body, back down again.

"You're trespassing," he grunts, sitting back on his legs. There are freckles sprinkled across his nose, and even though I'd guess this man to be in his early thirties, they somehow make him look younger, boyish. The heavy scruff on angular cheekbones counteracts the boyishness of it.

"You should be wearing sunglasses." I have no idea why that's the first thing to come out of my mouth.

"Huh?" He pushes shaggy hair out of his eyes, squinting up at me. Apparently, he agrees that it was a stupid thing to say. Even if he *should* be wearing them.

"Sorry." I shake my head. "I live next door." I toss my thumb over my shoulder at the house. "I heard you over here, and it sounded like you were struggling, so I thought I better check on you."

"I'm fine." His voice is deep, rich, with a timbre to it that sends a shiver down my spine. "You can go now."

I narrow my eyes on him. "Are you supposed to be here?"

His lips twitch with the tiniest hint of amusement. "This is my house, so yes. Are *you* supposed to be here?"

We both know the answer to that.

"Oh." I take a step back. "I ... no ... I suppose not." I blunder over my foolishness. "I'm sorry."

He ignores me, already turning back to his laborious task. Based on the state of the yard, it's going to take a long ass time for him to clear everything out on his own, but maybe he plans on getting help later. Right now he needs to exact his frustrations on the yard himself.

"I didn't mean to intrude," I ramble, backing up toward the open gate in the corner. "I was concerned." He ignores me, tossing more greenery behind him. "Anyway, if you need anything, feel free to knock on our door."

I realize he's not going to say anything at all, so I rush back through the gate and cross onto our driveway.

The side door opens, and my mom pokes her head out. "I was just coming to check on you. I was worried."

Shaking my head, I scurry up the steps into the house. "Sorry, I just met our new neighbor."

"Oh." Surprise colors her tone and she peeks around like she might spot someone. "I didn't know they'd moved in already."

"He doesn't seem very friendly."

She frowns, locking the door. She's already removed the cupcakes from the pans and lined them on the counter. "That's unfortunate."

"Mhmm," I hum.

"He could be in a bad mood. Moving can be stressful."

I shrug indifferently, but my eyes drift to the window above the breakfast nook that overlooks his yard. I can't see him, but I imagine him over there in his crouched position.

"Maybe."

Somehow, I doubt it, and even with his less than kind behavior, I can't help but be curious about our new neighbor.

CHAPTER TWO

The new neighbor—it's been three days and I still don't know his name—works methodically on tending to the yard. He's made decent progress and yesterday he was aided by a few others.

He hasn't noticed me sitting on the roof watching him.

My mom would call it spying if she caught me, but I don't like that term.

I've always liked to watch other people—not in a Peeping Tom sort of way—and think about their lives, who they might love, what they might be worried about. So many people, so many intersecting lives, and yet we all pass by without a thought for each other.

Watching him work in the yard, aggressively tearing at weeds, wiping sweat from his brows, I find myself wondering what demons haunt him. It seems like he has a lot of pent-up anger, and I wonder what put it there.

But I can't ask him.

So, I watch instead.

Watch, and wonder.

The curiosity is eating at me. Climbing back through my window, I shut and latch it before giving Binx a scratch on his head and bounding down the stairs.

No one else is home at the moment, so I have no one stopping me as I pull out one of each of the cupcakes we made the other day, as well as a glass of my mom's fresh lemonade.

Carrying everything next door, I say a silent prayer that

he's in a better mood than he was the other day, but after watching him work for the last hour something tells me not to get my hopes up.

"Hi," I call out in a chipper tone.

The man stops digging up a bush, his eyes narrowing upon me.

He's not wearing a shirt today, and up close I can see the sweat clinging to his muscular chest. His shoulders are wide, with his waist tapered in. Based on the muscles this guy is sporting, he has to spend a lot of time in the gym when he's not working.

He wears a baseball cap today, shielding his eyes from the sun. My lips twitch with amusement when I think about my sunglasses blunder. It must've had some impact on him.

His eyes drop to the tray in my hands, and he flips his cap around backwards.

"Trespassing, again?"

I roll my eyes. "I'm being neighborly. Cupcakes and lemonade." I hold the tray out triumphantly. His tongue slides out the tiniest bit, wetting his lips. He makes no move to take it. "It's not poisoned," I cajole. "The cupcakes are cookie dough, lavender and honey, and lemon with mint frosting. My personal favorite is the cookie dough."

"You talk a lot."

I shrug, unbothered by his observation. "I've been told."

Hawthorne Mills, Massachusetts has a majority of chilly days in the year, but the summers can be sweltering. Today's definitely one of those days. Just in the short time of trekking across our two yards and standing in front of him, I can already feel sweat dripping down my back. I eye the pool to my right, wondering if he plans to clean it out and open it up before the end of the summer.

With a sigh, he wipes his fingers on his shorts. "Which one is the cookie dough?"

I nod at the one in the middle and long tanned fingers reach out to take it. "You don't want the others?"

He shakes his head. "No." He starts to turn back to his work.

"What about the lemonade?"

He hesitates and takes it, setting it down on a flat piece of ground.

I wait, hoping he'll say something, like you know, maybe a *thank you*. But he picks up the shovel, ready to dig again.

"Is there something else you need?" He switches his cap back, so the brim is low, hiding his brown eyes.

"No. That was it."

Defeated, I turn to head back to my house. When I get to the gate, I yell back, "You're welcome!"

The faintest chuckle echoes behind me.

***

As I walk into the antique shop located on Main Street of our small town, the bell chimes happily, signaling my arrival.

A Checkered Past Antiques is my mom's pride and joy. While she loves baking at home, she never had dreams of owning a bakery. No, this is what she always wanted. A cute little shop filled with pieces she's chosen herself. Some she's done nothing to, others she, or I, have given a bit of a facelift in the garage behind the back of the building.

"Hey, Mom," I call out, heading toward the back. I set down my bag behind the counter.

"Hi, sweetie." She looks up from a display she's rearranging for the fourth time this week.

Some people might hate working for their mom, but I love it. Chatting with customers, sprucing things up, watching people fall in love with old things ... all of it is so magical.

It's also nice that my mom lets me sell the candles I make. It started as a small hobby, a suggestion made by my therapist to help me channel my anger and depression into something productive. Well, candles weren't her specific suggestion. She said things like painting, photography, or sports, but somehow, I landed on candles. Now, they've become popular in our small town, and I even sell them online. I need to start making the fall scents, so they'll be ready come the autumn season.

"Do you need help?" I approach the table.

She shakes her head, adding one of my candles with the Salem & Binx logo—a small black cat with S&B—to the display. "Almost done here and then I'll head out."

I'll man the shop on my own for the afternoon before I close up and head home for dinner in the evening.

My mom doesn't stay long after my arrival and heads out after giving me a hug.

A few people stop in, some locals, some tourists, and I'm not surprised when I've been there about an hour and my boyfriend, Caleb, stops in.

"Hey," he greets, holding up a bag of food from a local diner. "I hope you're hungry."

"Starved." My stomach rumbles in agreement.

Caleb Thorne is the quintessential All-American boy. Descendent of our town's founder, star of our high school football team, and blessed with wavy blond hair, icy blue eyes, and cheekbones you only see on models.

And he's all mine.

He sets the food down on the counter, leaning over to kiss me. "Missed you." He gives me the grin he reserves only for me.

"I missed you, too." He's been in Boston the past few days, getting a feel for the city since he'll be moving there to attend Harvard in the fall.

"Anything exciting happen while I was gone?" He starts unpacking the bag while I reach beneath the counter and pull out drinks from the mini fridge my mom keeps there.

I think about my mercurial new neighbor but decide to skim over that. "Nah. I sat on the roof and people watched. Brainstormed some new scents for my candles." Holding up my arm marred with scratches, I add, "And I gave Binx a bath because he snuck outside and smelled like ass when I found him."

"Ouch." He inspects my arm carefully. "It looks like you went to war."

"I practically did."

He chuckles, releasing me before leaning in to steal another kiss. "I'm happy you survived." He pops open one of the Styrofoam containers and passes the turkey club inside to me.

"How was Boston?" I pop the tab on the Diet Coke.

"Fucking amazing." He can't help but smile, a wistful expression on his face. Caleb has been dreaming of attending Harvard since we started dating our sophomore year. He was convinced he wouldn't get in, but I knew better. "You'd love it there."

I frown. This is an issue we've been facing as of late. Caleb thinks it makes perfect sense for me to move with him and live off-campus. While I think that's silly. I don't even like the city all that much and Caleb's going to be busy with school. What would I do? Sit in an apartment and twiddle my thumbs? I mean, logically I'd get a job somewhere, but I have one here—one I love—and I can continue to build my candle business.

"I'm sure I will when I visit you."

He sighs, shaking his head. Picking up a fry, he spins it around in his fingers. "You really won't go, will you?"

"Caleb," I sigh, exasperated, "I wouldn't be happy there."

"Babe, you don't know that."

I pick up my sandwich, taking a bite. I'm too hungry for even this topic of conversation to steal my appetite. "And you don't know that I would." My tone is firm but not argumentative. "I need to stay here. Figure out what my next step is."

His shoulders sag. "I know, I just..." He glides his fingers through his hair. "I'm going to miss you, that's all."

"I know, and I'll miss you, too. But Boston isn't that far. I can still visit you and vice versa." Boston is only a three-hour train ride from our little town. He acts like it's a world away, but it's really not.

"You're right."

By some miracle, no customers come in while we eat and catch up. When the food is gone, Caleb gathers everything up and gives me a kiss goodbye with plans set for us to see a movie this weekend.

The rest of my shift goes smoothly, and I head home after locking up behind me, surprised to find the neighbor's truck still parked in the driveway. Normally he's gone before five, but it's pushing six o'clock.

With a shake of my head, I start up the driveway to the side door, pausing when I see something on the steps.

It's the glass for the lemonade and beneath it is a ripped

piece of paper with something scrawled across it. I squint, trying to make out the handwriting.

It's one word, but I can't help but give a small laugh.

Thanks.

CHAPTER THREE

There are nights where no matter what I do, I can't sleep. It doesn't happen as often as it used to, but when it does, I've learned not to fight it. It's a little after five in the morning when I slip from my bed. Binx cracks one large green eye open and glares at me for disturbing his slumber before closing it and going back to sleep.

Changing out of my pajamas into my running gear, I quietly tiptoe down the stairs, so I don't disturb my mom or sister. Scribbling a note to let them know I've left for a run, I step outside and inhale the early morning air. Dew coats the blades of grass as I stretch my legs for a few minutes before I take off in a light jog.

I never listen to music when I run, partly for safety reasons, but also because I don't like the distraction. Emptying my mind, steadying my breaths, and reconnecting myself with the world around me is what I *need* when my insomnia hits.

My breaths are even as I enter the small downtown area, running around the gazebo in the center of town—this time of year it has ivy and crawling flowers growing up the sides—past the antique store, and back toward home. It's a three and a half mile loop by the time I make it back to my street.

The gray pickup truck turns down the street from the opposite end as I slow to a walk. It stops in front of the house and our new neighbor hops out. He pauses on the sidewalk, hands on his hips as he stares at the house like it's some mighty obstacle he needs to overcome.

It's not a stretch. The siding needs to be painted, the roof replaced, and several of the shutters are hanging on by a thread. But with only a few days' work, the yard is starting to look like—well, an actual yard and not a jungle.

He turns his head at the sound of my footsteps, those shrewd eyes narrowing upon me.

"You're up early." His voice is gruff as he turns back to his truck, opening the passenger door. He procures a travel coffee cup and is closing the door when I reach him.

"I'm up early a lot."

He sips his coffee. "You're young. You need to be careful out there."

I snort, the unflattering noise lingering in the air between us. "Don't worry about me. I'll be fine."

I don't tell him, but everyone worries so much about monsters lingering outside they forget about the ones that can haunt you behind closed doors.

"You went for a run." He finally notices my attire. I guess he thought I hung around outside early in the morning for funsies.

It's not a question but I answer like it is anyway. "Yes. When I can't sleep, I go for a run. It clears my head."

He gives me a funny look. "You don't sleep?"

"Sometimes." I shrug, noting that the back of his truck is filled with fresh mulch. "Insomnia is a bitch."

He cracks a tiny smile. "I better get to work."

"Right, of course." I start to walk away, but turn back around. "You're my new neighbor, but I still don't know your name."

He raises a brow. "Thayer."

I dip my head. "Nice to meet you, Thayer. I'm Salem."

He doesn't say anything, so I start walking again. I've made it a few feet onto our driveway when he says, "Do you have any more of those cookie dough cupcakes?"

I glance back with a smile and nod.

***

We didn't have any cupcakes left, but for some reason I hadn't been able to tell Thayer.

Thayer.

I've never heard such a name before, but it perfectly suits the rugged man next door.

My mom and sister have both left for work, so that's how I find myself in the kitchen whipping up cupcakes. I know my mom will be curious about why I made them, so I'll have to come up with some other excuse than giving them to the grumpy neighbor. Something tells me she wouldn't understand.

The house is quiet as I bake, but I don't mind it. I like being alone, crave it. When I'm alone I don't have to fake anything, paste a smile on my face if I don't feel like it or participate in conversation when I'd rather be silent.

Binx circles through my legs, and I smile down at the cat. He really is my best friend—not that I'd tell Lauren that. She'd be greatly offended if I told her I ranked a cat above her.

As if conjured by my thoughts alone, my phone starts ringing with a FaceTime from her. With a sigh, I wipe my fingers on the apron I tied around me and prop my phone up before answering her call.

"Hellooooo!" She yells a little too loudly when I answer.

"Hey," I reply back, adding frosting to a bag.

Her nose wrinkles, her red painted lips pouting with

contemplation. "Are you baking?"

"Yes." I twist the bag shut.

"Huh." She hums, swishing her long dark brown hair over her shoulder. "Anyway, I was calling because Oscar is throwing a pool party this weekend and we're going."

"We are?"

She rolls her eyes at me. "Of course, we are. This is like our last summer to goof off. Parties, too much alcohol, sex, it's all happening."

I shake my head at her. "You're insane."

"But you love me."

She's right, I do. Lauren can be a bit over the top at times, but she's the best kind of friend you could ask for. Fiercely loyal and protective.

"I need a new swimsuit," I admit, thinking about the rough shape mine is in after the last few years of use.

"Perfect." She claps her hands eagerly. "We can go shopping this afternoon."

"I work." I turn the light on in the oven to check the progress on the cupcakes before clicking it back off.

"Tomorrow, then?"

"Tomorrow."

"I'll pick you up at eleven? We can get donuts and coffee before we hit the mall."

"Sounds great."

"All right, see you then."

She ends the call without a goodbye. That's Lauren. Always in a hurry.

An hour later, I'm walking over a batch of freshly frosted cookie dough cupcakes. I kept six, and I'm giving Thayer the other six.

When I reach his yard, he's crouched in the front, knees in the dirt as he installs some sort of plastic thing in a swooping shape. I notice half of the mulch is already gone.

"I come bearing cupcakes," I say by way to announce my appearance.

He glances over his shoulder before rising to a standing position and yanking off his gloves. "I've been dreaming about these."

He seems to be in a better mood today than the previous times I've encountered him. I wonder what's changed—or more importantly, what put him in such a foul mood.

"They're pretty dreamy."

He takes the container and pops it open, he sniffs them, then pulls out one before putting the top back on. He unwraps the cupcake and takes a massive bite, eating about half in one go.

"Delicious." Some crumbs go flying out of his mouth and he gives a boyish laugh, swallowing the bite. "Sorry about that."

Unbothered, I shrug. "I'm glad someone else likes them." Before I can stop myself, I blurt out, "You're in a better mood today."

His nose crinkles. "You noticed that, huh?" He finishes the rest of his cupcake.

"Kind of hard not to when you've been a bit of an asshole."

He flinches, and a part of me wishes I could take back my words, but another part is glad I said them. I think people need to get called on their bullshit more. "Sorry about that." He glides his long fingers through the waves of his hair. "Just a lot of shit going on." He glances over his shoulder at the house, and I'm sure that's *some* of this so-called 'shit' but definitely not all of it. I'm not one to pry, though, so I dip my head.

"Enjoy the rest of the cupcakes."

He nods back, and I turn to walk away.

"Thank you, Salem."

I pause at the sound of his voice, my name on his tongue sending a shiver down my spine I don't understand.

One foot in front of the other, I keep walking.

CHAPTER FOUR

"These are all hideous." Lauren plucks my swimsuit choices out of the dressing room. "You wait here, I'm going to pull a few."

"Nothing too scandalous."

She throws up her hand in an I *know* gesture.

Sitting on the bench in the dressing room, I wait for her to return. The walls are covered in bright tropical wallpaper, and the store boasts loads of neon signage with loud pop music blasting through the speakers.

Lauren returns a few minutes later and holds up three options. I pick the plain black one with a bikini top and high waisted bottoms that fully cover the butt.

Lauren laughs. "I knew you'd choose that one."

"The other two are..." Well, they leave little to the imagination. I don't care how other girls choose to dress, but I like to have more of my body covered. It's just personal preference.

"I know, I know." She pushes me into the dressing room with the black choice. "You change into this and I'm going to see what else they have."

"I only need one," I argue, already hopeful this will work just fine.

"Blah, blah, blah," she cajoles in a playful tone.

I change into the bikini and look at myself in the mirror. Thick blond hair hangs down well past my breasts, but thanks to the horrendous lighting in the dressing room it looks more like an awful shade of pink. I've already formed a light tan this summer, freckles sprinkled across my chest despite lathering myself in sunscreen.

The curtain swishes open. "God, you're hot," Lauren compliments, making my cheeks turn red.

"I could've been naked!"

She rolls her eyes. "I've seen you naked."

"We're in public!"

"Stop being dramatic. All your bits are covered." She looks me up and down. "Only you could make a bikini that plain look so good. I found it in this color too." She holds up a pink one.

"Fine. I'll get both." I swipe it from her. "Now get out of here so I can change."

"So dramatic," she jokes, leaving me be.

I check out with my swimsuits while Lauren continues to browse the store.

"I'm having so much fun." She loops her arm through mine as we head out of the store into the mall. "Are you?"

"Absolutely," I fib, not wanting to rain on her parade. Malls and shopping aren't really my thing.

She throws her head back and laughs. "You're such a little liar, but I'll let it pass." She tugs me toward another store. "Let's see you *absolutely*," she mocks, "enjoy this store too."

Great.

***

Caleb's hand is entwined with mine as we trek toward the backyard of Oscar's house. Lauren skips ahead of us, a tote bag large enough to fit a small child on her shoulder. She glances over her shoulder at us, a tiny pair of sunglasses perched on the end of her dainty nose. Those are way too small to actually protect her eyes.

"Hurry up, you slow pokes."

Caleb chuckles, squeezing my hand. "She's never going to change, is she?"

"You mean, stop bossing people around?" I crack a smile. "No, never."

I know Lauren can be a bit much for some people. She can be bossy and abrasive, though I never think she purposefully means to be that way, because the girl has a heart of gold. A lot of people aren't blessed enough to see that side of her, but I am, so I consider myself lucky.

Oscar's family owns a massive new build and when we round into the back, my breath is stolen at the beautiful, luxurious space. You can tell that it's been professionally landscaped. The pool is a curving work of art, complete with not one, but *two*, slides.

This is nothing like the rubber ducky plastic swimming pool I had growing up.

Caleb seems to be just as in awe as I am. His house is an old historic mansion. It's beautiful, but it's not *this*.

The only high school parties I've ever attended were field parties after games and the occasional basement one. Those looked nothing like this one.

"There are literal waiters," Caleb mutters lowly so I'm the only one who can hear.

"Is that—?"

"Yep. Pretty sure that's champagne."

"Wow. I didn't know Oscar had ... well, this." I sweep my hand at the palace in front of us.

"Me either. I don't hang out with the guy much."

While Caleb might be a golden boy, he doesn't relish in the limelight and usually avoids these kinds of things unless he's with close friends or me. In which case, I suckered him into coming with me today.

There are a good amount of people here, which makes my anxiety spike. I don't particularly like big crowds and small talk.

Caleb knows this, and bless him, he makes a beeline for a lone chaise lounge off in the distance that no one has occupied. It's in a less populated area of the backyard since most of the guests are either in the pool or hanging out by the food and drink table.

I set down my bag, looking around for Lauren and spot her by the table speaking with Melanie, a girl from our class. I raise my hand in a wave when Melanie looks over. She waves back, her smile forced as she eyes Caleb at my side.

That happens a lot. Girls were jealous that he chose me, acting as if I stole him or performed witchcraft to get him to fall in love with me.

I duck my head in embarrassment and turn back to the chaise. Caleb is oblivious to the exchange. "I'm thirsty, you want anything?"

"Diet Coke if they have it."

He nods. "Be right back."

I pull a towel out of my bag—much smaller than Lauren's—spreading it out onto the chaise. Kicking off my flip-flops I reach for the hem of my oversized shirt, the Coca-Cola label on it. Caleb got it for me as a gag gift since I like the diet kind so much. Rolling up the shirt I stuff it inside my bag. I reach for the button on my shorts and hesitate a moment before I take them off.

Caleb returns just as I'm putting my shorts away and sits down on the chaise, setting our drinks on the ground beside him. He motions for me to take the spot between his legs. I do, resting my back against his chest. I let out a sigh as he rubs his hands over my arms. "Did you put on sunscreen?"

"Ugh, no." I groan, reaching for the bottle in my bag. I spray it onto myself and pass it to him.

Once we're both fully protected from the sun, I lean against him and close my eyes.

His lips brush against the top of my head and I can't help but smile. "I feel like I've hardly seen you since graduation."

"We're busy," I sigh sadly. Between my job, Caleb's job, and him preparing to go off to college in a few short months—*weeks*, really—there hasn't been a lot of 'us' time like there normally is. "Are we still on to see a movie tomorrow?"

He winces. "Fuck, I forgot to tell you. My mom needs me to clear out the garage. I think since I'm going to be moving out, she's finding every job she can that requires my help."

I laugh, picturing Mrs. Thorne scouring her house for things that need to be fixed that she knows Caleb will be better help with than her husband. Sure, she could hire someone, but where's the fun in that?

"I'm sorry," Caleb says, bringing my attention back to him.

"It's okay." I'm not bothered. I understand that things are changing. Soon, I won't see him at all unless I go to Boston, or he comes home for a weekend. My chest pangs. He's been a constant in my life the past three years. It'll be strange for him to be gone, but I think, maybe, good for me. It'll force me to focus on myself. My wants and needs. Hopes and dreams for the future. Whether that's college or something else.

"It's not." His lips touch tenderly to the exposed skin of

my shoulder, already warmed by the sun. "I want to spend time with you."

"We'll do something else. Maybe you can come over for dinner," I suggest.

He frowns, thinking. "We'll see."

I don't feel like talking about this anymore. Looking around at the party, it seems as if everyone from our graduating class is here, even some underclassmen. It's not like we have a lot of kids at our school anyway. The town is small, the population even smaller.

"You want to get in?" Caleb points to the pool.

I shake my head. "You can if you want."

"Nah." His arms tighten around me. "I'm fine right here."

I smile, but he doesn't see it since he's behind me, and sink further against his body.

"Bleh," Lauren fake-gags, as she walks by, setting her stuff up on the pavers beside us. "You too are so sickeningly sweet you make me sick. Sick, I tell you."

"You need to get a boyfriend," Caleb tells her, to which she pulls a disgusted face.

"No thanks. I'm okay not tying myself down right now."

"Suit yourself." He wraps a strand of my blond hair around his finger. "Don't forget your drink."

"Oh, right." I lean over and pick up the glass, taking a sip and letting the bubbles hit my stomach. I know I should stop drinking soda, regular or diet. It's awful for you, but I haven't been able to curb the habit.

"You two losers can keep hanging out here—" Lauren adjusts her bikini bottoms. "—but I'm going for a dip in the pool. Keep an eye on my shit for me." She doesn't wait for a response, heading straight for the pool. I expect her to take the stairs and walk daintily down into it, but instead she shouts, “Cannonball!” and plunges inside. When she surfaces, she glances around frantically. “Where’d my top go?”

CHAPTER FIVE

The purple, orange glow of sunrise filters in through my blinds as I tie my shoelaces, securing my running shoes onto my feet.

Binx watches me through slitted eyes from the bottom of my bed, irritated at me for leaving early again.

"I'm sorry, Binx."

I swear he huffs before his eyes shut completely. Cats. Can't live with them, can't live without them.

Pulling my hair into a ponytail, I glance in the mirror above my dresser smoothing out any bumps. Satisfied my hair won't fall out mid-run, I swipe Chapstick on my lips, give Binx a scratch behind his ears, and quietly head down the stairs. I have to take my time since the old stairway creaks like an achy back.

Scribbling down a note, I slip out the door. I take a moment to stretch and fill my lungs with the crisp early morning air before it heats up in just a few short hours.

Walking to the end of the driveway, I stifle a groan when I see Thayer at the back of his truck, the bed lowered and filled with all kinds of plants and shrubbery.

He sets the flowers on the sidewalk, his gaze catching my shoes. He looks up quickly.

"Another early run?"

"Yes," I drawl.

His eyes narrow. "Don't you own a treadmill or something?"

"No. Even if I did, I prefer running outside."

"Do you carry pepper spray with you?"

"No."

He shakes his head, settling his hands on his hips. "It's not safe."

"I'm not asking you for permission to run in my own town. I've been doing this long before you graced us with your presence." I nod my head at his house.

"Sorry for being concerned about your safety."

"I can look out for myself."

"Are you sure about that? You seem young."

"I'm eighteen." Admittedly, when I say it out loud it does sound, in fact, young and does nothing to prove my point. Trying to change the subject, I point to one of the plants. "You're planting jasmine?"

"You know plants?"

"Some." I swish my hand back and forth.

"Hmm," he hums, looking mildly impressed. "Since I can't stop you, you better get started."

I shake my head. This man is baffling.

"See you later, Thayer."

"Have a good run, Salem," he replies, already turning back to his truck to continue unloading.

My run goes a long way to help clear my head and when I reach our street, another truck has arrived and a whole crew is working at Thayer's house now.

Interesting.

I ignore the men, some who stare blatantly at me as I walk past.

"Stop staring and work!" I hear Thayer yell at them in a disgruntled tone.

Shaking my head, I check the mail and walk up my driveway, my eyes narrowing upon something left on the steps.

Bending, I pick up the object with a shake of my head.

"Pepper spray," I say aloud, in disbelief, turning the black cylindrical tube over in my hands. There's a price sticker on the back from the convenience store down the road.

"If you're going to go on runs so early, you need to carry some with you."

I look over at Thayer who stands right behind me. For someone so large and with heavy boots attached to their feet, he moves quietly.

"Look who's trespassing now."

His lips twitch the tiniest bit. "You caught me."

"Thanks for this." I hold up the can like he doesn't know what this is.

"You're welcome."

We stare at each other, silence hanging between us, but neither of us makes a move to change it. Not for a full minute at least.

Then, he shoves his hands in the pockets of his cargo shorts, glancing over the fence that separates our two houses. "You don't by any chance need a job do you? It wouldn't be full-time or anything ... just twice a week, maybe a few hours some weekends."

I hesitate, curious. "What kind of job? I'm not sure I'm cut out for landscaping. My plant knowledge is mediocre at best."

He chuckles, shaking his head. "No, not that. I need a babysitter, nanny, something, whatever, for my son. Once I get this place fixed up, he'll be staying here with me some."

"Oh." I wasn't expecting that. "You have a kid?"

He laughs. "Yeah, Forrest. He's six."

"That's cute." I smile. I love kids. They're fun, so openly curious about anything and everything. Sometimes, I envy them for that, because my childhood was ripped so cruelly away by a monster. "I have a job already," I admit, his face turning immediately crestfallen. "But I do work for my mom—she owns an antique shop in town—so I might be able to work something out." It's the best I can offer him.

"All right." He nods, running his fingers through his hair. "Okay. I'm hoping to have this place ... livable in the next few weeks. Not that it's worthy of being condemned, but some things have needed to be rewired, the plumbing," he rambles. With a shake of his head, he chuckles. "Sorry. We'll revisit this conversation soon."

"Sure," I agree. "We can talk whenever."

He doesn't say anything else, just turns and walks back to his house.

Head down, I open the side door and kick off my sneakers. Peeling off my socks I stuff them inside. I need to shower. I'm sweaty and smelly, but I can't help taking a moment to inhale the scent of pancakes.

"Mmm, Mom, those smell delicious."

She smiles gratefully, flipping over a pancake on the griddle. "Thanks. Are you hungry?"

"Starving," I admit. "But I should really shower first."

She rolls her eyes, adding pancakes to the already growing stack on a flowered patterned plate to her left. "Your stench hasn't sent me running for the hills yet," she jokes. "I think I'll survive."

"Mom," I laugh.

"Just eat." She points to the kitchen table. "Your shower can wait a few minutes."

Georgia's feet sound on the stairs, and she enters a moment later. Her long blond hair is pulled back into a ponytail, her makeup expertly applied. Her scrubs are a navy blue color and somehow they hug her curves.

"I've gotta go. I'm running late." She swipes a pancake from the plate, shoving half in her mouth while turning to the coffee pot. "Morning, sis." She turns to me with a smile while pouring coffee into her travel mug and then dumping in a heaping spoonful of sugar and creamer.

"Hey."

"Love you, guys." She plasters a kiss on my mom's cheek and gives me a quick hug before swiping another pancake and dashing out the door.

That's Georgia for you. Always late. Always in a hurry.

But somehow, she manages to be perfectly on time to everything. It's baffling.

Her car rumbles in the driveway, tires screeching as she peels out of the driveway.

My mom shakes her head, smiling with amusement. "That girl."

I'm sure she says those same two words to Georgia about me at times.

After stuffing my face with pancakes, I head upstairs to shower, the ancient pipes creaking and groaning. My shower ends up being colder rather than hot, but it's okay, I need the cool down anyway. Thank God it's not winter though, or I'd be halfway to sick.

Brushing my hair out after my shower, I change into a pair of shorts and a tank top before slipping out my window. I lay down on the roof, closing my eyes and letting the heat warm my skin. The noises next door soothe me, and I find myself dozing off.

Only a short time passes before I crack my eyes open.

Sitting up, I rub my tired eyes. I glance at my phone, cursing under my breath at the time, and hurry back inside.

I'm supposed to meet Caleb at the mall for lunch at one of our favorite places before going to work, so I change my clothes and put away laundry. By the time that is done, I need to make the thirty-minute drive to the mall.

When I arrive, Caleb is already there. Somehow, he makes a basic pair of khaki shorts and a white shirt look good and I plant a kiss on his lips when I reach him, having to stretch on my tiptoes. He wraps his arms around me, smiling into the kiss.

"What was that for?"

"I missed you, that's all." I settle back on my feet. "I'm also starving. Feed me."

The two pancakes I had this morning weren't enough.

He chuckles, wrapping an arm around me. "Your wish is my command."

He steers me into the restaurant, and we're quickly seated at a table. We catch up on little things that we haven't talked about over text the past few days and when our food arrives, we both dive in like we haven't eaten all day. I know Caleb is spending a lot of his free time at the gym or on the field working with his old coach to prepare for college, but I miss him, so it's nice to get to spend this time together.

Taking my hand as we leave the restaurant, I browse some stores as we venture back to the parking lot. "Ooh, hold on." I tug him toward a sunglass kiosk.

"You need new sunglasses?" He questions, brows furrowed.

"Uh ... yeah," I lie. I don't know what makes me lie about it and not tell him that I'm looking at them for my new neighbor, but I try not to think about the reasons why that might be.

I pick up a pair of men's and look them over before putting

them back and grabbing another.

"Those are for men," he points out.

"I know. I want them for when I run so I want something more sporty."

Another lie.

In the span of less than a minute I've lied to my boyfriend twice. I'm a horrible girlfriend.

But I know if I explain, he'll read into it and think it's something it's not.

I purchase a pair and we say our goodbyes in the parking lot.

As I drive back to town to the antique shop, I keep glancing at the bag from the sunglass kiosk. I couldn't resist, not after Thayer got me the pepper spray. I'm not sure he'll find it as amusing as I do, but I don't dwell on that. I think it's funny and that's all that matters.

Parking, I head inside the store to find my mom chatting with Thelma about the bake sale. Thelma glances my way, lighting up, and I try to hide my cringe.

"Oh, good, there she is. Just the girl I was looking for." Oh no. "I volunteered you to work one of the game booths at the bake sale."

There are game booths too?

"You did?"

"I knew you'd say yes so I didn't see the big deal."

Over Thelma's shoulder my mom stifles a laugh, shaking her head. She knows I would've never said yes. Thelma knows it too.

"Of course," I agree, no point in arguing. "Can't wait."

Thelma gives a self-satisfied nod. "Good girl."

Why do I feel like I just got a verbal pat on the head?

My mom gives a soft laugh and says something to return Thelma's attention to her. Bless her. I scurry to the back storeroom and set down my bag. I linger a few minutes before poking my head out.

"She's gone."

"Oh, thank God."

She gives a soft laugh, picking up her purse and tossing it over her shoulder. "Marcy Hill is coming by to pick up that serving buffet in the front when her husband gets home with his truck. Other than that, just man the store."

"Okay." I go over to the floor to ceiling shelving unit that houses most of my candles, straightening them.

"I'll see you for dinner."

"See you later," I call after her.

I haven't mentioned Thayer asking me to nanny some. I'm not even sure why I haven't told her.

In fact, I'm not quite sure she's even met our new neighbor.

CHAPTER SIX

"Isn't this fun?" Lauren leads me to her basement, Caleb trailing behind me.

"I didn't know the fun had started yet."

Lauren gives me a playful swat as we round the corner to the theater like set-up in her finished basement. There's a screen that pulls down with a projector, a drawer full of snacks and candy, and even a working popcorn machine.

"The fun always starts as soon as you see me," she quips, flipping her hair dramatically over her shoulder for extra flare.

"Hey, man." Caleb fist bumps Dawson, Lauren's flavor of the week.

She doesn't have boyfriends. She has dates.

Long-term isn't for everyone, especially at our age, and that's fine.

"What movie are we watching?" I follow Lauren over to the massive stack of DVDs that belong to her dad.

"I was torn between these." She holds up three different choices.

"That one." I point at The Hitman's Bodyguard. "There's action for the guys and Ryan Reynolds for us."

She snaps her fingers. "I like the way you think."

She puts the movie in and pops some popcorn.

The four of us settle on the giant bean bag like chairs in the middle of the room, two of us in each one.

Caleb wraps his arm around me, picking up a handful of

popcorn.

"Are you okay?" He whispers in my ear. "You seem a little tense."

I press my lips together, trying to think of an excuse. I'm happy he's here, but I'm not happy he told me he lied to his mom to be able to come. He shouldn't have to lie to her to see me. That's ... not right. I've always thought she liked me fine, but now it seems like she's trying to fill his time with everything else, so he doesn't have any left for me. I don't like that it leaves me feeling needy.

"I'm fine," I lie instead, not wanting to bring up my insecurities. "Just happy you're here." At least that part isn't a lie.

"Shush, you lovebirds," Lauren hushes from our right.

Caleb chuckles, burying his face into the crook of my neck. He presses a kiss there and I relax against him, doing my best to let the tension leave my body. I want to enjoy whatever time we have left before summer ends. I know time will fly by.

Snuggling my body further into Caleb, I focus on the movie, but my eyes grow heavy—perhaps sleep senses that I feel safe for the moment—and I drift off.

***

I jostle awake to Caleb carrying me out of Lauren's house and to his waiting car outside.

"I can walk," I mutter sleepily.

His chest rumbles with a laugh against my ear. "I've got you, babe. You're not even heavy."

"I'll get the car door for you." Lauren's voice is near and I hear the cheery beep of Caleb's SUV getting unlocked. The vehicle is brand new, a gift from his parents for graduating.

He sets me in the passenger seat and secures the seatbelt across my body.

"Sorry I fell asleep."

Caleb starts up the car. "Babe, it's fine. You must've needed the sleep."

He has no idea just how much. It becomes even more evident when I fall asleep again on the way home. Caleb jostles me awake when he gently pulls me from the car and back into his arms.

"I'm the worst girlfriend ever," I groan into his neck.

He gives a soft laugh. "No, you're not."

"No, I am."

"Hey!" A sharp voice sounds from nearby. "What the fuck is going on here?"

Oh no. I know that voice.

"Uh ... who are you?" Caleb asks.

"Neighbor," Thayer replies. "What's wrong with her? You didn't drug her, did you? I'll fucking beat your ass."

"What?" Caleb gasps offended. "Are you kidding me? No!"

"It's a legitimate question. She's passed out in your arms."

"Thayer," I groan. "I'm just sleepy. That's all."

"You know this prick?" Caleb looks down at me in his arms.

"Neighbor, remember?" Thayer interjects.

"I wasn't talking to you." Caleb sounds angrier than I've ever heard him, though I'm sure I'd feel very much the same way if I'd been accused of drugging someone.

"Are you okay?"

It takes me a moment to realize Thayer is talking to me. "Yeah. Just tired. You don't need to worry. Caleb is my boyfriend."

"Even more reason to worry." He glowers at Caleb while I struggle to keep my eyes open.

"Thayer," I groan.

"Fine." He finally lets us pass, me still carefully cradled in Caleb's arms.

"Your new neighbor is a fucking psycho."

I don't agree or disagree. Thayer is ... well, *Thayer.* Or so I'm learning.

My mom lets us inside and Caleb finally sets me down, kissing me goodnight before departing. I trudge up the stairs, take a quick shower, and dive into bed.

But the sleep that was so easy with Caleb becomes non-existent.

***

I'm not surprised when I leave for my run and Thayer's outside. I should be pissed at him, and I am a little peeved, but I know he was genuinely concerned when he saw what appeared to be my unconscious body being unloaded from a teenage boy's car.

The sunglasses case is clasped in my hand as I walk over. He sits on the steps of his front porch eating a sausage McMuffin and sipping a coffee. He looks up at the sound of my approaching feet.

"Good night of sleep?"

"No," I snort.

"Hmm," he hums, chomping into his sandwich.

I take it we're not going to acknowledge last night. Whatever. Suits me fine. I'm not one for confrontation.

"I got you something."

He arches a dark brow. "That so?"

Thayer is a man of few words.

"Yes." I hold out the case, trying not to smile in amusement.

He wipes his hands on a napkin before taking the case. His lips curl with amusement before he even lifts the hinged lid.

Pulling out the sunglasses, he fits them on his nose tilting his head up at me. "How do I look?"

Hot.

Ice runs down my spine at the unbidden thought.

"Great ... you ... they look great."

He chuckles, slipping them off. It's still dark out and not necessary to wear them yet.

"Thanks. You didn't have to do that."

"You didn't have to get me pepper spray, either." I point to the can clipped to my shorts.

"That's for your protection," he argues, going back to his breakfast.

"So are those."

He fights a smile—I don't understand why he battles against them instead of letting one shine through. What does he have against smiling? "You have a point."

"Of course I do."

He shakes his head. "Enjoy your run, Salem."

"I will." I start to walk away, already warmed up and ready to go. "Oh, and Thayer?" I look over my shoulder at the man that's too handsome for his own good.

"Yes?"

"Don't threaten my boyfriend."

CHAPTER SEVEN

July comes in with a blast of heat that our small town hasn't seen in recent years, and everything seems to be happening at once.

A moving truck is parked on the street, unloading furniture into Thayer's house. Sitting on my roof with my knees drawn up to my chest, I watch them carry in everything from a couch to a child's bed. I need to broach the topic of nannying again for him, because I do actually have the time to spare and wouldn't mind the extra money.

The bake sale is this weekend, but unfortunately, I won't make any extra cash manning the booth Thelma volunteered me for.

Thayer's made great progress on the house, at least on the outside. I can't speak for the inside since it's not like he's invited me in. Why would he?

But the pool is a crystal clear shiny blue, the bushes and flowers are carefully manicured, and the once patchy grass is now lush and full.

Thayer has a green thumb, that much is obvious.

His little boy runs around with unleashed excitement. It's the first time his son has ever made an appearance here. Thayer's never mentioned his ex or the situation with his son, but I'm not stupid. It's obvious it's complicated.

I know I should crawl back into my room and stop 'spying', but I can't help it. Curiosity gets the best of me so I stay out as long as I can until I grow too hot. Besides, my mom will be home soon, and I can't have her catching me on the roof. She's never said it, but I'm pretty sure she's afraid I sit out here and contemplate jumping. I'm not suicidal, and even if I was, the fall wouldn't be enough to kill me. Break some bones? Sure. Death? Not likely.

When my mom arrives home that afternoon, we get to work on the cupcakes, so we'll have enough for this weekend. The store was closed today, and she spent her time hanging up flyers and talking to locals about the bake sale—as if they probably haven't already heard about it from busybody Thelma.

"Thank you so much for your help," my mom says when I pull the last batch of cupcakes from the oven. We ended up adding a few more popular flavors on top of the more unusual ones. Cookies n' cream, vanilla, and red velvet.

"It's no problem, Mom."

"Still, I appreciate it. I'm sure you'd rather be with Caleb or Lauren."

"I like baking with you."

She smiles at that, pulling me into a hug. "I love you."

The side door into the kitchen opens then and Georgia walks in. "Aw, am I missing out on the love fest?" Mom laughs, opening up her arm to beckon Georgia into our embrace. "Well, how can I resist that?" Georgia sets her tote bag down and joins us. My nose wrinkles at the scent of antiseptic clinging to her hair and skin.

"Go shower," my mom tells her, "and we'll start on dinner."

Georgia narrows her eyes. "Is that your way of telling me politely that I stink?"

My mom shrugs, her lips twitching with amusement. "You smell like a hospital."

Georgia sighs, bending to scoop up her bag. "What are you

guys making?"

We exchange a look. "Haven't figured it out yet," I reply.

Georgia gives a small laugh. "All right, you two figure it out and I'll ... try not to stink when I return." Her footsteps creak up the stairs a moment later.

While my mom prepares the cupcakes to be frozen so we can frost them later, I scour the refrigerator for something to prepare for dinner. I end up settling on a salad and baked lemon chicken. Simple and easy—you can never go wrong with that.

When Georgia rejoins us, her hair is wet from the shower and she's wearing a pair of cotton shorts and a big holey shirt I know belongs to Michael.

"This smells amazing. Need help with anything?" She gathers her hair up, securing it with an elastic at the nape of her neck.

"Can you pop the garlic bread in the oven?" I point to where I have it ready to go in.

With the table set, we sit down a few minutes later to eat.

Sometimes, in moments like this, where I'm enjoying a peaceful moment with my mom and sister, I can't help but think about when there were never times like this. When we walked on eggshells, lived in fear of an outburst, or worse.

We don't have to worry about that anymore, but the scars are still there. They always will be. They cut too deep to ever go away fully.

We made it to the other side thanks to a simple twist of fate.

Others who are in our situation aren't as lucky, and that's something I never let myself forget.

CHAPTER EIGHT

My tank top sticks to my chest, my body already covered in perspiration. Despite the cover of a tent, the shade and the small portable fan set up on my table are doing nothing to help. Instead of a game booth, Thelma decided to have me do face painting.

Me? Face painting?

I don't know what Thelma was drinking that possessed her to think this was the perfect fit for me. I don't have an artistic bone in my body.

"What am I?" The little girl looks in the hand mirror I hold out for her.

"I ... um ..." *Isn't it obvious?* "A butterfly."

"Oh. That's cool." She flounces off, her dress swishing around her legs. Her mom sticks some dollar bills in the donation jar before running after her.

I motion the next kid forward, a boy with a mop of red hair and freckles on his nose.

"I want to be a lion," he declares proudly, pointing to his chest.

Turning to the paints, I sigh. "I'll do my best, kid."

I'd so much rather be with my mom selling cupcakes, but no, Georgia got the job of helping her. I swear Thelma has some sort of weird old lady vendetta against me.

Swirling the brush in the paint, I set about doing my best to make this kid look like a lion. All while making small talk and keeping a smile plastered on my face. The kids are great, really, they're nice and here to have fun. I just get annoyed getting dragged into things instead of someone extending the courtesy of *asking.* I would've said yes if Thelma had, but she just went ahead anyway and I find that to be extremely rude.

On and on it goes.

One kid wants to be a snake, another a unicorn, one wants to be Spiderman, the next a planet. Despite my lack of artistic capabilities, I do my best to meet each and every request.

A little boy jumps up to me, bouncing like a little kangaroo. "Hi." His voice is high-pitched and chipper. "I'm Forrest, like—"

"The forest?"

"Yeah." He nods enthusiastically. "Can you paint a dinosaur on my face?"

"I thought you said you wanted a car," a familiar voice speaks up, a big, tanned hand falling on the boy's shoulder.

"Dad," Forrest drawls, "I changed my mind. I'm allowed to do that."

Thayer cracks a smile at his son. "All right. Dinosaur it is. How are you, Salem?"

"Your name is Salem?" The kid asks, eyes wide. "Like the place where all the witches burned?"

I try not to laugh. "The very one."

"Wait," he pauses, nose crinkling with thought. "How do you know her, Dad?" He glances up at Thayer, willing him to fill in the blanks.

"She's my new neighbor."

"Oh, that's cool." Forrest seems appeased by this answer. "So can I have a pink dinosaur?"

"Sure thing." I dip my brush into the pink paint and set to work.

"You stick your tongue out when you do that."

"Huh?" I look up at the sound of Thayer's voice. "Shoot." I left a streak of pink paint on Forrest's cheek. I grab my damp cloth and wipe it away while Thayer explains.

"When you're concentrating. Your tongue. You stick it out."

"I didn't know."

He looks like he wants to say more but chooses not to. I finish the dinosaur—honestly it looks like a giant pink blob and nothing at all dinosaur shaped about it—but when I give Forrest the mirror he smiles with glee.

"Awesome! Thanks, Salem!"

Thayer shakes his head, a full-blown smile on his face. His teeth are white and mostly straight, but one of his canine teeth is chipped. It's sort of endearing.

He slips a twenty into the jar and I smile gratefully. "Be sure to stop by mom's booth. There are cupcakes."

His brown eyes light up. "I do love cupcakes. Have a good day, Salem."

"You too."

I watch him walk away, speaking with his son, and that's when I spot Caleb heading toward me. I wasn't sure he'd be able to get away from his family's booth selling pies and a few other things. He carries two cans of sodas and I sigh in relief at the sight of them. Caleb, however, is watching Thayer with a shrewd gaze.

"What's your neighbor doing here?" There's a sneer to his voice, not that I can really blame him since Thayer accused him of drugging me.

He passes me a can of Diet Coke and pulls out the plastic folding chair on the other side of the table while I motion the next child forward.

"Well, this is a bake sale in the center of town open to everyone..." I trail off, letting him fill in the blanks. When he doesn't say anything, I add, "And he has a son, who wanted face painting."

He takes a swig of his regular Coke. When he sees I'm too busy to open the top of my can, he reaches over and pops it for me, the soda fizzing excitedly inside.

"Thanks."

"Something about that guy rubs me the wrong way," Caleb continues while I start on another unicorn request. He wears a funny expression, a cross between confused and disgusted. "He's just ... odd."

"I don't know about odd. Grumpy, though? Definitely that."

"That too."

"How's it going at your mom's booth?"

"Almost sold out."

I'm not surprised. His mom makes the best pies around. "Did you snag a peanut butter pie for me?"

He chuckles. "Yeah, babe. Put it away first thing."

"Thank you. I would kiss you if I wasn't otherwise occupied at the moment." I wiggle my paint brush in the air. "Have you seen Lauren?"

"Yeah, she's working a ring toss booth. I thought this was a bake sale, so what's with all these random booths?"

I give him a look. "Since when does anything Thelma does make any logical sense?"

"Good point." He runs his fingers through his hair. It's gotten even lighter from all the sun he's getting this summer, his skin a deep tan.

We're down to *weeks* now before he leaves for Harvard and

a full week of that he'll be gone on vacation with his family. My heart aches. Even though I don't want to go to college, or move to Boston, it doesn't mean I'm not going to miss him.

Time is a precious treasure, limited in quantity, and it can be squandered so, so easily.

I do a few more kids before the line, thankfully, begins to dwindle.

"I'm starving. Do you mind grabbing me something to eat? I have cash in my wallet." I nod to my bag hanging over the back of the chair he sits in.

"I don't need your money, babe. I got it." He finishes his soda and gets up. "I'll be right back."

He's only been gone a minute when I feel a presence behind me. Thinking he's come into the tent from behind me, I turn around, already saying, "Wow, that was fast."

But it's not Caleb behind me. It's Thayer. His son is at his side holding a paper bag filled with my mom's cupcakes—I know because I spent a good hour last night putting stickers on them for the antique shop. "*Free advertising*," my mom said.

"What are you doing back?" I inspect Forrest's face to see if the horrible dinosaur painting smeared or something, but it's still the same weird shape it was before.

"Brought you something." Thayer reaches into the bag and pulls out one of the boxes that contains a single cupcake.

"You said your favorite is cookie dough too, right?"

I can't believe he remembered that.

"Yeah." I take the offered box.

"Thought you might need a snack."

"Thank you." I mean it. It's a thoughtful thing for him to have done.

He dips his head in acknowledgment and leads Forrest

back out of the tent.

Caleb returns a few minutes later with a box of treats. His eyes narrow on the cupcake I haven't eaten yet.

"Where did that come from?"

"My mom." The fib comes to my lips before I even make the conscious decision to lie about the origin. "She thought I might be getting hungry."

Does he notice the shake in my voice? Why am I even nervous?

He glances around, his eyes falling back to the box. He swallows before his eyes meet mine.

He doesn't believe me.

"Okay." He sets the box down on the table. "I have to go help my mom."

"Caleb," I call after him, but he ignores me, disappearing into the crowd.

Shit.

CHAPTER NINE

On the roof again, watching the sunset, I notice an unfamiliar car turn onto the street and park in front of Thayer's house. My eyes are pulled from the beauty of the sun going down for the evening to the woman who climbs from the SUV. A girlfriend? His ex?

From this distance, all I can tell is that she's thin—the kind of thin that's almost willowy in a way—and has dark brown hair. She walks toward the front door, but before she even reaches the porch steps the door opens and Forrest runs out with arms wide open.

"Mommy!"

Well, that answers that.

She squats down, opening her arms for the boy. He hugs her fiercely and lets go, running back into the house calling for his dad. I watch as she hesitates outside, and Thayer appears a few moments later, barefoot in a pair of shorts and a plain cotton t-shirt. He sets a small bag on the ground by his feet and crosses his arms over his chest. His lips move rapidly as he speaks to his ex and then Forrest reappears, a teddy bear clasped under his arm. It's a chestnut color with a red ribbon around the neck.

The two of them speak for a few minutes, and I can tell from their body language that it's a bit heated. Finally, she takes Forrest's hand and leads him to her car parked on the curb. Thayer follows with the bag and puts it in the trunk. Crouching down, he hugs a teary-eyed Forrest goodbye and helps him into the car. He closes the door and turns to his ex. They say something more and he walks back up the front pathway, pausing to turn around and wave at Forrest as they leave.

"Bye, Dad!" Forrest calls out the window, his little hand waving. "Love you."

"Love you, bud!" Thayer calls back, watching the car disappear. When it's no longer in sight his shoulders sag with sadness. He turns to head back inside but he pauses, his head jerking up. His eyes lock with mine and my heart gives a jolt at being caught. He squints up at me before turning back around and walking through his front gate and into our yard.

"What are you doing up there, Salem?" His hands slide into his pockets and he rocks back on his bare heels.

"I was watching the sunset."

"Was," he repeats. "And what distracted you?"

"My neighbor." He glances to his left where his house is, lips thinning. "You were fighting."

His mouth twitches. "Why do you think we got divorced?"

I shrug, wrapping my arms around my legs and resting my chin on my knees. "Couldn't agree on the best cupcake flavor?"

A full smile cracks his lips, and I feel like I've won some sort of victory. "Yes. That's typically what makes or breaks a marriage. Disagreeing on a cupcake flavor."

"You never know."

"Hmm," he hums, cocking his head to the side. "You hang out up there a lot?"

"Yes."

"Why?" The question is a low drawl.

"Because I like it."

"And your mom lets you?"

I resist the urge to roll my eyes. I know the immature move wouldn't help my argument. "I'm eighteen."

"And you live with your mother," he points out.

"She doesn't like it," I admit, figuring he won't let it drop until I give him more. "But I ... out here I'm free."

God, it sounds so dumb coming out of my mouth, but that's how I feel.

"Free. Like a bird? Do I need to worry about you trying to fly off the roof?"

"No."

"That's good." He glances at his house, taking a step backwards. "You're welcome to use the pool any time you want. Your sister, too."

"You've met my sister?"

He pauses in his retreat, his face scrunching. "Yes."

"You said that funny," I accuse.

He rubs a hand over his stubbled jaw. "She yelled over the fence at me when I was weeding."

Oh, God. There's no telling what Georgia said.

"What did she say?"

"Well, after she said 'nice ass' she asked if I was single."

"Sounds like Georgia," I try not to laugh. "She has a boyfriend."

He arches a brow. "Trying to warn me off?"

I pale, realizing I *am*, because the idea of Thayer and my sister? I don't like it. Not one bit.

"No," I say, but there's no confidence in the word.

Suddenly I'm flushed, frazzled, downright *confused*.

Thayer's eyes drop to our driveway, staring at his bare toes. "About nannying—"

"Yeah?" I latch onto the change in subject, wanting to get

my mind off why I'd possibly be bothered by my sister flirting with Thayer.

"Are you interested?"

"As long as it doesn't interfere with my job at A Checkered Past."

He nods, like he expected this. "We'll make it work."

He doesn't wait for me to respond with anything else. He gives his back to me and returns to his house, not looking back at me once.

CHAPTER TEN

I swing my tote bag over my shoulder—filled with snacks, water bottles, Diet Coke, a swimsuit, and other odds and ends—and set off to make the short trek next door for my first day watching Forrest. When I told my mom Thayer had asked if I could babysit some, she thought it was a great idea. It's a new experience and extra money for me to stow away for whatever comes next for me.

The porch is freshly painted. The white is bright, almost blindingly so. Tilting my head back, I notice he's painted the ceiling of the porch a light blue color. Interesting.

Pressing the doorbell, I wait. I hear fast-paced steps running toward the door and the rumble of voices.

It swings open, revealing Thayer with his hand on his son's shoulder, holding the boy in place who hops up and down excitedly.

"Hi, Forrest." I smile down at the child. He has something dried around his lips, syrup from his breakfast maybe.

"Thank you for doing this." Thayer looks ready to dash out the door. "I have a big project and I..." He glances down at his son. "Taking him with me isn't easy."

"My dad owns a landscaping company. Right, Dad?" He looks up at his father for confirmation.

"That's right."

"Oh." I look over at his truck, now parked in the driveway instead of the street, taking in the name. "Holmes Landscaping,"

I read aloud. "Is that your last name?"

"Thayer Landscaping has a nice ring to it," he quips easily, rubbing his jaw. I give him a look and he chuckles. "Yes, Holmes is my last name."

"Interesting," I muse, rocking back on my heels. Arching a brow, I point past him. "Are you going to invite me inside?"

"Oh." He shakes his head rapidly. "Sorry, yeah." He steps aside, pulling Forrest gently alongside him.

I step into the foyer, the smell of fresh paint clinging to the walls that are painted a muted gray color. The floor looks newly redone and there's a beige runner on the stairs. That's about it. No photos. No personality. Just a blank slate. But I guess this house is a work in progress for him. There's time to add more to it later.

"I'll only be gone a few hours, three tops," Thayer says, guiding me past what I assume will be the dining room on my left but currently looks like a makeshift storage area, and straight back to the kitchen.

"Wow." It's not a good 'wow' either. The appliances are missing, the cabinets, the counters, *everything*. There's a table set up against one wall with a microwave and a toaster oven.

"My dad's...what was the word you used, Dad?" Forrest looks up at his father for clarification.

"Renovating," he supplies, glancing at me. "I couldn't put off moving in any longer, my lease agreement was up on my apartment, but a lot of the things I ordered are on backorder. Like..." He waves his hand at the empty kitchen.

"The cabinets?" My lips quirk.

"Those, and the appliances, and all of it pretty much. At least it gives me a chance to redo the floors."

I notice several tiles laid out on the floor, like he's deciding between them.

"You could carry the wood through?" I suggest.

"Mmm, maybe," he hums in thought. "Anyway, I've gotta go. You have my number. Contact me if you need to. And you're welcome to swim, just keep an eye on him."

"Absolutely. Don't worry, I have things covered here."

His gaze flits over me and then his son. With a resigned sigh, he nods. "I'll see you in a few hours." He crouches down, opening his arms for a hug. Forrest gladly dives into his arms. "Love you, bud."

"I love you, too, Daddy."

I think my heart just melted.

Thayer leaves, the front door clicking quietly closed behind him.

"Well," I look down at Forrest, "what do you want to do?"

***

The pool is surprisingly warm, and I wonder if Thayer has it heated. Forrest climbs out for the umpteenth time and cannonballs right beside me. I think he loves soaking me.

"What was the score on that one?" His little head bobs up, goggles slipping off his nose. He takes them off, their imprint left behind around his eyes and bridge of his nose. Cleaning them off he slips them back on and gets ready to go again.

"Eleven out of ten."

His nose scrunches. "You can't get an eleven out of ten. That's not possible. It's out of ten so the most you can get is that."

"Ah, you caught me." I've learned pretty quickly that Forrest is smart—or maybe I haven't been around enough six-year-olds and they're all like this. "Ten outta ten then." I hold up all my fingers and wiggle them accordingly.

He dips his head in a nod. "That's better."

He goes to jump and stumbles, nearly belly-flopping into the water, but I catch him in time.

"Whoa," I set him down gently in the water, "careful."

"Sorry." He says sheepishly, kicking his legs. "My dad says I have no fear."

"I'm thinking I agree with him."

Forrest beams like this is something to be very proud of. "If your name is Salem what's your middle name?"

"Grace."

"Grace," he repeats with a laugh. "That's way different than Salem."

"It is," I agree, swimming backwards. "What's yours?"

"Xavier."

I wasn't expecting that. "That's a cool name."

"It sounds like a superhero, so I think so too." He floats on his back, looking up at the sky. A laugh shakes his chest. "That cloud looks like a cat licking his butt."

I glance up, but I don't see what he sees. "Totally." Lowering my head before I get dizzy, I add, "I have a cat."

"You do?" He brightens, swimming over to me. "What kind?"

"He's a black cat. His name is Binx."

"Can I meet him sometime? I want a dog, but my mom says they're dirty and my dad always says maybe one day. I think that's just parent talk for never."

I'm immensely amused by this kid. "Who knows. We can't predict the future. And sure, you can meet him any time."

"How'd you get him?"

I pause, thinking about how I discovered Binx in that alley. "He sorta found me, I guess." I can tell this explanation doesn't suffice for him. "Someone left him in the alley behind my mom's store."

"Whoa." His eyes get wide. "Your mom owns a store? That's so cool."

"I guess."

"What kind of store?" He dunks his head under the water and comes back up, pushing his hair out of his face.

"It's an antique store."

"Antique?" He fumbles over the word.

"Yeah, old furniture and stuff."

"Oh, that's not as fun as I thought."

I can't help but laugh. "What kind of store did you think she had?"

He shrugs his small shoulders. "I don't know. A toy store."

"That would be cool."

"Maybe I can have a toy store when I'm all grown up."

I smile, charmed by this kid. "You can do whatever you want."

"That's true. Maybe I'll be a firefighter, or fly a plane. Ooh or a dinosaur wrangler."

"The possibilities are endless," I assure him.

That's the beauty of childhood. You have the ability to dream up anything and have the belief that you can do it. And then you grow up and the world around you likes to crush those dreams and bring you back to reality.

Granted, dinosaur wrangler doesn't actually exist.

"I'm hungry," Forrest announces, swimming for the stairs that lead out of the pool. "Can you fix me lunch?"

"Sure." I have no idea what kind of food Thayer has, there

wasn't anything I could see in the kitchen when we passed through and there's no fridge so...

We wrap up in towels, and Forrest leads me inside to a small freezer plugged in a random side room. He tries to lift the lid, but it's too heavy for his bony arms. I grab it and push it up before he can hurt himself.

It's filled with microwave and oven-ready meals. Makes sense.

Forrest grabs some kind of kid's meal with dinosaur shaped chicken nuggets. "This please." He shoves it at me, and runs off.

I haven't explored Thayer's house yet—I'm nosey, but not that nosey—and since it's mostly still a work in progress I'm not sure if I could deduce anything profound about him anyway.

Back in the kitchen I pop Forrest's meal in the microwave, tightening my damp towel around my body, but it doesn't do much to protect me from the chill of the AC with my wet hair dripping down my back.

"Forrest?" I call, wondering where he ran off to. "Forrest?" Panic seizes me and I run out of the kitchen straight outside, nearly tripping on my towel in the process. "Forrest," I scream when I see him face down in the pool.

He pops up, giving me a funny look. "What?"

My heart beats a mile a minute, panic freezing me to the spot I stand. "You can't get in the pool without supervision," I practically shriek. "And definitely not without telling me." I press a hand over my heart, waiting for the organ to slow down but I'm not sure that's going to happen any time soon.

"I'm sorry," he frowns, looking ready to cry.

It's on the tip of my tongue to tell him it's okay, but I bite back the words. It's not. It's not okay at all and I want him to understand that.

"Come eat your lunch and we can swim after."

"Okay." His voice is small, chin quivering. He eats his lunch at a folding plastic table and chair set, avoiding looking at me for as long as possible. I munch on an apple I brought with me and sip at my Diet Coke, waiting for him to make the first move. He dips his chicken nugget in ketchup, munching on the end. "Do we have to tell my dad about this?"

I try not to crack a smile. "Yes, we have to tell him."

He hangs his head. "He's gonna be real mad. He told me not to, but I didn't think it was a big deal." He perks up, eyes round. His nose is reddened from the sun and I make a mental note to apply more sunscreen on him before we go out again. "I'm a strong swimmer. Real good."

Softening my gaze and my voice, I say, "It doesn't matter how strong of a swimmer you are, something bad can happen to anyone."

"Even you?"

"Even me."

"What about my dad?" He thinks he's stumped me with this one.

"Him too."

"Hmm," he hums. "So, he's not invisible like he says?"

"Invincible," I correct, not missing a beat. "And I don't know your dad well enough to attest to that. He could be entirely indestructible for all I know."

Thayer does have this larger than life, untouchable, persona about him.

Forrest nods at this. "He does have really hard muscles."

I throw my head back and laugh. I think I love this kid.

CHAPTER ELEVEN

I awake with a cold sweat sticking to my skin. Binx opens one green eye, deduces that I'm not dying and promptly goes back to sleep. My heart races in my chest from the nightmare.

The door creaks open.

Hands on my body.

Hands that should protect me, shelter me, only destroy instead.

The tears pour steadily down my cheek. Not a nightmare—reality, my past, always circulating back to haunt me.

My shaky feet hit the hardwood floor and it groans in protest like I've woken it up too.

I push my hair out of my eyes, it's damp.

Choking from lack of oxygen I stumble to my window and open it. I know in my current state I shouldn't get on the roof, but I need to feel the air on my face. I crawl out the window on all fours.

Normally the dreams—nightmares, memories, whatever you want to call them—don't affect me *this* badly. I saw my therapist yesterday for the first time in three months and it stirred a lot of shit up, and apparently, in my vulnerable state of sleep, my brain decided to attack me.

Gulping in lungsful of air, I try to slow my heartbeats back to a normal speed, but I'm not sure it's going to happen any time soon.

It's too early even for me to go on a run—when I opened

my eyes and glanced at the clock the numbers flashed two a.m.

But I can't imagine going back to sleep. Something stirs in the night, and my head whips to the side, spotting the small glowing ember of a cigarette. Fear spikes inside me at the realization that someone else is awake at this hour and might spot me, but then I realize—

"Thayer," I gasp.

The cigarette disappears and it's too dark for me to see anything. I keep telling my mom we need to install motion lights, but she hasn't listened.

Thayer suddenly appears in our front yard, looking up at me with fear in his eyes. I know I look crazy up here on my hands and knees, my hair matted to my forehead and eyes crazed.

"What the fuck are you doing?" His arms fumble through the air like he thinks he's going to have to catch me.

"Nightmare," I explain.

"And that made you think, "hmm, let me climb on the roof in the middle of the night?""

"I wasn't thinking clearly." My fingers dig into the shingles.

"Obviously," he snaps, still looking mildly panicked.

"Do you want me to climb down?" I start to crawl forward.

"No!" He cries out, arms flying in the air again. "Go back to your room."

"I don't want to," I confess. "I won't be able to go back to sleep."

He runs his fingers through his hair. "Well, you're not climbing down from the roof." He looks dismayed that I'd even think of trying.

"I've done it before." His eyes widen in horror. *Whoops, wrong thing to say then.* "Why aren't you asleep?" I ask, trying to distract myself and him.

"A lot on my mind."

"So much that you needed to smoke?" I inquire. I've never seen him smoke before, so I don't think it's a regular habit.

He sighs, rubbing a hand over his jaw. "Sometimes I need one when I'm more stressed than normal. It calms me down."

"Interesting." My hand slips from my sweaty palm and Thayer makes a noise below. "I'm okay." I steady myself.

"Get down from there right now. You're stressing me the fuck out and I'm already anxious enough as it is."

"Threats don't work on me."

"How about a deal then?"

"What kind?" I probe, cocking my head to the side.

He shrugs. "I can't sleep, apparently you can't sleep either, so climb back in your room and come down here and we can just talk or whatever. Just please get off the roof."

I press my lips together, thinking over his offer. "Deal."

"Thank God." He exhales a gust of air.

"But you wait right there." I wiggle a finger at him in warning.

He raises his hand. "I'll be in this spot."

Crawling on all fours, I turn myself around and quietly climb back through the window. I close and lock it before stuffing my feet into a pair of sneakers.

Sneaking down the stairs, I slip out the side door and run around to the front of the house where Thayer waits in the same spot he was in, just as he promised.

"I'm glad you didn't die climbing back in your window," he quips. He tips his head toward his house for me to follow.

I roll my eyes, falling into step beside him. "You're being dramatic, I was fine."

"You looked like you were having a panic attack."

I wince. I *was*.

"I had it under control."

He arches a brow, opening the gate that leads to his backyard. "Do you want something to drink?"

I mock-gasp. "Are you offering an underage girl alcohol, Thayer? How scandalous of you."

He lets out a gruff laugh. "I said a *drink*—that includes water and soda."

"You have Diet Coke?" I perk up.

"Yes."

"I'll have that then." I sit down on the back step, looking out at the pool. The water glimmers with the reflection of the nearly full moon.

He arches a brow. "You don't want to come in?"

I shake my head. "No, I need the fresh air."

"Ah, yes, hence you climbing out of your bedroom window at—" He checks his watch. "—two in the morning."

He waits for me to say something but when he sees that I'm not going to he just heads inside to get the soda. He returns less than a minute later, sitting down on the stair beside me. His leg brushes mine, sending a shiver up my spine.

"Here," he says gruffly, extending the bottle my way. "That stuff will rot your teeth, you know."

"Then why do you have it?" I retort, unscrewing the top. The soda fizzles and I take a sip.

"I keep a stock of all kinds of drinks and sodas for my team."

"Ah, your team. You're a football coach too?" I arch a brow, kidding around with him.

"My landscaping team."

"That's nice of you."

"A lot of the guys forget to hydrate, so I started taking a full cooler with me on jobs. I learned pretty quick most of them refuse to drink the right stuff." He wags a water bottle between us.

"This quenches my thirst plenty," I joke, tapping my bottle against his in an awkward cheers.

He shakes his head in amusement. "So, are you going to tell me what that nightmare was that sent you crawling out of a second story window at such an early hour?"

I drop my head, my blond hair swinging forward to shield my face. It's stringy from the sweat I broke out into in my sleep. "No." My voice is small. Frail. Cracked.

"You don't want to talk about it?" He doesn't wait for me to answer. "Fair enough."

"Are you going to smoke another cigarette?" I'm not sure what makes me ask the question.

"No," he sighs, rubbing his fingers over his lips. "I shouldn't have had one in the first place. My ex..." He pauses, flinching, like he didn't mean to let that slip. "Let's just say she knows how to push my buttons like no other."

"That bad, huh?"

He rubs a hand over his jaw. "I don't want to bad mouth her. We had good times, we made an amazing kid together, but sometimes people just grow apart and sometimes you start to see what you thought you had was all a very beautiful lie."

My eyes narrow in confusion. "What does that mean?"

He shakes his head. "Just manipulative bullshit I finally clued into, and when I started really looking at my life, I realized I was just ... not happy and life's too short for that. I never pictured myself divorced, and I was conflicted because of my son, but I decided he was better off growing up with parents who are separate and happy than together and miserable."

"Makes sense." I nod along. "That's what scares me—not being happy," I elaborate. "Settling. Being complacent."

"It happens all too easily." He drinks his water, his Adam's apple bobbing. "Be smarter than me." He winces. "Fuck, that sounds terrible. To be honest, I wouldn't take any of it back. Like I said, we did have good times, and got an amazing kid out of it." He runs his fingers through his hair. "I'm just digging a hole for myself."

I laugh, bumping his arm lightly with my elbow. "Don't feel bad. I understand what you're saying."

Silence settles between us, only filled by the music of summer's insects.

He knocks his knee against mine. "Does that happen often?"

I jolt from my runaway thoughts. "Huh?"

"The nightmares?"

I give a shaky nod. "It's why I don't sleep a lot and go for a run."

He presses his lips into a thin line, probably wondering what could've possibly happened to an eighteen-year-old to make her like this. But he doesn't press further.

Instead, he changes the topic of conversation altogether. "I'm going to install one of those fences around the pool itself. Hopefully that'll keep anything from happening again like the other day." I wince at the memory of discovering Forrest had snuck back into the pool. "I'm sorry he scared you. I had a long talk with him about it. I mean, we'd already had one so who knows how good it did a second time, but I'm trying. He's only six, but he thinks he's eighteen and can do whatever he wants."

I laugh at that. "Well, he's a great kid."

"He is." He nods. "I can't thank you enough for babysitting some. I like to spend as much time with him as I can, but sometimes—"

I bump his knee with mine. "You're a parent but you still have other obligations. It doesn't mean you love him any less."

He knocks his knee back into mine. "You better try to get back to bed."

"I know," I sigh heavily. "But I won't sleep." He gives me a sympathetic look. "It's okay," I wave away his concern, "I'm used to it."

"Do you ever take sleeping pills?"

I look into the distance, beyond the fence surrounding his entire yard. Behind it is a field of wildflowers that extends for an acre or so before it butts up against a forest. It's protected historical land which is why it was never developed—probably thoroughly haunted land if you ask me—but it is beautiful to look at.

"In the past I have," I admit begrudgingly, "but I hate how they make me feel. So much so that I'd rather go without sleep." Sympathy coats his face. "It's okay," I say by reflex.

His eyes narrow. "No," he shakes his head roughly, brows furrowed, "it's not."

Setting my half-drank Diet Coke beside me, I rub my hands on my legs before standing. "You're right. I better go back home."

"You know," he says before I move, "this doesn't help you with your sleeping problem?" He gives the bottle a light shake.

"Caffeine doesn't hype me up."

He doesn't stop me as I leave, but I feel his eyes follow me as I go.

CHAPTER TWELVE

I didn't fall back asleep after I returned home. Instead, I tidied up my room the best I could while everyone else was still sleeping, then went for a run. I don't know if Thayer saw me leave on my run, but he was getting in his truck for work when I returned, his eyes watching me shrewdly. I can tell he's worried I don't sleep enough. It's something I worry about too, but I hate sleeping pills and I can't force my body to sleep when it doesn't want to.

Out of my shower, I dress for the day in a cute summer dress with a floral pattern. I'll be working at the store all day today while my mom works in the back, preparing things for our big summer blow out coming in a few weeks for the end of summer.

Downstairs I find Georgia sitting at the kitchen table with a bowl of her favorite vanilla crunch cereal while our mom pours coffee into a mug.

"Morning," my mom smiles when she spots me, "did you sleep well?"

"Yeah," I lie, tucking a piece of hair behind my ear so she can't see any tells on my face. She'll be upset if she knows it's getting worse. I go to the fridge and pour a glass of orange juice. Popping a piece of bread in the toaster, I turn around as my mom slides into the chair across from Georgia.

Georgia's hazel eyes meet mine. "I was telling mom she should have you introduce her to the new neighbor since you're babysitting for him."

I give her a funny look. "Why?"

She mirrors my expression. "Because mom is a beautiful, single woman who deserves her second chance at love."

My mom blushes, staring into her cup of coffee. She confessed to me once that she feels undeserving of falling in love, not after how awful my father was, and she couldn't protect us. I told her she was being crazy. She's a victim too.

But Thayer?

"He's too young for me," my mom says my next thought, but she doesn't know that one I had right behind it.

That I can't stand the idea of her with Thayer, because I like him, and not in a platonic he's kinda-sorta my boss way.

Holy shit.

I have a crush on our neighbor who has to be in his early thirties.

I have a crush, a big one, and I have a boyfriend.

My stomach roils and when my toast pops up, I suddenly don't feel hungry, but I know after my run I have to force something in me.

Grabbing the butter from the fridge, I apply the thinnest layer possible, wrinkling my nose with distaste at the toast in my hand. My mom catches the gesture and frowns.

"Are you feeling sick, honey?"

"I'm fine." I force myself to take a bite. I don't want her making me stay home today.

Georgia finishes her cereal, drinking the last of the milk out of the bowl and rinsing it. "I've gotta get to the hospital." She grabs me and places a loud, dramatic kiss on top of my head. "Love you, guys." She kisses Mom's cheek.

Scooping up her bag and car keys, she's out the door and

gone.

Mom shakes her head. "That girl has always been a hurricane."

It's a good way to describe Georgia. Wild, unpredictable, a tad dramatic.

Sometimes I wish I could take a page out of her book and let go more. I know I can be too uptight at times.

"Are you sure you're okay?"

"Huh?" I jolt back to reality.

"You seem really out of it," she explains. "Are you okay?"

"Y-Yeah. Just a lot on my mind," I stutter, finishing my toast and brushing crumbs off my dress. My mom eyes the mess now on the ground and I give a small laugh. Grabbing the vacuum from the pantry I sweep them up.

"Is it about Caleb?" she questions when the vacuum cuts off.

I almost blurt out *no*, but I realize she's just given me an excellent out for my behavior. "It is," I lie, easily, too easily, "it just sucks that he's leaving so soon."

She doesn't remind me that I could've gone with him, or headed off to a college of my choice. We both know I've already turned down those options. She's never asked me why and I'm glad for that, because frankly, I don't know. I just know that I'm a little lost right now and I'm not going to find myself that way.

Her lips downturn sympathetically as I stick the vacuum back where it belongs. "I know it sucks, honey."

"I'll get over it," I mumble, hoping we can move on from this topic of conversation. It's not that I won't miss Caleb, I *will*, but I don't know that I'm going to miss him as much as I should.

She moves Georgia's bowl from the sink to the drying rack. "If you don't mind, go on over to the store and open up. I'll be there in another hour or so." Her shoulders fall tiredly.

I narrow my eyes at the gesture. "Is everything okay?"

She sighs, rubbing a hand over her face. "Yes."

I don't believe her, but I'm lying as well, so I'll let her keep her secrets too.

***

Iced coffee in hand, I cross the street to A Checkered Past Antiques and unlock the door, switching the sign on the door to OPEN.

I flick lights on as I go, setting my bag down behind the counter.

Luckily, my vanilla iced coffee tastes way better than my toast did.

Settling behind the counter, I flip through a magazine left there by my mom. You can never predict days at the store. Sometimes it's constant traffic in and out and other times it's dead to the world. I know my mom's been lucky that the store is popular enough that people from the city make the trek all the way here to seek out unique pieces for their homes.

My phone vibrates with a text, and I grab it in case it's my mom asking me to do something.

It's Lauren. A smiling selfie stares back at me as she holds up peace fingers, her eyes shielded by a tiny pair of sunglasses. The ocean reflects behind her. She's gone for the week on vacation, soon that'll be Caleb too. My mom mentioned maybe taking a short trip somewhere. I think she felt bad since all my friends are getting vacations, but I told her not to worry about it. Money is tight and I don't want her spending unnecessary dollars on a frivolous trip. She dropped it and didn't bring it up again.

Me: I hope you have so much fun!

Lauren: I wish you were here!

Me: Me too.

I'm sure a beach trip would be fun, but secretly, I'm glad to be here.

Home is where I want to be.

Where I need to be.

Besides, no matter where I go or what I do, the nightmares will always find me.

CHAPTER THIRTEEN

"Go Fish," Forrest says, and I grab another card off the coffee table, eyeing the massive amount of cards in my hands. Either I suck at Go Fish, Forrest forgot the rules, or the little devil is cheating.

From his coy grin my vote is on cheating.

Keys rattle in the front door and Forrest tosses down his cards, the much smaller amount than mine scattering everywhere. "Dad!" His feet pound on the floor as he runs for the foyer. I pick up his cards and stack them along with mine, putting everything back in the box.

"Hey, buddy, did you miss me?" I hear Thayer say in reply.

"Yeah! Did you bring me a pizza?"

"That's what's in my hands."

"You're the best dad ever."

Forrest runs past the archway of the living room, heading toward the kitchen, with a Pizza Hut personal pizza clasped in his hands.

I pick up a throw blanket from the floor and fold it, returning it to the back of the couch. Thayer clears his throat, leaning against the archway. Brown hair tumbles over his forehead messily, and not in the purposeful way like so many of the boys I went to school with tried to achieve. This is just pure mess and I love it.

Pressing a hand to my chest, I mock gasp. "And where is *my* pizza?"

He chuckles softly, rubbing the back of his hand. "Stolen by a pigeon."

"Damn carrier pigeons," I cluck my tongue. "Can't trust them."

"It's true," he shrugs, easily playing along. "They work for the government."

I throw my hands up in pretend frustration. "I hope the pigeon enjoys my pizza."

"I'll ask him if I see him again."

"Him?" I arch my brow. "How do you know it wasn't a girl pigeon?"

"Could've been," he concedes, stepping into the room. He drops his crossed arms to his sides. "Thanks for watching him."

I wave away his thanks. "No problem." He pulls out his wallet and grabs some cash, passing it to me. "Thanks."

He dips his head in acknowledgment.

"Salem," Forrest calls from the kitchen, "do you have to go home?"

I glance at Thayer. "I can stay a while longer," I whisper in case Thayer wants me to go. I totally understand if he wants time with his kid.

He shrugs. "You can stay if you want."

"All right," I say louder so Forrest will hear me, "I'll stay for a little while longer."

***

An hour later I find myself curling up on Thayer's couch with a bowl of popcorn. Forrest sits on one side of me, leaning his small body against mine, Thayer on the other, careful to keep six inches of space between us.

On the TV, *The Santa Clause* plays. Apparently, those movies are Forrest's favorite, and it doesn't matter that it's July, he wants to watch them anyway.

"Daddy," he asks, crunching popcorn between his teeth, "do you think I'm on the naughty or nice list?"

"Definitely nice," Thayer nods at this, "but that can always change. That's why you have to always be on your best behavior. Santa is always watching."

"This is true," I agree.

Forrest looks up at me with wide eyes while on the TV screen Tim Allen climbs up a ladder in his boxers. "Have you ever been on the naughty list? Does he really give you coal?"

I love that Forrest doesn't wait for me to answer the first question before adding the second, like he automatically assumes I've been on the naughty list at some point.

I shake my head. "Nope, always the nice list for me."

He frowns, dejected at not having a proper answer to his naughty list question. "Do you know anyone who was on the naughty list?" He tries again.

"Nope, sorry."

"What about—"

"I thought you wanted to watch a movie?" Thayer butts in.

"I do," Forrest replies enthusiastically.

"Then why aren't you watching it?"

"Oh, right." He fixes his gaze back on the TV screen.

The living room is in much better shape than the kitchen. The floors are finished, the walls painted, and the comfy sectional is obviously brand new. Thayer's even mounted the TV above the fireplace.

Thayer reaches over for popcorn, his fingers grazing mine in the process. Our eyes meet. I'm the first to look away, dropping my stare to the kernels. He puts another couple of inches between us. Almost a whole foot.

Interesting.

I force myself to focus on the movie and not the man beside me.

As the evening progresses, the popcorn moves to the coffee table and Forrest's head drops to my lap. Despite his soft snores, neither Thayer nor I make a move to stop the movie and get up. When the end credits roll, Forrest is still passed out. My fingers glide idly through his hair.

Thayer stands up with a groan, stretching his arms above his head and exposing smooth, muscular abdominals, deeply tanned from all his time in the sun.

Stop staring! He's practically your boss!

And much older than me. But I'm not sure exactly how much.

"How old are you?" I blurt.

Thayer gives me a funny look. "Thirty. I'll be thirty-one next month. Why?"

"No reason," my voice squeaks.

Thirteen years—almost fourteen. That's more than an entire decade.

My face heats at my thoughts, but if he notices he doesn't say anything. He bends down, scooping Forrest into his arms. He brushes my arm, glancing at me and muttering, "Sorry."

I hope he doesn't notice the shiver that rushes down my spine.

"It's okay." I tuck a piece of hair behind my ear and stand, grabbing the popcorn bowl.

Thayer heads upstairs, carrying Forrest. I dump the last of the popcorn in the trash and rinse the bowl in the downstairs bathroom sink since there's currently not one in the kitchen.

I'm headed for the door to let myself out when Thayer comes down. He runs his fingers through his hair, looking tired.

"You're headed out?" I nod in reply. "Have a good night." I press my lips together at that, thinking about how I rarely have a good night of rest. He notices my expression and adds, "Maybe you'll sleep."

"Maybe," I echo. There's always a chance.

CHAPTER FOURTEEN

A shrill scream wakes me up at eight in the morning. I didn't have any nightmares, but that's only because I didn't go to sleep until four in the morning. My eyes barely want to open, but I force them to.

"God, you're such a pain in my ass!" The yelling starts up again.

Yawning, I slide out of my bed. Binx is in the corner on his cat tree, craning his neck to peer out the window.

"I'm so glad I divorced you!" The same voice screams.

I open my window, poking my head out to find the woman I saw before who's clearly Thayer's ex, standing on his front porch poking him repeatedly in the chest. She's short, having to stretch her neck nearly all the way back in order to see him.

Thayer's voice isn't as loud, but it is still raised, and our houses are close enough together for me to hear him. "I asked for the divorce."

She throws her hands up. "You infuriating—"

"You're making a scene," he remarks, nodding his head across the street to where our elderly neighbor, Cynthia, has stepped outside on her front porch, sweeping the already immaculate stoop.

She looks over her shoulder briefly before focusing back on him. "I don't care. Let them hear. Let them all hear!" She throws her arms out wide.

Thayer merely shakes his head. He's in a pair of sleep pants and a cotton shirt, his hair messy like he hasn't been awake long. "You're making a fuss, Forrest asked for five minutes to get his stuff and I said to take all the time he needed."

"Exactly!" She cries like he's just proven the point of her entire meltdown. "You're trying to steal him from me! Manipulate him like—"

"Krista." His voice is a biting reprimand. "Do you hear yourself? He's a child. He's finishing packing his things."

She bites her cheek, glancing to her right where she spots me hanging out the window eavesdropping.

Shit, I've been caught.

I pop back into my room and close the window. Listening time is over.

"Well, Binx," I eye my curious cat, "that sure was interesting."

I take a hasty shower and put on a minimal amount of makeup. Caleb is supposed to pick me up for breakfast at nine, so it's not like I could've slept much longer anyway.

He doesn't know about my insomnia, the nightmares, restless sleep. It's not something I've wanted to burden him with. Caleb has enough on his plate.

I hastily dry my hair—well, half dry it—and pull it into a bun. I glance at the clock and I have less than ten minutes until he's due to show up. I swipe some mascara on my lashes and dot gloss on my lips.

My phone vibrates by the sink with a text.

Caleb: Be there in 5.

I head downstairs, sitting on the front porch. My shoelace has come untied on my right foot, so I bend down and retie it. A shadow falls over me and I look up, expecting to see Caleb, my smile ready for him. But it's Thayer. He's changed clothes—a pair of athletic shorts and a shirt with the sleeves cutoff. I try not to check out his biceps but fail immediately.

"Hi," I squeak at the man that towers above me.

His dirty tennis shoes toe the ground. "I'm sorry about this morning. What you overheard."

I arch a brow. "Are you going door to door apologizing to everyone on the street?"

"No," he admits. "Just you."

I place a hand over my heart. "Aw, I'm special."

He doesn't say anything, but his eyes say you are. I try not to read into that, in case it's my imagination playing tricks on me.

He looks away, shoving his hands in his pockets. He does that a lot when he's uncomfortable or nervous.

I draw a circle around a bruise on my knee. "I don't really understand why you're apologizing for someone else's behavior, though?"

He winces. "You're right, I shouldn't, but—"

"She's an adult. Her actions only reflect on herself. If she hasn't figured that out yet, that's on her."

Staring off into space, he nods woodenly.

Caleb pulls his car into the driveway, and Thayer narrows his eyes on the small vehicle.

"We're going to breakfast," I explain, even though I don't owe him an explanation.

"Well," he steps back, "enjoy your breakfast."

He throws his hand up in a wave at Caleb, though his expression is anything but friendly. Caleb raises his hand in response, also glowering. Men are so weird.

Hopping into the car, I lean over and kiss Caleb. "Hi," I say brightly. "Morning."

"Morning." His voice is still thick with sleep.

"You sound tired."

"A little," he admits. "Dad's running me ragged."

I frown. I hate that Caleb is so busy this summer, working, preparing for college ball, and not getting any break at all.

"I'm sorry."

He reaches over and entwines our fingers together on his leg. "At least we can have breakfast this morning."

"That's true," I brighten. His hand is warm in mine, rough from lifting weights and practice.

"You want the windows down or up?"

"Down." I bounce in my seat a little, eager to feel the air on my face.

He chuckles, accommodating me even though I know he hates having them down. Wisps of hair that escape my bun smack against my face. I ignore it, breathing in the fresh summer air.

A few minutes later he parks outside our favorite breakfast diner filled with greasy, artery clogging food. AKA the good stuff.

Maybe not good for your body, but delicious for your taste buds.

Caleb hops out and I follow him inside. The place is busy, like usual, but we find a table in a back corner and sit down. I swipe a menu from the napkin holder, perusing the items.

Caleb watches me with an amused tilt of his lips.

"What?" I look at him over top of the plastic menu.

"We come here all the time and you always look at the menu."

I shrug, flipping it over to scan the back. "You never know, I might change my mind and order something different one of these times. Plus, what if they add something new to the menu or get rid of—"

"If it isn't my two favorite people." Darla, our usual waitress, smiles down on us, tapping her BIC pen against her notepad. "The usual? Veggie omelet and Diet Coke for you," she points at me, "sausage, egg, and cheese biscuit with hash browns and water for you?" Her pointed finger moves to Caleb.

"Yes and yes," he tells her.

"You got it."

She heads over, already hollering our order out to the cook.

"What does your mom have on your agenda today?" I ask him.

He winces. It's subtle but I don't miss it. I didn't mean to make a dig at his mom, but it's a legitimate question.

"We're heading to the mall later. There are some things she wants to get before we go to the beach, and she's got this whole big ass list of things she says I need for school. I told her I don't think I'm allowed to have a toaster in my room, but she won't listen."

Darla drops our drinks off and I mouth *thank you*, already ripping off the paper from my straw. I take a sip. Sweet sustenance. Some people rely on coffee—and don't get me wrong I like that too—but Diet Coke is my drug of choice. Okay, probably a bad way to phrase that.

I ball up the paper wrapper. "I wish I knew why your mom hates me."

"She doesn't hate you." I give him a look and he lowers his head. "Maybe a little, but it's nothing personal. I think she's scared that you're going to take me away from her, but she'd feel that way with any girl I dated."

"Any girl, huh?" I joke. "Are you saying I'm not special?"

He chuckles. "That's not what I'm saying at all."

"Good." I toss the wrapper at him playfully. He peels it off his shirt and slides it back across the table to me. He knows I play with my wrappers through every meal.

"Have you thought any more about what you're going to do?" He pulls the sugar dish closer to him, reorganizing the multicolored packets.

"What do you mean?" I look up from the balled-up piece of paper in my hands.

He raises a brow. "Salem, you can't work at your mom's shop forever."

His words sting. I love working there. What's so wrong with that? "No, I don't know, and that's the whole point of not going to college. I need time to think."

"And what if you still don't know then?"

"Why are you giving me the third degree?" I demand, feeling defensive. He's my boyfriend. He's supposed to be on my side, right?

His shoulders sag. "I'm not trying to be a hard ass. I just want you to find something that makes you happy."

"I am happy. I love making my candles and working for my mom. It's nice babysitting Thayer's son, too."

Caleb frowns at the mention of Thayer. I'm not sure he'll ever like my neighbor after their horrific first encounter. "I just wish you knew what you wanted to do."

He's known since practically forever that he wanted to play football and go to law school. He can't fathom someone not knowing what they want to do with their life. Just like I can't relate to someone being so certain. I'm not the same person I was a year ago. I can't imagine settling into a plan and trusting it to work, not when future me is a stranger. I'm trying to get to know her, so I know she'll be happy. That's all.

Darla sets our plates down, refills of our drinks as well. "Enjoy, guys."

I dig in immediately, not having realized how hungry I was until the food was placed in front of me.

"Hungry?" Caleb smiles in amusement.

"Starving. I'm pretty sure this is the best thing I've eaten all week." I point my fork at the omelet.

"So, you're saying I need to be a better boyfriend and feed you more often?" He jokes playfully.

"Definitely. Food is the way to my heart."

"Man, I wish I would've known that before I got these." My brows raise at his segue. He slides his hand into his pocket and pulls out two rectangular pieces of paper. He slides them across the table to me and I pick them up, squinting at the tiny print.

My mouth drops. "Concert tickets? For Willow Creek? Are you kidding me?" I gape at the tickets, shocked. They're one of the biggest bands in the world right now. Selling out whole stadiums. I tried to get tickets and got kicked off the website for some stupid reason. "How did you even get these?"

He grins, pleased by my reaction. "I have my ways."

"If we weren't in the middle of a restaurant, I'd kiss you right now."

He chuckles. "Kiss me anyway." He leans across the table, and I do the same, our lips meeting halfway. His hand cups the back of my head, holding me there a little longer before releasing me.

"This is," I stare at the tickets in my hand, "amazing. Wow." His grin says everything. "Thank you."

"You don't have to thank me, babe."

I look at the date on the tickets. It's a few days before Caleb moves to Boston. It's a bittersweet feeling knowing we'll get to go together but that he'll be leaving so shortly after.

But that's life.

It's fluid, always moving, always changing. You either flow with it or you drown.

CHAPTER FIFTEEN

"Michael! What are you doing here?" My sister's shrill shriek, not a happy one, echoes through the house. I glance at Binx who sits on the desk in my room while I flip through a magazine.

"Babe," I hear Michael's pleading voice on the other side, "I'm sorry. I'm really sorry."

"That's the problem," my sister volleys, "you're always sorry for something. How about you don't do something to be sorry about in the first place?"

The door slams and then Michael immediately hits the doorbell.

I should be used to the fact that these two constantly fight and break up then make up a week later, but it's exhausting. I wish they'd either break up for good or stay together. It can't be that difficult.

"Ugh, what?" Georgia must swing the door open again.

"I got you flowers."

I ease out of my desk chair, poking my head out the door to try to peep down the stairs. Michael stands there with a bouquet of white daisies—Georgia's favorite—clasped in his hands. It's a big bundle too, not one of those cheap bouquets from the grocery store.

"They're beautiful." Her voice begins to go all lovey dovey.

"I swear I wasn't looking at that chick's ass."

I snort and both turn to look up the stairs, but I think I

manage to pull my head back inside fast enough. Not that they won't know it was me anyway.

"Let's talk outside," Georgia says to him, the door closing behind her.

Alas, my entertainment has disappeared.

I return to my desk and magazine. My notebook rests beside it with candle scent ideas as well as possible names. I turned my attention to the magazine when my brain started to get tired.

Scratching Binx behind his ear, I tell my beloved cat, "I'm so happy Caleb and I aren't like those two."

He purrs in agreement. I tug my notebook closer to me, pop my earbuds in, and get back to brainstorming.

***

"You made dinner?" My mom gasps, setting her bag down by the door. "I was going to suggest we order pizza."

I shrug. "We had stuff we needed to use up in the fridge." I slide the casserole out of the oven, tucking the mitts under my arm. I grab the rolls I heated up and start plating.

My mom grabs the plates and puts them on the table. Glancing at me over her shoulder, she suggests, "Why don't you ask the neighbor if he wants to come over for dinner? He got in at the same time as me. I'm sure he's hungry and this is already made. Besides, Georgia is with Michael tonight."

"Thayer?" I ask stupidly.

"Yes," she says slowly, giving me a funny look.

I almost ask *why*, but I realize she's only trying to be nice. "Um, okay," I hesitate, my fingers curling against the counter. "I'll go ask him."

She's already making an extra plate, like it's a given that he'll be joining us as I head next door. Head down, I shuffle hurriedly down our driveway and over to Thayer's house, bounding up the front porch and knocking, since I know the doorbell is disabled at the moment since he's replacing it.

I don't have to wait long before I hear heavy boots thudding against the floor. The door swings open and—

Oh my God.

The plaid shirt he wears is unbuttoned revealing a tanned, well-muscled chest speckled with chest hair. I'm staring, God am I staring, but I can't look away. Thayer is the perfect specimen of man. I have to force my hands to stay at my sides, so I don't poke him to test if he's real or not.

"Hey," he says, sounding tired.

"Hi." My voice sounds smaller than normal, an octave higher.

"Did you need something?" He prompts when I stand there stupidly.

"Oh, yeah, my mom wanted to invite you over for dinner. I made a casserole. There's plenty, so it's no trouble."

He cocks his head to the side, thinking over my proposal. "All right."

For some reason I didn't expect him to agree so easily. He starts rebuttoning his shirt and I try to hide my frown at the disappearance of his perfect chest.

You shouldn't be staring at him. I silently scold myself. You have a boyfriend.

Tucking a piece of hair behind my ear, I take a few steps back as Thayer shuts the door behind him.

"Casserole, huh?" He seems amused by my meal choice.

"There were a lot of random things in the fridge, so a

casserole seemed like a safe bet."

"Do you like to cook?"

I nod. "Yeah, I do actually." I open the side door and wave him inside first, but he insists on waiting for me.

"Oh, good!" My mom claps her hands together. "I hoped you'd agree to dinner."

Thayer dips his head. "I appreciate the offer. I've been living off McDonald's and frozen meals."

My mom frowns. "That's awful. Well, it's no trouble at all. You're welcome to have dinner with us anytime or Salem can run leftovers over to you so you don't have to eat with us."

"You don't have to do that."

"It's no trouble at all. Plates are on the table. What would you like to drink? We have," she opens the fridge, "water, Sprite, Diet Coke, there's some beer too."

"I'll just take a water. I don't need the caffeine this late or I'll be up all night."

She laughs, filling a glass of water for him. "Man, I wish Salem was like that, but this girl can drink copious amounts of caffeine and be perfectly fine."

"What can I say?" I shrug, grabbing a Diet Coke. "I'm blessed."

Thayer watches me, amusement sparkling in his brown eyes. He follows me to the table and for some reason I'm surprised when he pulls out the chair beside mine and sits down. I expected him to take the one on the end.

My mom pours a glass of wine, a rarity for her, before joining us at the table. I study her appearance, noting the dark circles beneath her eyes. I wonder if, like me, she's not getting much sleep.

"Thank you for having me over," Thayer says before we all

dig in, "it's really nice to have a home cooked meal."

My mom waves her hand away. "It's no trouble at all and we always have plenty."

This is true. I always seem to make an abundance of food. Especially pasta—I can't seem to get the serving size down and just keep adding more noodles to the water.

We eat our first couple of bites in silence before my mom asks him a question. "Where are you originally from, Thayer? Do you have family nearby?"

He shakes his head. "My folks are in Florida, they moved there after they retired, and I have a brother out in Colorado. If you count my ex-wife, she's just a few towns over."

"You have a brother?" I blurt.

It's not like Thayer and I sit around and paint each other's nails, having lengthy conversations about our lives, but this serves as a reminder of how little I truly know about him.

"Mhmm." He nods, taking another bite of food.

"Is he older than you?" I find myself curious about this brother I've never heard of. He doesn't have any personal photos in his home, either, at least not yet, so I haven't been able to get an idea of his family life other than his ex and son.

"No," he chuckles, like the idea of his brother being older than him is preposterous. "Laith is twenty-six."

"Do you see your family often?" I'm thankful for my mom taking over the conversation. I drop my eyes to my plate of food, pushing it around with my fork.

"When I can. I try to take a trip down to Florida every winter to stay with my parents for a bit."

"That's nice," my mom smiles, "I'm sure they're always happy to see you."

He jerks his head in a nod. "They come up here some too.

Usually in the fall. They make a road trip out of it because my dad hates to fly." He gives a sudden laugh. "He'll tell you it's my mom that hates flying, but nah, that's all him."

"Men love to blame their wives for their fallacies." My mom pales, realizing her blunder. "Not all men, of course, but some—"

Thayer cracks a smile. "I understand what you're saying."

Her cheeks color. "My husband—he's passed—but he was..." She flounders, searching for the right words to say in front of a relative stranger.

"Not the best," I finish for her.

Thayer's eyes ping-pong between us. I'm sure he's taking in that a lot is being left unsaid. "I'd say I'm sorry for your loss, but I'm not sure that's the right thing to say here."

My lips thin, trying not to laugh.

"Oh, uh, it's all right. Sorry is fine, or not sorry, either or." It's rare for my mom to get so flustered. "I'm going to see if we have any dessert." She shoves her chair back and scurries over to the refrigerator.

I feel Thayer's eyes on me, but he won't dare ask something, not with my mom present. I'm sure he's formulating plenty for another time. I push my food back and forth some more and then his big warm hand settles atop mine.

"If I have to watch you push your food around for another minute, I'm going to force feed you." My jaw drops at his statement. "Good, you're halfway there already." He tries to take my fork from me to, no doubt, shove food in my mouth.

"Okay, okay," I say, getting his point. "I'll eat." I heap casserole onto my fork and put enough in my mouth that it's overfull.

My mom returns to the table with a defeated expression.

"We don't have any dessert. I haven't made any lately and—"

"Mom," I quiet her, "it's fine."

She gives me a grateful look and takes her seat once more. She finishes eating at the same time we all do and goes to gather the plates.

"No, let me." Thayer stands, taking her plate from her and stacking his and then mine on top.

"Oh, you don't need to do that," she insists. "You're our guest."

"It's no trouble." He's already walking toward the sink.

"I'll help. You can go on up to bed," I tell her, worried about those dark circles beneath her eyes.

She doesn't argue so it's only further confirmation that she's truly tired.

Thayer carries everything over to the sink, thanking her again for the dinner invite. We wait to speak until her footsteps disappear upstairs.

"Dinner was delicious," he says, running water in the sink.

"Thanks. My mom's not kidding. We always have plenty, so feel free to pop over anytime."

"Are you worried I'm not eating enough?" He arches a brow as if to say he's the one worried about me.

"We always have extra, that's all." I shrug off the real question he's asking.

He cleans the plates and passes them to me to dry. My mom would love a dishwasher, but every time she finally thinks she's getting one something invariably happens that she has to use the money for instead.

"Your dad," he prompts, and I immediately begin shaking my head, not wanting to delve down that path. "There's more there, I know it."

"There is," I confirm, "but I don't want to talk about it."

"Salem—"

My fingers curl against the counter, knuckles turning white. "I don't want to talk about it," I bite out. "He's dead, gone, and that's all that matters."

Thayer studies me through narrowed eyes. I can see the words on the tip of his tongue, how he wants to ask what happened, to demand answers from me. Instead, he ducks his head and utters one word. "Okay."

He lets the water out from the sink, turns his back on me, and walks right out the door.

CHAPTER SIXTEEN

"You look thirsty." I hold out a bottle of water to Thayer. Sweat clings to his tanned skin, dampening his hair. The extended plastic bottle is a peace offering. We haven't spoken in days. I don't like it one bit. Somewhere, along the way, Thayer has become my friend. It feels weird not speaking.

He hesitates, eyeing the bottle and my hand, refusing to meet my eyes. I almost think he's going to reject my offer and ignore me all together. The rejection stings and I start to pull the bottle back toward me, but he reaches out with quick reflexes and swipes it.

A gruff, "Thanks," leaves his lips.

I toe my worn shoe against the deck. "What are you doing?" I eye the wooden pieces scattered around him. I can deduce what he's building on my own, but I want to make him talk to me. Something more than one word.

"A swing."

Well, at least it was two words.

"Why?"

He doesn't look at me, searching the deck for a specific piece. "Because I want a porch swing."

I lean against the column. I'm not going to allow his dismissive tone to force me to leave. "What are you going to do with this porch swing?"

Yes, I'm pushing. For more words, more anything.

He pauses, screwdriver in hand. "Swing on it."

I sigh, crossing my arms over my side. "Are you mad at me?" I cringe as soon as the question leaves my mouth. It sounds so juvenile.

He arches a brow, settling his hands on the top of his thighs. "What gave you that idea?"

"You're in a bad mood," I state, but I make no move to leave.

He lets out a gruff laugh. "I'm usually in a bad mood." He's quiet for a moment, searching for a piece on the ground. "It's nothing to do with you."

"Do you want to talk about it?"

He glares at me. "Do you?"

Translation: If I'm not sharing, he's not either.

"I never want to talk about my dad," I supply, looking away.

"And I," he groans, stretching to reach something else, "don't like talking about my ex. I guess we're even."

"I guess so." I bend down and pass him the piece I think he's looking for. His glare settles on my hand, and he swipes it from me without a thank you. I don't let his grumpy attitude ruffle my feathers. "Do you want any help?"

He opens his mouth, I'm sure to say no, but he sighs and runs a hand through his hair. "You want to help?" He sounds entirely doubtful.

"Sure."

"All right." I think it takes a lot for him to concede.

I make myself comfortable—well, as comfortable as I can get—on the porch, settling in to help him.

We don't speak except for when he asks me to pass him something. I'm fine with that. I don't need conversation. It's nice to exist with someone without the need to fill every silence. It's taken me a long time to become comfortable with my own thoughts.

Thayer finishes putting the swing together faster than I'd think possible.

He already has metal hooks drilled into the ceiling and he lets me help balance the swing as he attaches some sort of thick rope to the hooks.

When it's all done, he steps back to assess his handiwork, hands on his hips.

"It looks good."

He jerks his head down once, the nod the only acknowledgment he gives of his handiwork. He turns toward his front door, and I expect him to go inside without saying anything more to me, but he pauses, waiting.

"You coming?" I smile, following him inside. He leads me to the kitchen and opens the mini fridge. He pulls out deli meat, mayonnaise, and lettuce. "Do you want a sandwich?"

"Sure," I reply, taking in the base cabinets that have been installed. They're missing the doors, but at least it's progress.

"What do you want?"

I shrug, pulling a chair out at the card table. "You can make it the same as yours. I'm not picky."

He makes the sandwiches in silence and plops a plate down in front of me without ceremony, pulling the chair out across the table.

"Thanks."

"Mhmm."

I eye him before taking a bite of my sandwich. "You're a man of few words, aren't you?" He gives me a funny look. Brows furrowed, nose scrunched. "That must've driven your ex-wife crazy."

He sighs, running his fingers through his hair. "I don't want to talk about her. And need I remind you, that not everybody is perfect."

I wipe a crumb from my mouth. And think about what I'm going to say next. "Nobody is perfect," I agree, nodding at my own words. "But that doesn't mean that we shouldn't be aware of our flaws. If we're not mindful of them, then we can't improve on them."

Thayer grunts an unintelligible response. "You're wiser than me."

I don't know about that. I look away. "Some days I feel so much older than I am, and some I feel so much younger than I am." I don't think that he realizes how big of a confession this is for me. It took a lot for me to admit that.

He studies me with narrowed brown eyes. I think he sees more than I want him to see. Maybe even knows more than I've said or thought or confessed. I wonder idly if perhaps I could share the darker parts of myself with him. But it's terrifying to think about letting somebody in like that. Not even Caleb, who I've been with for years, knows everything. Lauren does, but she's my best friend. You can't not tell your best friend all the pieces of you. I know I should tell Caleb. He deserves the truth. But for some reason I can't bring myself to. It makes me sick to think that I might share those parts of myself with Thayer and not him. Maybe it's because Thayer is older that I feel like he could handle it better. I guess that's a backwards way of thinking, since Lauren is the same age as Caleb. But I can't help but feel that Caleb just couldn't handle it. The last thing I want is for my boyfriend to look at me differently. To see someone who's not whole. I just want to be Salem to him. That's who I want to be to everybody. I know, though, that this truth can always change how people think of me and how they see me.

I'm lucky to have a friend like Lauren because she never, not once saw me as broken or less than anyone else.

"Where did you go?" He asks softly.

"Just lost in my thoughts." I force a smile, but I know there's a shadow in my eyes. And from the way he looks at me, I know he sees it too.

Maybe one day, I think to myself. *I'll tell him.*

Someone else in this world should hear my truth.

CHAPTER SEVENTEEN

"Cat!" Forrest screams, running out of his dad's truck.

Ever since I told him about the cat in *Sabrina the Teenage Witch* named Salem, he's taken to calling me Cat. I think it's cute, and I like that we have a thing that's just ours. Thayer shakes his head at his kid.

Forrest barrels into me, hitting me full force in the legs with his body weight. I rock back, steadying myself. "Whoa, bud."

"Hi." He tilts his chin back, taking me in. "Are you coming over today?"

I glance at Thayer, unloading Forrest's bag from his truck. "I don't think your dad needs me today."

"Dad!" The little boy shrieks. "Can Salem come over? I want her to swim with me."

Thayer's eyes meet mine, trying to silently communicate with me if I'm okay with that or if I want him to tell Forrest I'm busy. I don't have anything better to do. Caleb's at the gym and then going out with his friends. Lauren is with her boyfriend of the week.

I shrug. "I don't mind."

Thayer nods. "Head over when you feel like it."

Forrest tosses his hands in the air, letting out a whoop of joy. "Let's go swimming, Cat!" He grabs my hand, trying to yank me forward.

"Hold up," I tell him, taking my hand back. "I have to put

my swimsuit on."

"Oh." His face falls.

I tweak his nose. "I'll be right over after I change."

"Wait!" He brightens again. I've already taken two steps away from him. "Can I meet your cat? Binx, right?"

I look to Thayer. "I don't mind," I say.

"If you're okay with it. I'm going to unload the groceries."

"My dad got me more Kid's Cuisines," Forrest whispers conspiratorially. "He told me I'm going to turn into a dinosaur chicken nugget if I keep eating so many, but I don't think that's possible."

"There are worse things you could be than a dinosaur chicken nugget."

"True," Forrest follows me in through the side door, "I could be a murderer."

I glance back at the child. "Should I be afraid of you?"

"I don't know." He stares at me with large round eyes. Then he lifts his hands in a clawing gesture. "Rawr!"

I pretend to be terrified. "Come on, this way." I curl my finger for him to follow me upstairs to my room. Binx sits perched on his cat tree, watching us with careful green eyes. "I brought you a friend, Binx. Say hi."

"*Meow.*"

"See, he said hi," I tell Forrest.

"Hi, Binx." Forrest waves. "Can I pet him?"

"Sure." I step away and let Forrest take my place. He reaches up, letting Binx smell his hand before he scratches him behind the ear. My cat immediately starts to purr. "Aw, he likes you."

"He does?"

"Yep." I open my dresser drawer, pulling out my bathing suit. "You hang here with Binx, and I'm going to change in the bathroom."

"Okay." He's too taken up with Binx to care much about anything else.

After I've changed, I return to find Forrest sitting on my bedroom floor with Binx curled up in his lap.

"I wish my dad would let me get a cat," he says, patting Binx's side.

"Maybe one day. You never know." I pull my hair back into a ponytail and yank on some shorts over my swimsuit.

"True. I'll keep asking."

"Are you ready to head back to your house?"

He frowns down at Binx. "I guess so."

Hands on my hips, I say, "Well, jeez, don't sound so excited to go swimming with me."

He brightens. "Oh, right! Swimming!"

I lift Binx off his lap and put him back on his tree. "Come on, Forrest," I hold my hand out to the child, "let's go swimming."

***

Thirty minutes into swimming and the back door opens. Thayer steps out in only a pair of swim trunks hanging low on his hips, revealing every perfectly sculpted muscle in his chest and abdomen. He even has that V-shape so many guys work hard to achieve dipping beneath the band of the board shorts.

My thighs clench together.

Stop staring at your boss like that! He's thirteen years older than you!

The reminders do nothing to quench the desire pulsing through my body.

He slips a pair of sunglasses onto his face and joins us at

the pool edge.

"Having fun?"

"So much fun!" Forrest replies, splashing water when he lifts his arms in the air. "We've been playing Marco Polo."

"I wanted to play mermaids," I explain.

"That's for girls," Forrest repeats the argument he gave me from the start.

"And I am a girl," I retort, trying not to laugh.

Thayer shakes his head, but I can see his amusement in the slight uptick of his lips. "Mind if I join?"

I shrug, swimming backwards. "It's your pool."

Translation: I'm not going to stop you.

Thayer steps into the pool and I watch the water ripple against his waist when he reaches the five-foot section. My eyes trail up his toned stomach, the smattering of hair on his chest and around his naval. Then, to my horror, my boss splashes water at me and says, "Eyes up here, Salem."

I flush all over at being called out. He's smiling though, amused. At least he's not pissed, but I mean, talk about embarrassing. I want to hide my face behind my hands, but I make no move to do so because I feel like that would only please him more.

"Come on, Dad," Forrest tries to climb on his dad's back, "let's play."

Thayer scoops Forrest up easily, practically holding him upside down. His laughter fills the air, and Thayer dunks his hair in the water.

There's a newly installed pool fence around the perimeter now, but when I came out here with Forrest it did little to stop him. He flipped the lock and dove right in. The kid is fearless, and I think that's both a good thing and a bad thing.

Thayer lets Forrest go and the boy swims over to me, smacking a wet hand against my arm. "Tag, you're it."

"Oh," I laugh, already swimming after the little guppy, "we're playing tag now, huh?"

His laughter fills the air as I chase him, Thayer shaking his head as he watches us. I never imagined this was how I would be spending my summer, but honestly this is so much better.

An hour or so later, we climb out of the pool—a tired Forrest complaining that he's most definitely not tired at all—and Thayer towels off his chest, passing me one to dry with.

"Thanks." I take it gratefully and wrap it around my body.

"I'll grab you some cash."

My brows scrunch. "Why?"

He hesitates, giving me an equally confused look. "For hanging out with Forrest."

I shake my head. "No, no. This was just for fun. You didn't ask me to watch him."

"But—"

"No," I insist. "Seriously, Thayer."

He still looks hesitant, but he nods. "Okay."

"Forrest," I call out, since the little boy has already run inside.

"Yes?" He pokes his head out the door, Poptart in hand.

"I'm heading home, so I wanted to say bye. I had fun."

He takes a bite and says, "bye," around a mouthful.

I turn to Thayer and a moment I don't quite understand passes between us.

The way he looks at me feels like more and that both intrigues and terrifies me.

"I'll see you," I say to Thayer, already walking away.

His voice is soft behind me. "See you."

CHAPTER EIGHTEEN

Caleb's leg rests against mine, my head on his shoulder. We watch the sun go down on the roof outside my bedroom. It's something we do a lot, but our days together are dwindling. He leaves for vacation tomorrow, and then, we only have one week left together when he gets back.

Before school ended, we did talk about the possibility of breaking up, or at least taking a break once summer ends and he leaves, but we decided against it—wanting to try to make it work. I don't tell him, but some days I wonder if we're being silly thinking we can do this. We're so young. It's not right, not fair to him, to think that our end is inevitable, but—

"I'm going to miss this." He draws random shapes on my bare knee. "Sitting on your roof, watching the sunset, just ... existing with you."

"Me too."

And I will. Despite my fears and reservations of our longevity, I will miss Caleb so much. He has a piece of my heart I know I'll never ever get back.

"Do you have to leave tomorrow?"

He rubs his jaw. "Unfortunately. But I'll be back at the end of the week."

"And then we only have *days* together," I remind him.

He nods, Adam's apple bobbing. I know he's affected by this—maybe even more than me. Change is hard. "At least we have the concert."

I brighten. "I'm so excited about that."

I've wanted to see my favorite band in concert since I was in middle school, but tickets always sell out insanely fast or cost an arm and a leg. It was just never possible. This means even more to me because Caleb knew it would make me happy.

Guilt plagues me for only minutes prior thinking maybe we should break up.

It's all so complicated.

"We leave early in the morning. I'll text you every day, I promise."

"Don't worry about me." I want him to enjoy his vacation. He deserves this break before his big move to Boston. "I'll be fine. I have work and lots of things to keep me busy."

At my words his gaze drifts next door.

"Hey," I touch my finger to his jaw, bringing his gaze back to me. "Don't worry about him."

He frowns, and I worry that maybe I've accidentally told a lie.

The way Thayer looks at me...

The way I look at him...

It's more than it should be.

But nothing can happen, I silently remind myself.

Caleb jerks his head in a nod. "Sure."

He doesn't sound convinced. I loop my arms through his. "I love you."

And I do. Caleb has been my rock the past few years, the boy who healed the heart of a broken girl. I'll *always* love him, no matter where the future takes us.

He cups my cheek, leaning in to press a tender kiss to my lips. "I love you, too."

He looks at me like I'm something precious, fragile, a

treasure that's all his.

I cuddle closer to his side and close my eyes.

I don't want to break your heart.

CHAPTER NINETEEN

The sound of a lawn mower stirs me from a restless sleep. I got up and went for a run at five-thirty this morning, running until my limbs couldn't move one step further, exhausting myself to the point that I got back to my room and crashed on my bed with my shoes still on.

"Ugh," I groan, wiping drool from my mouth. "Gross."

Sitting up, I kick my shoes off the rest of the way and roll over onto my back. My body feels spent. I went too hard, pushed myself too far, but sometimes it feels like the only way to escape.

Get yourself moving, Salem, I silently scold. With a groan I pry myself off my bed. My running shirt lies on the floor in a heap. At least I managed to get one thing off.

Stifling a yawn, I glance at the clock and see that it's a little after ten. That means I got around three hours of sleep once I got back. It's better than nothing and at least it was a solid few hours, compared to all the tossing and turning I did before that.

Opening my window, I slip out onto the roof, searching for the source of the noise, not at all surprised when I see that Thayer is out mowing. What is a surprise is that he's across the street mowing Cynthia's grass. She watches him from her front porch, sipping a cup of coffee, and appreciating the view. And by view, I mean a shirtless Thayer, his chest damp with sweat, looking like a rugged sports magazine model—too good looking for our small little town.

Cynthia notices me and raises her mug in a cheers. My

cheeks flush at being caught, but I make no move to crawl back inside.

Drawing my knees up to my chest, I wrap my arms around them. Thayer's been working on building a greenhouse in his backyard so I haven't seen him around as much, and he didn't ask me to watch Forrest this weekend. It's been a bummer, because with Caleb gone, I could've used the distraction. Yesterday, I went with Lauren to the mall and bought an outfit for the concert. Even though shopping isn't really my thing, I had fun.

Thayer looks up, no doubt having noticed Cynthia's gesture, and lifts his hand in a wave. I wave back with a smile. He fights a tiny grin, shaking his head but he continues to mow.

I watch for a little while longer before my grumbling stomach demands I put something in it.

Binx swishes his tail lazily, watching me from the floor as I climb back inside.

"You know," I say to him, "you could've extended a paw in help, but no, you just watch."

He blinks his owlish green eyes at me, completely unbothered. Cats.

Kicking my shoes out of the way, I head downstairs. The house is empty—my mom's at the store, and I'll take over in a few hours—and Georgia is at work too. I pour myself a bowl of cereal and sit down at the kitchen table.

My phone buzzes with a text.

Caleb: Miss you. Can't wait to get back and see you.

I stare at the text, feeling a heavy weight in my chest and

tears prick my eyes. Everything is changing already. I feel it. Can't he?

I finish my cereal, rinsing the bowl out in the sink. There's a knock on the side door and my nose scrunches, wondering who it could be. Possibly Lauren, but...

I open the door and the smile that overtakes me when I see Thayer standing there is downright criminal.

Good, eighteen-year-old girls, *do not* smile at their thirty-one year old divorced neighbor like that.

"Hey," I say, the word breathy.

"I thought I'd see if you wanted me to mow for you guys while I'm out." He pulls a bandana from the pocket of his shorts, using it to wipe the sweat from his brow.

"Oh." I look around at the overgrown grass. We've all been too busy to mow like we usually would. "Um ... maybe, if you don't mind, that is?"

It's a big yard and he's already done Cynthia's.

"I don't mind." He tucks the bandana back and grabs a baseball cap from his back pocket, slipping it over his head. His eyes are shadowed from me, but I still feel their intensity.

"What can I do for you?" I cringe as soon as I ask the question. Maybe it's just my brain slipping into dangerous territory, but I thought it sounded dirty. "What I mean is, can I make you some cupcakes or something?"

"Or something," he repeats, his tongue sliding out and over his lips. He gives a soft laugh. "Cupcakes would be amazing."

I nod shakily.

Why does he make me so jittery?

He tosses his thumb over his shoulder. "I'll see you when I'm done."

"Mhmm." I close the door and face the kitchen. I need to

get to work on those cupcakes.

But first, I text Caleb back.

***

I'm in the middle of washing up everything in the sink, the cupcakes cooling on a rack, when Thayer knocks on the door.

"Come on in," I call out, up to my elbows in sudsy water. He opens the door and pokes his head inside. "Your cupcakes are almost done. I just have to put icing on them when they're done cooling." I look over my shoulder at him, watching as he takes a seat at the table. He's even sweatier than he was before. "Do you want something to drink? You can grab anything from the fridge."

He nods gratefully, and gets up and grabs a bottle of water. He doesn't return to the table, instead sidling up beside me.

"I appreciate the cupcakes, but I would've mowed without them."

"I know." I dry off the mixing bowl. "But I was happy to make them."

He walks over and picks one up, sniffing it. "They smell delicious."

"You can never go wrong with cookie dough." He starts to unwrap one and I squawk in fear. "You have to wait until they're frosted. It's sacrilege to eat a cupcake without one. A cupcake without icing is a muffin!"

He holds it above my head. "Just a little taste."

I jump up and down, not caring how ridiculous I look. I still haven't showered yet and since it was hot in the kitchen while I was baking, I didn't bother to put a shirt on so I'm still in my jog bra. Thayer's eyes drift down, like he's realizing this too.

My stomach clenches at the heat in his eyes.

I'm stepping into dangerous territory, but I don't know how to backpedal from this.

I stumble, Thayer's hand quickly landing on the small of my back to steady me.

Our eyes meet, his gaze heated with desire. I'm young, but I'm not stupid. He wants me.

I think I hold my breath as he stares at me.

Kiss me, the thought pounds through my brain unbidden. I want you to kiss me.

Like he can hear my thoughts, he lowers his arm that was holding the cupcake high, holding me with both arms now, and his head starts to lower.

Kiss me, kiss me, kiss me!

The timer goes off, the one I set to remind me to see if the cupcakes were cooled enough, and I curse silently.

Thayer pulls away from me, clearing his throat. He sets the stolen cupcake on the counter. "You're right. These need icing."

"Y-Yeah," my voice shakes, "I'll get them ready."

He scoops up his water bottle, heading for the door without looking at me. "I'm going to go shower. I'll come back for the cupcakes."

"Okay." My voice is small, shaky, but he doesn't notice because he's already gone.

CHAPTER TWENTY

I step out of my car, shrieking into my phone, "What do you mean you can't go?" Tears prick my eyes. I just got home to get ready for the concert and Caleb's telling me *now* that he can't go? We're supposed to leave for Boston in two hours! "Caleb?" I practically beg into the line, willing him to take back what he said.

"Fuck, I'm sorry, okay? I didn't know my mom—"

"You didn't know, but she knew we had plans," I hiss, my keys shaking in my hands. I haven't been able to move from my spot beside the car. I'm frozen, from anger, sadness, just a whole wave of emotions.

"Salem," he says remorsefully. "I can't say no to this."

I pinch my eyes shut, a tear leaking out the corner of my right eye. His mom got him invited to some sort of dinner with alumni from Harvard. I know, *I know* this is an amazing opportunity for him, but it doesn't lessen my pain, the sting of disappointment.

"You can still go," he insists over my silence, "Lauren can go with you. Or Georgia. Even your mom."

"Lauren's in New York," I remind him. She went with her two sisters for three days. "And Georgia's out with Michael."

"Your mom, then?" He insists.

"My mom..." I hesitate. "She's been really tired lately. It's strange. But I won't drag her out all night to a concert, Caleb, and I'm not going all the way to Boston by myself."

"Salem," he says my name remorsefully.

"I'm mad," I tell him. There's no point in sugarcoating it. He can hear my pain in my words. "This was supposed to be a night for us."

We even have hotel reservations.

"I know, babe. I'm so sorry. I'll be in Boston anyway. You can go with us and just go to the concert by yourself."

"Do you hear yourself?" I argue. "I want to go, believe me, but I wanted to go with you." My tears are coming forcefully now. I hiccup, wiping at my wet face. "Don't worry about it. I'll be fine."

"Salem—"

I hang up and when he immediately calls back, I silence my phone, stuffing it into my pocket. I don't even feel sorry for it.

Covering my face with both hands, my keys fall to the ground. I feel like throwing up, and I'm made even more upset by the fact that I hate that I'm being so dramatic. But I was looking forward to this so much. Caleb and I haven't had much alone time this summer, and it's left me feeling confused and lost. I thought tonight would help me reconnect with him, to feel surer of where we stand with him leaving in just a few days.

And now...

"Are you okay?"

Are you kidding me? The last person I want seeing me breakdown like this stands at the front of my car.

"Ugh." I wipe my snotty nose. "I'm *fine*," I bite, more harshly than I normally would, but with Caleb's news, plus the fact that things have been awkward with Thayer since the day in my kitchen, I just don't have it in me to deal with this.

"What happened?" His eyes narrow upon me, voice gruff.

"Did someone hurt you? I swear to God if it was your preppy pretty-boy boyfriend I'll—"

"He hurt me, but not like you think," I confirm, walking away from him.

"What did he do?" He growls behind me.

"It's none of your business, Thayer."

"You're sobbing on the public street, so that makes it my business."

I give a short, humorless laugh. "No, it doesn't."

"Hey." He grabs my arm, his hold gentle enough for me to pull out of, but I don't bother.

"What?" I look up at him, chin lifted defiantly.

"Tell me what's wrong."

"Give me one good reason why," I argue. I know my face has to be red and splotchy from crying, but I make no move to hide myself.

"Because I care about you."

Dammit, I told him to give me a good reason and he did.

"I was supposed to go to a concert tonight with my boyfriend and he canceled. That's it. I'm being stupid." I drop my gaze, shrugging my shoulders like it's no big deal.

"You're allowed to be upset, Salem." His voice is soft, more gentle than usual. "You're allowed to *feel*. Don't let anyone ever let you think otherwise."

I wipe away fresh tears. "It sucks," I explain. "I was really excited. It's my favorite band, and we were going to spend the night in the city."

He looks me over, his jaw ticking. "I'll take you."

Stunned, I blink at him. "What did you say?"

"I'll take you," he repeats.

It's not possible I heard him right. "I ... you're going to take me to a concert? In Boston?"

"Sure," he shrugs, his shirt pulling taut over his muscular arms and chest, "I don't have anything else going on."

"You have work," I remind him.

"And I own the company, so I call the shots. I can take off tomorrow. We can spend the rest of the day in Boston and come home in the evening. I'll drive us."

"You're serious."

It's a statement, but he answers anyway. "Yes. Do you have both tickets?"

I nod. "Yeah, he gave both to me."

"Good." He releases my arm and takes a couple of steps back. "When do we need to leave?"

"Two hours."

He nods to himself at this timeline. "Okay. Be at my truck then."

"This is seriously happening?"

I can't believe Thayer is swooping in like some knight in shining armor to save the day. It feels too good to be true.

"Seriously," he responds. "You're not missing out on this."

Tears spring to my eyes once more, not like they'd really dried up to begin with. "Thank you."

"You don't have to thank me for this."

"Believe me," I say, getting a little choked up, "I do."

He nods, backing further away. "I'll see you in two hours."

CHAPTER TWENTY-ONE

I'm riding in Thayer's truck.

On our way to Boston.

Together.

I pinch my arm, and sure enough, this is real.

The AC blasts cold air in my face, but I don't mind, and a rock station plays on the radio. The leather interior is a chestnut color, warm and rugged just like Thayer. He drives with one hand on the wheel, his eyes shielded by the pair of sunglasses I bought which makes me smile every time I look at him.

We've been on the road an hour already. My phone continues to blow up with text messages from Caleb.

"Your boyfriend?" Thayer asks, not bothering to take his eyes off the road.

"Yes." I silence my phone, looking out the passenger window.

"You're ignoring him?"

I sigh. "It's petty, I know, but I need to cool off and I can't do that if I talk to him right now, so it's better if I just ignore him. Besides, it's not like we can say anything that hasn't already been said."

Thayer nods, rubbing his jaw with his free hand. "Relationships can be complicated, but I want you to know it's okay to be hurt and upset. Feel what you need to feel."

"I know." I pull the mirror down, checking my makeup. I'll touch it up when we get to the hotel and change into the outfit I got for the concert. Originally, Caleb and I planned to be ready when we left Hawthorne Mills, but we were taking the train which adds time onto the trip. With Thayer driving we'll have time to change at the hotel. Well, I'm changing. Who knows with him. Right now, he's in his usual attire of cargo pants and a t-shirt. If he doesn't change it's no big deal. I mean, he didn't have to do any of this at all. I could be missing out on the concert all together.

"Thank you," I say for what feels like the millionth time since I climbed in his truck.

He grunts. I think it's either another *you're welcome* or *stop thanking me*. I'm not versed in caveman speak.

He turns the volume up on the radio, and I think that's code for he's done talking. That's fine with me. I watch out the window as we approach the city. It's so vastly different than our small town. A whole world apart.

Thayer glances at me every so often as we drive through the bustling streets toward the hotel that's only a few blocks from the concert venue.

"What are you thinking?" he asks, curiosity in his voice.

I crack a small smile. "Probably not what you think I am."

"Enlighten me."

I pick up my bottle of water and take a sip, carefully screwing the cap back on. "I was thinking about how unappealing I find all of this." I wave my fingers at the horde of traffic congestion. "I much prefer our small town."

He rubs his fingers over his lips, trying to hide his smile. "I would think most kids your age would idolize the big city life."

"I'm not a kid." I don't say it defensively, just matter of fact. "And I'm not like most people."

"That you're not."

***

"Where the fuck is the other bed?" Thayer curses, following me inside the hotel room. He sets our bags down. "I'm going to go talk to the concierge."

I grab his arm. "Calm down. I was staying here with Caleb, remember? And they're all booked, I called before we even left home. I'll sleep on the couch."

"You're not sleeping on the couch," he grumbles.

"Well, you're not either," I argue back, flicking on the light in the bathroom. "You're doing me a favor, so you can get the bed."

"I can't believe we're arguing about this." He pinches the bridge of his nose like I'm giving him a headache.

"We can share the bed," I volley back, and before he retorts, I add, "It's a king size bed, Thayer. I can keep to my side, can you?"

"Yes," he growls, eyes darting to the bed. "You got one bed with your boyfriend?"

"Yes." I open my overnight bag on the floor. "He's my boyfriend." His eyes narrow upon me and I roll mine back. "Yes, Thayer, I planned on fucking my boyfriend tonight, but he bailed."

His face reddens. "Don't ... don't say that again."

I laugh, shaking my head. "Men are so weird. Obsessed with sex, but God forbid a woman be open about it."

He wets his lips. "That's not ... just ... *fuck*." He puts his hands on his hips. "Just get ready." He waves me toward the bathroom.

"Are you shooing me away, Thayer?"

"Yes," he huffs.

I shake my head. Flustering Thayer might be my new favorite thing. "You'd think I was talking about murder, not sex. Don't be such a baby."

"Salem." My name is a warning, a threat on his sharp tongue.

I look over my shoulder at him, getting way too much enjoyment out of torturing him. "You didn't think I was a virgin, did you?"

He looks up at the ceiling and I'm pretty sure he says a prayer.

I decide to give the big guy a break and take my clothes to the bathroom. I change out of my jean shorts and tank top into a pair of fake black leather skinny jeans and a black bustier top. The outfit is out of my comfort zone, but I wanted to wear something different tonight. There's also the fact I thought Caleb would be the one taking it off of me at the end of the night.

I fluff my hair up, giving the strands more body, and touch up my makeup. Opening the door, I keep my head down as I hurry into the room and grab my heeled boots. I look up before slipping them on and my breath catches.

Thayer watches me with heated brown eyes, desire evident in the way he looks at me. He scans me from head to toe and my stomach rolls over.

Caleb has never looked at me like this.

Like I'm something precious, a treasure meant to be worshiped. With him staring so unabashedly at me, I stare back. While I was in the bathroom, he changed into a nice pair of jeans and a white v-neck that, like most of his shirts, clings to him like a second skin. It looks like he's even brushed his hair. I wish I could turn my attraction for him off like a switch, but

I can't. It's a curse. But I know this isn't one-sided, not with the way he's looking at me right now.

He clears his throat. "You look nice." He looks away hastily, rifling through his bag like he's just realized he was looking at me for too long.

"So do you." I sit down on the edge of the bed and yank my shoes on. "I'm not used to wearing shoes like this." I wiggle my foot before I zip the shoe. "You might have to hold me steady tonight."

"Whatever you need."

Unbidden, one word comes to mind.

You. I need *you.*

Thayer grabs his wallet from his shorts and stuffs it in the pocket of his jeans. Glancing over his shoulder, he asks, "When should we head over to the venue?"

I check my phone, ignoring the string of text messages from Caleb. I'll reply back to him soon, just not right now. "We can go now. It'll give me a chance to get any merch I want to grab."

"Are you hungry?"

I shake my head. "I'm too excited."

He chuckles. "That means you'll be starving later."

"Exactly." I grab the crossbody bag I packed, stuff some cash, my ID, and phone inside. "Okay, I'm ready now."

He opens the room door, nodding for me to head out first. "Let's go."

CHAPTER TWENTY-TWO

The line is long, snaking around the arena. We stopped and got a bite to eat on the walk over, Thayer insisting, "You might not be hungry, but I am." I ate anyway, because what he said before we left the hotel was true. I might not have been hungry then, but I would've been.

Thayer looks around, hands in his pockets at the gathered crowd of girls ranging in age from about fourteen to late twenties.

"This band ... it's really popular, huh?"

I beam, nodding eagerly. "Yeah. They're amazing."

"I've probably heard some of their stuff, right?" He scratches the back of his head.

"On the radio, I'm sure."

"They're a boyband?"

A girl behind us gasps. "Willow Creek is *not* a boy band. They're a *band*."

"Band ... that consists of *boys*, correct?" Thayer argues. I'd be irritated if he didn't look so genuinely confused.

The girl behind me sighs. "A boyband usually just sings. Willow Creek is a band—with a lead singer, guitarist, bassist, and drummer."

"I got it," he says, but I think he's just placating her. She seems satisfied enough, nodding her head like a job well done.

Thayer runs his fingers through his hair, the line moving forward at a more rapid pace now.

When we near the entrance, I open my bag and search for the tickets.

I pale.

ID, phone, cash ... no fucking tickets.

"Oh my God," I turn to Thayer with horror-filled eyes, "I left the tickets in the room."

"No, you didn't," he insists with a shake of his head. "Salem," he growls my name.

Tears pinch my eyes. This is the *worst* day ever. "We have to go back to the hotel." My chin quivers with the threat of tears. "We have time."

Not much, not since we stopped to eat, but we can make it work. I'll miss the opening artist, possibly even Willow Creek's first few songs, but I won't miss the whole concert and that counts for something.

Thayer shakes his head and grabs my hand, pulling me out of line and over to the ticket booth. "Wait here," he instructs in a growly tone, walking up to the window where SOLD OUT blazes.

"Thayer," I beg. "We're wasting time. Let me get an Uber."

He ignores me, tapping on the window forcefully.

I cover my face with embarrassment while he speaks to the person. He's wasting precious time. His name is on the tip of my tongue, to beg and plead for him to hurry up so I have some sort of chance of seeing the show. I watch him nod and take something before returning to my side. "We're good to go."

"Huh?"

A door suddenly opens and the person he was speaking to at the ticket booth waves us hurriedly inside.

"What's going on?" I hiss at Thayer, letting security look through my bag.

He pulls two tickets out of his pocket.

"Thayer," I practically whine his name, "I had tickets, what did you do? Buy two more? It said they were sold out. How did you even...?" I trail off, my eyes zeroing in on the tickets. "Those are pit," I state.

The tickets Caleb purchased were *good* tickets, nothing to complain about, but these are amazing—what dreams are made of.

"I know." He says it so calmly, so assuredly.

"They had to cost a lot of money."

The man beside me shrugs. *Shrugs.* Like, "No biggie."

"Thayer," I continue, "this had to cost thousands."

"It doesn't matter what it costs. I want you to be happy." His forehead creases at this admission, like he didn't mean to say it out loud.

"We could've gone back to the hotel," I point out, looking through the glass doors we came through.

"And you would've missed part of it."

"It wouldn't have been the end of the world."

"Salem?"

"Yes?" I arch a brow, curious.

"Just say thank you."

I smile up at him, at this man who I realize has become my friend. "Thank you."

He dips his chin. "You're welcome."

His warm hand settles on the small of my back, steering me toward where we need to go. I'm glad one of us is paying attention.

We pass the merch booth and I study the items, trying to figure out what I like so I can grab something during intermission. "I love that shirt." I point to one hanging up at the top. It's navy blue with the band's logo of a Willow Tree with a tire swing all in white with neon blue outlining it.

Thayer grunts out a response.

As we search for a good viewing spot in the pit, girls run around screaming, shrieking with excitement. I don't join in their theatrics. I'm sure I will later, but right now I'm too stunned.

"Wow." I try to take it all in, letting Thayer tug me along. With his big body he moves much easier through the crowd of people. Some people give dirty looks, but I ignore it.

I'm at a Willow Creek concert—something I've dreamed of for years.

Sure, I was supposed to be here with Caleb, but...

Guilt settles inside me when I realize I'm happy I'm here with Thayer.

I eye the man at my side, wondering why I have to be so taken with him. Why can't I look at him like everyone else? Why does he, of all people, have to stir something inside me? It's not fair.

Thayer finally reaches a spot he must deem good enough because we stop walking and he looks down at me. "Stay *right* here. I'll be back."

"I—" He's already gone before I can say another word.

Pulling my phone from my pocket, I turn it back on and read through the string of texts. I had let my mom know I made it to Boston, so I text her again to tell her I'm at the concert and will let her know when I'm back at the hotel. It'll be late, but I know it'll make her feel better to have me check in, even if it wakes her up. I told her Thayer was bringing me and when she asked why he would do something like that. I lied. I said he had business he needed to handle in Boston, so it wasn't out of his way.

Now, not only have I dragged this man to the city and to a hotel overnight, but he's had to buy new tickets. Pit tickets at that. I know they weren't cheap, not for a band of this caliber. My stomach roils. I'll never be able to pay him back for this—literally or figuratively.

Scrolling through Caleb's texts, mostly 'I'm sorrys' and 'I'll make this up to you', I figure out what to say.

Me: School is important to you. Football too. I get that. Don't worry about me. Enjoy the dinner and make connections.

As soon as I send the text, reply dots appear, but I shut my phone off. I want to enjoy tonight, and Caleb needs to focus on his.

The lights begin to dim, the opening act getting ready to take the stage. I worry Thayer won't be able to find me, but I promised I wouldn't move, so I don't.

The band starts up, and I lose myself in the music. It's a small indie band, and I love that Willow Creek is giving their platform to a smaller artist to help them build their own career.

They're on their third song when I feel a hand on my elbow. I look up into brown eyes, glowing blue, then pink, then green from the neon lights.

"For you," he says in that rough tone he uses a lot.

"What?" I blink at him.

He holds out a bag and a bottle of water. He keeps the other bottle for himself. "For you," he repeats.

I open the bag hesitantly, like something might jump out at me. I can't make out any of the lyrics of the song being played because I'm too zeroed in on what's in the bag.

"Thayer," I say his name softly, I doubt he hears it, tears rushing to my eyes. Inside is the shirt I pointed out along with a tote bag and beanie. "You didn't need to do that," I tell him, speaking loud enough for him to hear me. "But thank you." I don't want him to think I'm not grateful, because I am. Extremely so. "This is ... way more than I ever expected. Thank you."

"You're welcome." He's nodding along to the music, not paying attention to me, and I'm not sure if that's because to him it's really no big deal or because he's trying to give me a moment to rein in my emotions. I wish now I had brought a bigger bag, and as if he senses my thoughts, he scoops the plain black bag out of my hands. "I'll hold onto this."

I flash him a grateful smile.

The opening band plays three more songs before they exit the stage. Excitement pulses in the air, the energy electric.

"It's happening!" I clap my hands excitedly, grinning up at my broody companion. The lights go dark and then one spotlight comes on. From somewhere an electric guitar starts playing. "Oh my God!" I put my hands around Thayer's muscular arm and give it a shake. Then Joshua Hayes comes into view in the spotlight. It's like the crowd isn't even there as he completely tears it up on the guitar. "That's Hayes," I scream, pointing like Thayer can't see him.

The guitar cuts off and he fades into the darkness when the light goes out.

Then the drums start, and I jump up and down, screaming like the girl beside me. She starts crying. "Maddox! Oh my God, I love you!" When the spotlight reveals him behind his drum set, I worry she might faint.

Like with Hayes, the light cuts out the sound of the drums ceasing.

Next is the sound of the bass and the light cuts to Ezra strumming lazily at the instrument, his curly black hair flopping over his forehead.

The lights cut out again and a hush falls over the arena.

My hand is still clutched around his arm, but he makes no move to shake me off.

It feels like we're all collectively holding our breath, then the music starts up again, all the lights exploding at once and revealing the entire band.

Matthias Wade—the lead singer and twin brother of the drummer—croons into the mic and I think I swoon a bit. The brooding, intense singer is my favorite. I steal a look at Thayer. Maybe I have a type.

He bends down to my ear, his lips brushing my sensitive skin when he speaks. "This is pretty good."

"I told you!" At least, I think I told him. I start dancing and Thayer smiles—a big, blinding, too good for this world smile. "This is the best night of my life!" I give him this truth and he takes it, pleased to have given this to me.

Thayer Holmes might not realize how special he is, but I know.

CHAPTER TWENTY-THREE

I'm on a high as we walk into the hotel room.

I spin in a circle, my arms outstretched as I sing one of my favorite Willow Creek songs in a very out of tune voice. But I don't care. Tonight was amazing. Out of this world.

"Out of this world, huh?" Thayer asks, locking the door up behind us.

"Did I say that out loud?" My cheeks are flushed.

"Yeah." His eyes sparkle with amusement.

"Well, it's true." I collapse on the bed. "Can you help me get these off?" I lift one leg, wiggling my foot.

He shakes his head but doesn't argue. He takes hold of my foot and unzips my boot. "Damn, that's really on there." He wiggles it back and forth and finally my foot is free. He sets my boot down on the ground and grabs my other foot. That one comes off easier.

I already texted my mom when we got back to the hotel, and she replied right away that she was glad I was safe and had fun.

There was one text from Caleb.

Caleb: You're important to me too. I love you.

Guilt settled inside me, and I texted back that I loved him too.

"My feet hurt," I whine, sitting up and rubbing the heel of

my right foot. “I’m never wearing shoes like that ever again.”

He chuckles. “I don’t blame you. These never fail me.” He points at his work boots.

Standing up, I grab my pajamas from my bag. “I’m going to shower, if that’s okay.”

“Take your time.” He sits down, removing his own shoes.

“Need any help with those?” I joke.

He gives me a half-smile. “I’ve got it.”

“If you’re sure.” I wink and shut myself in the bathroom.

Oh my God! Salem! Why did you wink at him?

Ugh. I hate myself.

I turn the shower on and while it warms, I remove my makeup. Despite my lack of skill, it managed to hold up decently through the night. My mascara did smear beneath my eyes a bit, but it could’ve been worse.

Hopping in the shower, I use the shower gel the hotel provided to lather up my body. It smells strongly of orange and vanilla. When I feel like all the sweat has been washed off my body, I turn off the shower and step out on the small towel, drying my body and slipping into my pair of sleep shorts and an oversized t-shirt.

“Your turn,” I tell Thayer, exiting the bathroom with a trail of steamy air following me.

He stifles a yawn. “Thanks.”

He’s already turned the bed back and clearly picked a side, so I take the other. A soft sound leaves my lips when my body sinks into the comfy mattress. Tonight was amazing, but I’m exhausted. I stifle a yawn, waiting for Thayer to come to bed before I crash.

When the shower turns on, I try not to think about Thayer being in there naked, but it only makes me think about it more.

I cover my face with my hands, groaning. "Hormones," I mutter, the sound muffled. "This has to be out of control hormones."

It's the only thing that makes sense.

Scooting down into the bed, I grab my phone and check my social media. I don't post a lot on my personal account, but I've been trying to build the one I have for my candles in case one day I decide to turn that into something bigger. Five new followers and I haven't even posted this week. Not bad. I've only been working on building the page for a year and it's already nearing two-thousand followers. It's nothing compared to other accounts, but I'm pretty proud of my little venture.

The bathroom door opens, and Thayer asks, "Do you want me to leave the bathroom light on?"

"It doesn't matter to me."

He decides to leave it on and closes the door so only a thin stream of light leaks into the bedroom.

His bare feet pad across the floor and he removes his watch from his wrist, laying it on the table and then plugging his phone in to charge.

I stifle a yawn, trying not to ogle Thayer in the pair of sweatpants he wears. It's practically indecent the way the fabric hugs his...

"See something you like?" His tone is surprisingly flirty and a flush heats my cheeks.

"No." I lie, sinking beneath the covers and pulling them up to my chin.

"Sure," he grunts, eyes narrowing upon me. "Are you going to jump me if I sleep without a shirt?"

"No shirt I can handle."

Fuck. I want to facepalm myself. I just implied that if he removed his pants I *would* jump him. Ugh.

He yanks off his t-shirt and settles onto the bed. Since it's a king size there's plenty of space between us, enough for a whole other body, maybe two.

"Thank you for tonight," I tell him for the millionth time. "You have no idea what it meant to me."

"You don't have to keep thanking me."

"I know, but—"

"But nothing," he responds. "I was happy to do it."

My voice is practically a squeak when I ask, "Why?"

Why would he do this for me? A man that's over a decade older than me. He's my neighbor. My boss. He owes me nothing.

He's quiet for a moment. I can sense him struggling with something. Finally, he hands over his answer like he's giving me something precious to cherish. "Because I wanted to." His eyes flicker over me. "I don't do things I don't want to, Salem. I'm a selfish man."

Man. He lays that word between us like a grenade, reminding me gently that while we might be lying in the same bed, he's thirty-one and I'm eighteen.

He doesn't wait for me to reply. He turns the light out on his side of the bed. "Night, Salem."

I whisper back, "Goodnight."

CHAPTER TWENTY-FOUR

"N-No! No! NO!" I thrash my arms and legs, fighting off an adversary that feels so very real.

"Salem," a familiar voice speaks past the terror crawling through my body. "*Salem.* I have you. You're safe. *Wake up, dammit!*"

I feel warm hands on my face, the weight of something against me.

"Don't touch me!" I scream. "Stop," I beg the body pressing against me. I throw my arms around, nails ready to claw. "Get off of me! I'm your daughter," I sob, begging and pleading though I know it'll do no good, it never does, "stop, I'm your daughter."

A gasp penetrates my nightmare, and the weight vanishes. "Wake up," the same voice begs. "*Please*, wake up."

My eyes fly open, my body drenched in sweat. I cry, tears wetting my face.

"Hey," Thayer says, his hand hovers above me and then he gently, hesitantly, brushes my sweaty hair off my face. "You're okay. You're safe with me."

He doesn't just say that I'm safe, he makes sure to emphasize that I'm safe with *him*.

My whole body shakes and I can't stop crying.

"Is this okay?" He continues to stroke my face, his body above mine. One of his knees rests between my legs. I nod, my bottom lip trembling. "Your nightmare..." He pauses, closing his eyes. A pained look punctures his face. "It was real, wasn't it? A memory?"

I nod brokenly. It seems to be the only thing I can do in the moment.

"Fuck," he growls. "Salem."

I shake my head back and forth roughly. I don't want him to say it. I don't want to talk about it. Therapy has helped me so much, but there are those residual things that haven't gone away—like my nightmares. Some scars don't heal as quickly as others.

"What can I do?"

"Nothing," I gasp, struggling to get enough oxygen into my lungs.

He can't fix this. No one can. I just have to deal with it.

Thayer stares down at me, a haunted look in his eyes as he sees the demons swirling in mine.

"I'm sorry," he says, his fingers still stroking my face gently, with so much reverence. "I'm so sorry, Salem. That should've never happened to you." He clears his throat and tears swim in his eyes. "Fuck, I'm just so sorry."

It's on the tip of my tongue, to say those words that we all say to try to make things okay, but if I say "I'm all right" it would be a lie and we'd both know it.

"Can you hold me?" My voice sounds so small, so incredibly broken.

Beneath the window, to my right, the AC kicks on and I jump.

Thayer nods, swallowing thickly. "I'll hold you as long as you want me to."

He rolls back onto the bed, gathering me into his arms. My leg wraps around him. His warmth seeps into me, and I soak in every ounce of comfort. My hand splays on his bare skin, my fingers rubbing against the chest hair smattered across his pectoral muscles. He has one of his hands curled around my arm and rubs his thumb in small circles, around and around. With his other hand, he cups the back of my head, gently massaging. I try my best to get my breath under control. If I keep hyperventilating it won't end well.

"Breathe," he murmurs, as if sensing this.

I squish my eyes closed. "I'm trying." I rub my damp face against his bare chest.

I'm *cuddling* Thayer. Holy hell. It's like I've stepped into some sort of alternate universe. Granted, I'm not all up in his business for any sort of fun reason, but it doesn't matter. I'm in his arms. He's holding me.

"I'm right here," he soothes, his fingers stroking through my hair. "I'm not leaving you. You're not alone." The reminder that I'm not alone sends relief coursing through my veins. "I've got you." I jolt at the gentle press of his lips against my forehead. I'm not sure he even realizes he's done it. He's too busy trying to calm me down and comfort me.

"I'm so sorry," I hiccup.

"For what?" I can feel him tilt his head down my way, and I reluctantly open my eyes.

"Waking you up."

"Salem," he growls, his chest rumbling with the two syllables of my name. "Don't be fucking sorry. I can't fucking take you being sorry for *this*."

I don't think it sunk in before now that I was talking in my sleep. That means he *knows*.

Oh, God. I stiffen in his arms, and he senses this, trying to pull away because he thinks I don't want to be touched. I quickly latch back onto him like a koala bear. I don't want his warmth, his comfort, going anywhere.

"Please, don't look at me differently after this. *Please.*"

He holds me tighter. "Never."

Somehow, some way, in the sanctuary of his arms, I drift back to sleep.

***

"Oh my God!" I wake up, crying out with pleasure, my hips undulating against something hard. My orgasm hits me so forcefully that flashes of light shimmer across my eyes, blocking everything else out. I moan, coming down from the high, but my hips continue to rock and rock and—

"Oh my God," I gasp for an entirely different reason, everything coming into focus around me.

The hotel room.

My nightmare.

Thayer holding me.

Mortification reddens my face as I take in the situation. My crotch pressed against his muscled thigh, hands splayed on his chest, and his brown eyes watching me in awe.

Panic surges in my veins.

I can't believe that happened. I know I was still half-asleep, but that doesn't change the fact that I just got myself off on his leg. I cover my mouth with my hand.

"I didn't mean to," I mumble around my fingers.

"It's—"

Yanking myself from his body, the blankets, from the bed itself, I tumble to the floor and grab my bag, secluding myself in the bathroom where he can't see me, but I can't escape my embarrassment.

I grip the edges of the granite counter in my hands, leaning forward. I'm out of breath, cheeks flushed, hair a mess. I look exactly like I just had a good fuck which is apparently what I was attempting to do in my sleep.

And if that wasn't bad enough, I had a nightmare he had to comfort me from. I brought one of my sleeping pills with me, intending to take it so I'd be knocked out and that wouldn't happen. Since I normally don't take them it slipped my mind.

Grabbing my toothbrush, I wet it under the water and slather on a ridiculous amount of toothpaste in my haste. I'm a mess.

After braiding my hair to the side, I change out of my pajamas into the fresh pair of shorts I packed and a cropped t-shirt that says All Love on it.

I keep expecting Thayer to knock on the door and ask if I'm okay, or to demand I talk about what happened, but I realize that's not really his style.

Smoothing stray hairs away from my face, I take a deep breath, burying my embarrassment down deep.

I open the door and step out to find Thayer already changed, snapping his watch into place on his wrist.

God, he has nice hands.

SALEM! You just orgasmed on the man's leg, now is not the time to be thinking about his hands! Get a grip!

There's a tray on the table with coffee, orange juice, water, and various breakfast items ranging from a muffin to a bagel with cream cheese and a few cereal options.

"I went downstairs," he says by way of explanation. "Wasn't sure what you might want so I grabbed a bit of everything."

I take the blueberry muffin that has some sort of streusel

concoction on top. "Thank you."

Don't think about what happened, I chant to myself, or else I'll lock myself in the bathroom again.

Carrying the muffin and orange juice over to the chair in the corner, I sit down to eat.

"After you eat, we'll head out." Thayer's already scanning the room, even getting down to peer under the bed to make sure nothing has dropped there. As if we've been here for a whole week and made a mess of the place.

"Okay." I brush crumbs off the arm of the chair to the floor. I feel his eyes on me, watching and appraising my behavior.

The adult thing would be to talk about what happened, but in this moment, I feel very much eighteen. Young and stupid. Finishing my muffin, I down the rest of the orange juice and grab my bag.

"All right, I'm ready." He effortlessly slides the bag down my arm, throwing it over his own shoulder. "You don't need to do that."

"It's fine, Salem." His eyes are soft, no hint of walls being put up after what happened this morning and last night. In fact, he seems more open than usual.

I dip my head. "Okay."

Thayer loads the car, and I check us out since the room is in my name. When I exit the lobby, his truck is parked at the front, and he messes with the radio.

When I open the door and climb inside, a song from Willow Creek is playing. I can't help it, I grin. He notices, because Thayer misses nothing.

"What?" He asks innocently. "They're not so bad."

I shake my head, still smiling, and strap the seatbelt across my body.

CHAPTER TWENTY-FIVE

I jolt awake when the engine to Thayer's truck cuts off. "We're home," he announces unnecessarily.

"When did I fall asleep?" I rub my eyes, stifling a yawn.

We ended up heading straight home instead of hanging around Boston for the day.

He looks at the clock on the dashboard. "About thirty minutes ago."

Not too long then.

I open the door to get out, and he follows suit. "I'll take your bag to the door."

"I've got it." I brush a strand of blond hair behind my ear. "It's not heavy."

"I'm carrying your bag, Salem." His tone brooks no room for argument. I walk side by side with him down the driveway, pausing at the side door. He waits for me to slide the key in the lock before he sets my bag down.

"I owe you all the cupcakes for this." I open the door wide, standing on the top step.

He watches me carefully and I wish I knew what he was thinking. "You don't owe me anything."

With that, he turns and walks away, leaving me alone with my thoughts.

***

The doorbell rings sometime after two and I'm not surprised to come downstairs to find Caleb on the front porch.

Opening the door, I give him a small timid smile. "Hi."

"Hey." He clasps his hands in front of him, his smile as thin as mine. His shoulders sag and he runs his hand through his hair. "Fuck, Salem, I'm so sorry. I'm an ass." He drops his head. "You have every right to hate me."

"I don't hate you. I was hurt—*am* hurt," I amend. "But I don't hate you."

He rubs a hand over the side of his nose, a nervous gesture. "My mom knew we had the concert. I don't know why she signed me up for the dinner. I—"

I hold up a hand silencing him. "It was an opportunity you couldn't pass up. I understand."

As I've had time to cool down, I know it was too good for him to say no to. Does that make it hurt any less? Not really, but I won't stand in the way of Caleb's dream. It would be selfish of me, and I won't be that girl. Besides, I orgasmed on my neighbor's leg so it's not like I'm a saint in this situation either.

He nods, but it seems wooden, like he's not sure. "Are you going to come in?" I ask him, and he gives me a genuine smile.

"I thought maybe I wasn't allowed."

I roll my eyes playfully. Grabbing him by the shirt I yank him inside. "Get in here."

***

"Do you want to stay for dinner?" I watch Caleb pull his shirt back on, covering his chest from my eager eyes. I search the floor for my bra and slip it on. He spins his finger, motioning for me to turn around. He clasps my bra back into place. His lips press a tender kiss to the back of my neck.

"Do you want me to?"

I laugh, scooping up my tank top. "I wouldn't ask if I didn't want you to."

"All right." He buttons his jeans. "Are you cooking it? I can help."

I nod. "I'd love that."

Both fully dressed, we make our way downstairs and I dig through the fridge searching for something I can throw together to make a meal. I set a pack of chicken breast out from the freezer and then find a frozen bag of veggies. Caleb grabs the chicken and pops it in the microwave to defrost.

I set out some seasoning for the chicken, turning to find Caleb leaning against the counter watching me.

"What?" I ask, tying my hair back in a ponytail.

He smiles, his eyes lighting up. "I can't watch my hot as fuck girlfriend?"

"Caleb," I laugh, shaking my head in embarrassment. Turning to the sink, I wash my hands. I realize we really do need to talk. In hindsight, I shouldn't have pulled him straight up to my room for sex, but I still felt out of sorts after what happened this morning with Thayer.

I needed to erase the memories of getting myself off on Thayer's thigh from my brain.

Only now I'm thinking about it again.

Ugh.

Rubbing a hand over my face, I blow out a breath. "I want to move past this," I start off with, and Caleb cocks his head to the side listening. "I'm not the best at talking things out, but I know we do need to talk."

"Okay," he hedges.

"I said I accepted your apology and I mean it," I insist, opening the bag of veggies and spreading them on a pan, adding some olive oil, salt, and pepper. "But I need to be honest, that it did hurt me. It *does* hurt me, when you do this." He opens his mouth to speak, but I hold up a hand, begging him to let me finish what I have to say. "You're leaving," I remind him. "In just a few days you'll be gone and I just ... wanted to spend as much time with you as I could." Treacherous tears sting my eyes. "It feels like everything is changing. *We're* changing. And it scares me."

"Salem," he murmurs, reaching for my arms and tugging me into his body. He's leaner than Thayer, a little bit shorter, but his body is warm and full of comfort. "I love you. This isn't going to change us."

I squish my eyes closed, holding on tighter like I can make sure he doesn't disappear.

But something tells me that no matter how snug I hold on, things are going to change anyway.

CHAPTER TWENTY-SIX

Lauren and I swing our legs back and forth, soaring into the air on the swing set at our local park. There are no kids around, so it's not like we're hogging them from the children. In fact, as it nears sunset, it's eerily quiet. There's an older couple walking their golden retriever and us. That's it. It's like everyone's gone... just like Caleb. He left for Boston yesterday. He FaceTimed me last night, showing me his dorm, and despite feeling sad at his absence I couldn't help but be genuinely happy for him. This is what he's always wanted.

"How are you feeling?" Lauren asks, interrupting the quiet between us.

I know she means about Caleb. "I'm okay," I assure her. "Sad, of course, but I knew this was going to happen."

She bites her lip, twisting the swing around. "I've been thinking."

"That's dangerous," I joke.

"Ha." She leans over, pushing my shoulder. "I know it's crazy, but I need a change of scenery. An adventure."

"Okay?" I hedge, urging her to go on when she doesn't elaborate.

"I want to move to New York. *City*," she adds. "I ... I don't know. When I was there with my sister I felt like that's where I'm meant to be."

"Wow." Her confession is unexpected. She hasn't mentioned this at all.

"I know, I know," she chants, shaking her head. "This wasn't my plan at all. I'm supposed to start community college next week." Her voice squeaks at the end. "But ... I won't be happy, Salem. I know I won't. I want bigger things. I already talked to my advisor, and I can take my classes online. I don't want to give up on college completely, but this way I don't have to stay here."

"You've given this a lot of thought, haven't you?" She nods, pumping her legs to gain more height as she swings.

"I hate leaving you like this. That's why I want you to come with me." She brightens, slowing to a stop. "We can be roommates. Get jobs waitressing and be discovered by some awesome talent scout."

"And what are our talents exactly?" I joke.

She wiggles her nose. "I haven't figured that part out yet."

"I'm excited for you. If this is what you want, I won't stop you. But I ... I'm staying here, Lo."

She ducks her head, dark hair shielding her face. "I understand."

"Are you looking at apartments?"

Her gaze drops. "I already put a deposit on one. It's small, of course, but it's going to be mine and that's all that matters."

"I don't want you to go." She already knows this, goodbyes suck. "But I'm so happy for you. You deserve to do whatever your heart wants and if it's moving to New York, do it. I'll always be your cheerleader."

She smiles. "You've always believed in me."

I roll my eyes, fighting a smile. "It's not a big deal. I know you'll succeed at whatever you set your mind to." I pause, rubbing my lips together in thought. "When do you leave?"

Her smile falls. "Next Wednesday."

I drop my head. “I thought it might’ve been even sooner.”

“The offer will always stand for you to move in with me. Like I said, it’s small, but there’s a loft for an extra bed.”

“You never know, I might take you up on it.”

She reaches over, squeezing my hand. “I hope you’ll go shopping with me. I want to buy a few things for the apartment before I go. New bedding, some dishes, stuff like that.”

I squeeze her hand back. “Of course.”

Leaning back, I start swinging again, letting the last of the sun’s summer rays warm my face.

Everybody kept telling me this summer would be different from all the previous ones. I didn’t quite believe them, but they were right. It’s been full of change. It’s scary, exhilarating, but I realize this has been the first step into our adult lives. Of course change was inevitable.

Caleb’s in Boston, Lauren is moving to New York City, and me?

I don’t know what’s in store for me, but for the first time in a long time, I’m excited to find out.

CHAPTER TWENTY-SEVEN

I pause in surprise at the end of my driveway. It's a little after five in the morning, so I guess it's no surprise really that I'm up for a run. What *is* a surprise is Thayer leaning against the lamp post in a pair of long jogging shorts and an old t-shirt with his company's logo faded on top.

"What are you doing?" I bend down, tightening the laces on my right shoe.

"What? I can't hang out against the street light at five in the morning? Isn't this normal?" His lips lift into a smile.

"Is that a joke?" I know it is. I stand up straight, hands on my hips. "Are you making jokes with me now, Thayer?"

He shrugs. "Sure, why not?" He moves away from the light, stretching his arms above his head and gracing me with a sliver of his stomach. My core clenches at the sight. "I thought I'd join you on your run."

"Am I that predictable?"

He frowns, a dark look stealing over his face. "Yes."

Stretching my legs, I look up at him skeptically. "You've never run with me before, so why now?"

He looks away, jaw taut. "It'll be good for my health."

"Sure." I don't believe him one bit, but I also have no reason to suspect him of lying.

I arch a brow. "And you think you can keep up with me?"

He grins. "I think I can."

***

"You do that every morning?" Thayer huffs, trying to catch his breath. We're stopped outside his house stretching.

"Pretty much. Except when it gets too cold, then I use my membership for the twenty-four-hour gym over by the grocery store."

His brows furrow deeply. "You're too young to be going to a gym like that at any hour."

"When I need to run I don't have much choice," I argue, stretching my calves.

He shakes his head. "I don't want you going there so early on your own."

I give him the stink eye. "I've been doing it for years."

He makes a sound like he tried to swallow his own tongue. "Worrying about you is going to be the end of me."

"All right, Dad."

He glares. "Do not ever call me that."

I pale. "Sorry, it was a joke." Color quickly returns to my cheeks when I remember that I *humped* his leg.

He shakes his head. "I didn't mean to sound so harsh."

"It's okay." I walk away from him, toward my house.

"Wait," he calls, his hand wrapping around my arm.

I look over my shoulder at him, biting my bottom lip. "Come inside. Please?"

I can't resist his warm brown eyes. I'm a complete sucker for this man. "Why?"

I want him to give me a good reason—a reason to say yes, even though I should most definitely say no.

"Because I want you to."

Damn him.

I give a tiny nod. It's barely a shake of my head, but with the way he's staring at me, he doesn't miss it. Tipping his head at his house for me to follow, I fall into step beside him. His arm brushes mine, sending my heart tripping over itself.

Unlocking the front door, he lets me in first. "I'm going to make breakfast. You want any?"

"Sure."

In the kitchen he grabs a carton of eggs from the mini-fridge and some bread for toast. He's added a portable stovetop to his smorgasbord of temporary appliances.

"When are the appliances due in?" I take the bread from him to pop some in the toaster.

"They're telling me this week." He grabs a cup to crack the eggs into. I watch his movements, the way his biceps work, and unbidden my eyes drop to his athletic shorts and the way they cling to the shape of him.

"You sound doubtful." I push the button down, watching the bread disappear and forcing myself not to look at Thayer's dick. At the thought of his dick my stupid, treacherous eyes dart back to his crotch.

He clears his throat and I redden at being caught. I look away hastily.

He scrambles the eggs together. "They said the same last week, so I'm not trusting their understanding of how long a week is. I think they're just trying to appease me."

"It's looking beautiful, though." The cabinets are a sage green color and he picked white counters with streaks of gold running through it. I find the combination to be unique and beautiful.

"Thanks." He pours the eggs into the hot skillet. I keep my eyes on his hands which is *almost* as bad. He has nice hands.

"Seriously, you're doing a great job with the place."

He gives a half-smile. "I knew it would take a while to get it where I want it, but it'll be worth it in the end."

"The best things take patience and time."

He chuckles. "I guess that's why I love puzzles so much."

I take this morsel of information he's handed to me, cradling it into my palm gently, holding onto it like a treasure.

"You like puzzles?"

"Mhmm," he hums, using a spatula to move the eggs around. The toast pops up and I grab plates and butter.

"Like puzzles you buy in a box, in a bunch of little pieces, put them on a table, kind of puzzle?"

He laughs—truly *laughs*. I think it might be my new favorite sound in the world. "Yeah, I'm working on one right now." He motions to the card table. "I can only do small ones at the moment, which isn't as enjoyable for me, but it's a nice decompressor in the evenings."

With the toast slathered in butter, I walk over to see the puzzle he's working on. It's a field of lavender. "It's beautiful."

"I know that's a lavender field, but it reminded me of all the wildflowers behind our houses."

The wildflowers are one of my favorite things about living here. Before Thayer moved in I used to wish my room overlooked them, but Georgia got that space. "I love the wildflowers," I murmur, picking up a piece of the puzzle and eyeing the shape of it.

"You do?"

I look at him over my shoulder and give him a nod. "Yeah, why would I lie about that?"

He shrugs, adding the eggs to the plate. "It's just ... I guess I would think a girl your age would find them ugly, a nuisance.

In the way, I suppose."

"No." I put the piece back with the others. "Wildflowers are strong. Resilient. They can grow under most conditions. I want to be like that." I let my hair down, his eyes watching my movements. "I want to have the confidence of wildflowers—to never give up, to flourish, and thrive."

He rubs his stubbled jaw. "I've never thought about it like that. I like your way of thinking." He sets our plates down on the table. "Orange juice?"

"Yes, please." He pours two glasses, and we sit down to eat. "Thanks for running with me this morning."

He waves away my thanks. "It was nice to run again."

"I expected you to be huffing and puffing."

He narrows those chocolate-colored eyes on me. "Are you implying I'm out of shape?"

I look over his muscular build. "Well, no. Certainly not that. But a lot of people are in shape and can't run. Cardio is hardio."

His lips twitch like he wants to laugh but doesn't want to give in to the temptation. "*Hardio*," he mouths with a shake of his head like he can't believe such a stupid made up word came out of my mouth.

"It's the truth." I take a bite of eggs. "Wow, these are really good."

"I add cheese."

"Really? I didn't notice."

Another twitch of his lips. "You were too busy staring at my..." He pauses, the bastard. "Puzzle."

Now it's my turn. "It's a very nice ... puzzle."

"You like puzzles, huh?"

The fact that puzzle has suddenly turned into a euphemism

for package doesn't escape me. Or at least I *think* that's what's happening here.

"Some of them."

He rubs his fingers over his lips. There's been a line between us, a blurry one, but it's been there. I feel like the night in the hotel blurred it even more, and now we're more willing to toe past it. I've never been attracted to guys much older than me. With my trauma, that was never something I could stomach, but I'm attracted to Thayer for so many different reasons and his age isn't one of them.

"Eat your food," he says in a gruff voice, and I swear there's pink in his cheeks.

I let him take another bite of food before I ask, "Are we not going to talk about the fact that I orgasmed on your leg?"

He chokes, pieces of egg flying out of his mouth. "Fuck, Salem. Warn a guy before you say something like that."

"Why?" I smile brightly. "This was way more fun."

He wipes up the mess with a napkin. "You are a menace." Recovering from my surprise attack, he asks, "Do you want to talk about it?"

I shrug. "Not really, but I thought the mature thing to do would be to talk about it."

His eyes narrow. "If you want me to forget it ever happened, I will. After ... *fuck*, Salem, after your nightmare, what I learned, I didn't want to bring it up and frighten you or something, okay? I wasn't trying to brush it under the rug."

I tuck a piece of hair behind my ear. The shorter strands never stay in my ponytail when I'm running. "It's okay, I was just joking around. It was embarrassing." Normally I wouldn't be bold enough to bring it up, but I haven't been able to get the incident off my mind.

"Hey." The tip of his finger lifts my chin. "Don't hide from me. Ever. I see you. I want to see you. All of you." I bite my lip, tears stinging my eyes. "I know I can be a dick, but I would never push you to talk about anything you don't want to."

"I know." And I do know it. Thayer isn't the pushy type. Quiet and broody? Yes. But not pushy. Changing the subject, I ask around a bite of toast, "Are you running every morning now?"

Today was the first time I've had a nightmare since we got back from Boston, so I can't be sure when he started.

He shrugs. "Just when I feel like it."

"Hmm," I hum. Searching for the coffee pot, I ask, "Did you make any coffee this morning?"

He shakes his head, cringing. "I'm out."

I mock gasp. "Out of coffee? That's a crime."

He arches a brow. "We can go get some."

I wave away his words with a flick of my hand. "It's no biggie. I'll get some later."

"I have some Diet Coke if you want that?"

I perk up. "I'll never say no to that." With a shake of his head, he gets up from the table and returns with a bottle. I take it gratefully. "Thank you." Popping the top, I take a generous sip. "This is better than coffee."

He groans. "I don't know about that."

"Well, *I* think it is."

Finishing my breakfast, I wash my plate up in the kitchen sink—yes, there's finally a sink. Thayer is moving on up in the world.

He steps up beside me, his body heat radiating against me. My eyes close, and I bite my lip so I don't moan. Everything about this man draws me in.

Caleb, I chant. *You have Caleb. You love him. You can't hurt him.*

Even though this summer wasn't ideal with Caleb, I do love him. I care about him so much. Being attracted to Thayer? I can't be. I need to stop.

Stepping away from him, I force a smile. "Thanks for running with me."

"Salem," he calls after me, but I don't stop.

I close the front door behind me and inhale a breath.

Get a grip, Salem.

CHAPTER TWENTY-EIGHT

Binx meows from the corner of the workshop behind A Checkered Past Antiques. "I know, buddy," I croon from across the room, pouring wax into the glass jars I use for my candles. "We'll go home soon. I'm almost done."

I'm working overtime to keep my fall scents out in the store. It's only mid-September but several have already sold out. I'm happy people love my candles because making them gets my mind off of other things.

I bring Binx with me from time to time. I think he appreciates getting out of the house and in a new environment for a while.

My phone rings, startling me and I curse when some of the hot wax hits my fingers. I finish pouring and swipe to accept the call.

"Hey, babe," Caleb's voice comes over the line.

My chest aches from missing him. "Hey. How are things?"

I can't believe he's already been gone a month. Lauren left two weeks ago. She's insistent that I come visit soon.

"It's school," he says like that's the only explanation needed. "I wish I could see your face."

"You could FaceTime me?" I laugh. "I look like shit, though."

When I make candles, I toss my hair up in a messy bun and wear old clothes so it doesn't matter if I ruin them.

"You're always beautiful." He switches the call to FaceTime

and I swipe to accept it.

"I warned you." I blow a piece of hair from my eyes.

He grins, his eyes sparkling. His dorm room sits behind him. I can tell he's at his desk, his bed behind him. "Nah, you look hot." I roll my eyes. "You do," he insists. "It's getting kind of late. When are you going home?"

I shrug, pouring more wax. "Soon." He looks doubtful. He knows I tend to get in the zone and overwork myself. "Promise."

He shakes his head, not believing me one bit. With the last of the wax poured, I carry my phone with me over to another one of my stations where wax has already hardened in the jars so I can start adding the sticker labels.

"Make sure you're taking care of yourself."

"I am, please don't worry about me. You have enough on your plate. I don't want to be a burden."

He blows out a breath. "You're not a burden. You never could be."

I drop my eyes, pretending to be focused on the stickers. I wonder what he'd think if he knew the truth about me. About what my father did to me. To my sister. He knows he was physically abusive to my mom, but he doesn't know the worst of it.

"You need to focus on school," I remind him.

"Hey." His voice is tight. "Something's wrong. Talk to me."

"Nothing's wrong." I force a bright smile. And really, there isn't. Not anything he can concern himself with, that is. Sometimes I just get in these ruts.

"I love you," he says softly. "You can talk to me."

I don't think he'd like me very much if I told him about my very complicated feelings for my neighbor. Caleb is perfect—well, as close to it as you can get. He's a *good* guy. A great guy, even. Our relationship is easy. He makes me happy.

But something has to be off for my thoughts to constantly stray to Thayer, right?

Or maybe there's something off with *me*.

"I know I can," I finally say. "It's just hard. Missing you. Lauren." This feels like a good enough excuse to get him off my back.

"I miss you, too, babe. Maybe you can come down for a weekend soon."

"I might."

I won't.

I can feel his stare through the camera. "Did I do something wrong?"

"No!" I rush to say. I don't want him thinking he did anything, because he hasn't. This is all my fault—the way I'm feeling. "God, no." I shake my head roughly. "I'm just distracted." I hold up a s'mores scented candle.

"All right." He doesn't sound quite believing. "I love you. I'll talk to you later."

"Love you."

I hang up first.

And then I cry.

I don't break down often. It's been a while since the last time it happened, a good six months or so, but the emotions flood over me. I think about my therapist, things she has said about coping with trauma, and I let myself feel. Let myself mourn for the little girl who had to be so strong when she should've only had to be a kid.

***

It's raining and I'm drenched as I stand on Thayer's front porch with Binx in my arms, meowing angrily over being wet.

I knock on his door, then ring the doorbell over and over.

I don't know what possessed me to walk up to his door instead of my house, but I'm here now and I can't make myself leave.

The door swings open and reveals Thayer standing there in nothing but a pair of sweatpants. No shirt. Just his package front and center—and we've already established how much my eyes like it, so of course they zero in right on it.

"What the fuck?" He takes me in from head to toe, soaked from my walk from my car to here. It wasn't far at all, I mean I live right beside him. That's just how bad it's raining. "What the fuck?" He repeats, his eyes landing on the angry black cat in my arms.

"Binx doesn't like the rain."

"Then why is he in it?"

"I needed to talk to you."

"So, you brought your cat?"

I roll my eyes. "He was with me in my workshop. I was making candles."

He gives me a quizzical look. "You make candles?"

"Yeah, but that's not why I'm here." He seems to just then take in my state beyond being rain drenched. His eyes linger on my red-rimmed ones.

He tips his head toward the inside. "Come in." He closes the door behind me. "So, why are you here?" Shaking his head he curses under his breath. "Let me get you a shirt or something. I don't want you getting sick."

"I'm fine." And just to contradict me, my treacherous body shivers.

He chuckles. "Wait here." He jogs up the stairs.

Binx squirms angrily in my arms. With a sigh, I let him down, hoping Thayer won't mind the cat hair.

He returns less than a minute later with a gray t-shirt scrunched up in his hands. "This should work." He holds it out and I take it, tucking it between my legs. Without thinking, I take my shirt off. A choked gasp comes from Thayer. I quickly tug his shirt on and down over my body.

"It's just a bra, Thayer," I try to kid. "You've seen me in my bathing suit." Granted, I always choose one that covers a lot of skin, but still, it's not like he saw anything indecent.

He clears his throat, his eyes narrow and dark. "What did you want to talk about?"

"Do we have to do it right here?" I look around this foyer. This doesn't exactly feel like the kind of conversation you have with someone by the front door.

"We can go to the living room." He starts walking, expecting me to follow. He pauses, glancing back at me. "Where did your cat go?"

"Oh—"

Sighing, he waves a hand. "Never mind. Maybe he'll find some mice and kill them. Might as well make himself useful while he's here."

Thayer takes a seat on the couch, motioning for me to sit wherever I'd like. I pick the end of the same couch, tucking my legs under me. I pull my damp hair away from my face, securing it with an elastic. Now that I'm here, I'm not as confident as I was before.

"Do you need a drink or something?"

I nod eagerly at the momentary reprieve. He doesn't ask what I want when he gets up, returning all too quickly with a

Diet Coke. Wrapping my fingers around the bottle, I unscrew the top and take a fortifying sip.

"Not many people know the truth about my dad," I begin, and his eyes widen in surprise. He didn't expect the conversation to go in this direction. "My mom and sister. They both lived it. Lauren, because I told her. My therapist. And now you."

"Your boyfriend?"

I shake my head. "He knows my dad was abusive but not the other stuff." I can't bring myself to say it. I might never be able to properly say those words, but my therapist said that's okay. I'm not avoiding what happened. "It's not something I share with others. I don't want them to look at me differently. My sister is the same way. I didn't know I talked in my sleep."

"Salem—"

"Let me get this out," I beg, fighting tears. "Call me crazy, but I'm kind of glad you know; that there's someone else out there in the world who knows the truth."

His face has darkened. "When you said what you did in your sleep..." He rubs his jaw. "Fuck, if he wasn't already dead, I would've killed him myself."

I give a weak laugh. "He wouldn't be worth going to jail."

Those warm brown eyes stare me down, looking, searching. I don't know what for, but finally he says, "But you are."

"Huh?"

"You're worth it, Salem."

"Oh." I duck my head. "I ... anyway ... I'm not saying I want to go into details or that I'll ever bring it up again but I'm glad you know the truth. That's ... that's all I wanted to say."

"There's something I've wondered," he muses softly. "If it's okay to ask?"

"I don't have to answer." It's the only go ahead I'll give him.

"Why didn't your mom leave him?"

I eye him, feeling more than a tad annoyed. "You know, it always amazes me that that's the first question people ask." I inhale a breath. "As if the blame lies on my mom and not on the man responsible. The man who beat his wife, snuck into his daughters' rooms at night," I rant, feeling my blood pressure rise. "It's *never,* 'Wow, what an awful human being he was. Your poor mom must have been terrified.'" I let him absorb this before I continue. "The blame always gets put on the victim or victims. Why is that?" I can tell I've stumped him. "It's because," I gather everything I have inside me so I can say this last bit, "society never wants to accept that monsters are real—just weak women."

His lips are parted, and he blinks, taking in what I've said. "Fuck, Salem. I never thought about it like that."

"Well, now you can." I play with the hem of his shirt that dwarfs my much smaller body. "She was scared to leave him. I've heard the threats. Ones where he said he'd hunt us to the end of the world or kill us and himself if she even tried. Sometimes I used to lie in bed and wish he would—that death would be better than *that.*"

"I can't imagine what you went through and I'm a selfish fucking prick because I also can't imagine a world without you in it."

"I just wanted you to know. I mean, since you kind of already did. I felt like you deserved to know more."

His jaw ticks. "I would've never asked you to share more."

"I know." And I do. "But you deserved to understand."

"I want you to know," he begins, sounding a bit choked up, "no one, no child, should've ever had to endure what you and your sister did. As a parent, I can't ... well, I don't know what kind of sick fuck you have to be to do that."

Wiping a tear that's escaped, I whisper hoarsely, "Thank you." Binx hops up onto the couch and into my lap. He curls up and lays down, knowing I need the comfort. I pet his head, feeling calm fill me. "I don't dwell much on the past anymore," I say softly, staring down at the cat in my lap. It's easier to look at him than Thayer. "But sometimes it creeps up on me and tonight was one of those times."

His warm hand curls around the top of mine. Tipping my head up, I meet his eyes. There's no judgment. In fact, he doesn't look at me one bit differently. I'm still Salem.

And that's all I ever want to be.

Me.

I hear my therapist in my head again, reminding me that my father can't take my identity if I don't let him.

CHAPTER TWENTY-NINE

I'm more than a little surprised when the bell chimes over the door in the antique store and Thayer strides in, moving his sunglasses to rest on his baseball cap.

"Hi," I say warmly, trying not to smile like a fool. "What brings you in here?" He clears his throat, looking around at the chandelier section.

"My parents are going to come up for Thanksgiving and I know it's over a month away, but I want to get them a gift. I thought I might find something for my mom here."

"Sure." I slide off the stool. "What does your mom like?"

"Flowers." He smiles sheepishly. "I guess she's where I got my love for plants and nature."

"We have some unique vases she might like." I lead him around through the maze of odds and ends. "What about this?" I hold up a classic blue and white design.

"She hates blue."

"That's out then." I put it away quickly. "What about this one?" I pull out a crystal one.

"Too stuffy for her taste."

"Hmm." I bite my lip. "Hold on." He follows after me as I go over to the display where my candles are. There's a vase there with fresh flowers inside. "What about this?" I hold it up so he can see the cream vase with tiny hand painted flowers.

"That," he takes it from me, spinning it around so he can see it from every angle, "is perfect."

"Good." I smile, pleased I could find something so easily for his mother. I set the vase behind the checkout counter, returning to where he still stands at the candle display. "What about your dad?"

He shakes his head. "Antiques aren't his thing."

I laugh, taking the vase back from him. "I'm not surprised."

He picks up one of the candles, reading the details on it before unscrewing the lid and taking a sniff. "These are yours."

It's a statement, not a question, but I answer anyway. "Yes."

He picks up another and sniffs. "I'll get one for my mom. Which is your favorite?"

I beam. "All of them." He chuckles at my response. "I put a lot of love into each of them, but this is my favorite." I pick it up and hand it to him.

He reads the label, a smile threatening to lift his lips. "Cookie dough? Why am I not surprised?" I shrug, clasping my hands behind my back. "I'll take one."

"Just one?" I kid. "Don't get cheap on me now, Thayer."

This time he gives me a full-blown smile. "All right." He grabs up two more of the cookie dough scent. "Does this suffice?"

I smile back at him. "It'll do."

***

"I have big news. Huge. Absolutely out of this world." Georgia breezes into the house from her date with Michael—the sound of his motorcycle driving off echoing in the distance.

I look up from the cupcakes I'm making for Thayer—he didn't ask for them, but after he came into the store today, I figured we both could use some. My mom sits at the kitchen table, eyeing the mess I'm making but not saying a word. It's late so it has surprised me that she hasn't asked why I decided to make cupcakes now.

"What is it, dear?" My mom turns in her chair to face Georgia. Her eyes look tired, bags bigger than normal beneath them. She looks pale, too. I need to make sure she's eating every meal and drinking enough water.

Georgia looks radiant, glowing and happy. Maybe Michael is finally getting his shit together and treating her the way she deserves. He's not a bad guy, not really anyway, just a little misguided.

Smoothing her blond hair down and straightening her top, she meets each of our gazes. Before she speaks, she meets my eyes and taps her nose.

"Huh?"

"You have flour on your nose."

"Oh!" I wipe it away with the back of my arm.

"Anyway," she claps her hands together, "Michael asked me to move in with him."

"Wow," my mom blurts, surprise evident in her tone. "That's ... wow."

"I know! It's so exciting! I think we'll be engaged by Christmas!"

If that's what she wants, if *he's* who she wants, then I hope for the best. "That's amazing, Georgia." I smile at my sister. Michael might not be my favorite person in the world, but my sister is, and I want her to be happy.

"I don't have much to move into his apartment, so I think I'll be out by the end of the week."

Mom's eyes widen. "Really? That's so soon."

"I know, but it doesn't make any sense to wait."

Either that or she's afraid if she waits too long, he'll change his mind.

"I'm happy for you," I tell her, hoping to distract her from our mom's obvious worry.

"Thank you, sis." She moves behind the island counter and hugs me—well, half hugs me since she doesn't want to dirty her dress.

Mom stands up, adjusting the apron she wears. This one has multi-colored fall leaves on it. I love her collection of aprons, the fact she has one for every season, holiday, and pretty much everything you can think of.

"My little girl is growing up." There are tears in her eyes as she hugs Georgia. She looks at me over my sister's shoulder. "Both of you."

"Are you okay with this, Mom?" Georgia holds her hands between hers.

"Of course, I am. I'm going to miss you, but this is the natural progression of things. I knew you girls would fly the nest one day."

"I love you," Georgia says, and I think my normally in control sister might cry too. She hugs our mom again. "I'm so excited. It'll be nice to girl up Michael's bachelor pad." She sashays away, singing softly as she goes.

My mom snickers. "Poor Michael, he doesn't know what he's in for."

"Oh yeah," I agree, sliding cupcakes into the oven. "Georgia's going to feminize his man cave, and he's going to lose his shit." Her laughter is soft as she returns to the table. She winces a bit as she sits, a sigh leaving her throat. "Are you okay?"

She waves away my concern. "Fine. I'm fine."

I hesitate, biting my lip. I don't believe her, but I don't push it.

CHAPTER THIRTY

The next day, I keep an eye out for Thayer's truck to return home. When it does, I wait about an hour before I gather up the plate of cupcakes and head next door. The chilly weather is coming in now that we're in the middle of October. My jeans hug my legs and hips and I chose a fitted top. I wanted to look cute, but not like I'm trying to seduce him.

Which I'm not.

That would be bad.

A good kind of bad, but bad nonetheless.

The door opens and Thayer grins, eyes crinkling at the corners. I think he smiles before he means to, because he clears his throat and quickly sobers. Eyes dropping to the dish of cupcakes, there's another hint of a smile.

"Cookie dough?"

"There's no better kind."

He steps aside, his hair damp from the shower and curling at his nape. "Come on in." I step inside and he closes the door. "You want a drink?"

"Sure."

I follow him to the kitchen, and he pulls out a beer for himself and a Diet Coke for me. I trade the plate of cupcakes for the Diet Coke. He sits them down, removing the top and plucking one out.

"If you keep feeding me these, I'm going to gain fifty pounds."

I take in his trim, muscular build. I don't purposely mean to check him out, that's just what happens.

"I think you'll be fine." Clearing my throat, I step away from him.

His woodsy scent fills my nose, making me feel lightheaded. Or maybe it's just him that makes me feel that way. I make a mental note to try to replicate his scent for a candle.

"You want one?" He asks around a bite, pointing at the plate.

"No, it's okay. I saved some for myself."

"Do you need to go somewhere or...?" He waits for me to fill in the blanks.

"I don't have anywhere I need to be." With Lauren and Caleb gone, all I have is work and my candles.

"You want me to put a movie on or something?"

"That would be nice." I move closer to the doors that open to the back deck. "The greenhouse is coming along."

"It's a slow project since I only work on it when I have spare time, but it'll be worth it when it's done."

"What about Forrest's treehouse?"

He winces. "That kid doesn't stop talking about it, even though I told him from the get-go that I wouldn't be able to build it until next spring and summer."

"He's just excited." I take a sip of the soda.

"I know." He finishes the cupcake and grabs his beer. "Come on." I follow him into the living room and plop on the couch while he grabs the remote. "Is there anything in particular you want to watch?"

"Are you offering me the choice, Thayer? That's a dangerous game."

"Don't make me regret this decision," he mutters, but he

doesn't sound mad.

"What if we watch your favorite movie and then watch mine?"

He thinks it over. "All right."

"What is it?"

He turns the TV on. "What is, what?"

I roll my eyes playfully, tugging a pillow onto my lap. "Your favorite movie?"

I swear his cheeks turn the tiniest bit pink. "The Lord of The Rings trilogy, we'll only watch the first one, though."

Mock gasping, I ask, "Thayer, are you a closet nerd?"

He arches a brow. "I own a landscaping business and know a hell of a lot about plants and you're assuming I'm in the closet about my nerdoms? No, Salem. I'm very open about the fact that I'm a nerdy individual."

I laugh, curling my legs under me. "Tell me more."

"About what?"

"Your hobbies. Anything." I shrug. I sound so desperate, and I guess I am. I want to know everything there is to know about Thayer Holmes.

He opens an app on the TV and scrolls through for the movie. "Um, well I love camping. Does that count?"

"That's definitely a hobby," I concur, twisting the soda lid back and forth.

"And you know about the puzzles."

"I love the puzzles." I blush when the words come out as a sultry purr.

He chuckles, shaking his head. "You know all the dirt on me. I'm losing all my cool street cred."

"I highly doubt I know all there is to know."

"More than most." He hits play on the movie and takes a

seat, purposely putting a cushion's worth of space between us. I suddenly hate that particular cushion.

We watch the movie in silence, and I'm surprised to find that I actually enjoy it. When it's over, he stands up and stretches. If he hears my moan at the sight of the sliver of skin above the waistband of his jeans he says nothing.

"I'm starving," he says, picking up his empty beer. "Do you mind if I order dinner before we start another movie?"

"Not at all." I don't know why he's even asking me. It's his house.

"Pizza or Chinese?"

"Either is fine."

"Salem," he says in a warning tone.

I laugh. "Pizza then. Pepperoni," I add before he can ask.

"I'll go order. Use the bathroom if you need to." He scoops up his phone in his other hand, heading out of the room.

My bladder is screaming, so I head to the half-bath. Washing my hands, I open the door and hear him on the phone.

"Miss you too, buddy. I'll see you Friday after school." There's a pause. "Mhmm, I'll pick you up from school." Another stretch of quiet as I walk into the kitchen. Thayer's eyes meet mine as he says, "I'm sure Salem misses you too and will be happy to see you." I smile at that. Forrest is a good kid and I like hanging out with him. I never know what's going to come out of his mouth. "All right. I love you, buddy. Sleep tight. Don't let the bed bugs bite."

He hangs up, looking at me with a sad smile.

"I'm sorry," I say, because I don't know what else to say.

He runs his fingers through his hair, grabbing another beer from the mini-fridge. "About what?"

"That you can't be with him."

"It is what it is." He pops the top and takes a swig of the liquid.

I slide onto a barstool across from him. "How'd you meet Krista?"

He rubs his jaw. "You really want to talk about this?"

I shrug, picking up the notepad on the countertop. It's a grocery list. "Why not? We have time to kill before the pizza gets here and we start my movie."

"All right." He leans against the counter. "We met in high school. She was a freshman, and I was a sophomore. We were only friends at first. We started dating the next year."

"So," I draw random designs on the granite with my pointer finger, "you were high school sweethearts, then?" My thoughts stray to Caleb.

"Yeah." He nods, a glum set to his shoulders.

It seems like he's not going to say anything more. "When did you get married?"

He rubs his stubbled jaw. "During college."

I shake my head, fighting a smile. "You're a man of few words."

He sighs, seeming to fortify himself. "We were young and in love. Marriage seemed like the next logical step. We got married my senior year." He sips at his beer. "I guess, in a way, it seemed easiest. She was all I knew, and I was content. Things didn't seem so bad. My parents loved her, and I did too. Then we had Forrest and it seemed like everything should be perfect now, but as the years went on, I think we both realized we had settled. I wasn't the right fit for her and vice versa." He runs his fingers through his hair. "Growing apart, that breeds resentment. I think we both stayed in the relationship longer than we should have because of Forrest. But in the end, we realized he was better off having happy parents that are apart than miserable ones together." A haunted look overtakes him, and I wish I could wipe it away.

"I think that's admirable. I can't imagine it's easy with a kid involved." Biting my lip, I ask, "Do you think Caleb and I are doomed then? That if you fall in love young it's only destined to end in heartbreak?" I hold my breath, waiting for his response.

He slides his beer to the side, having only taken a few sips and grabs a water bottle.

"I'm cynical about a lot of things, love being one of them." He exhales a weighted breath. "I'm not saying you're doomed or anything. Plenty of others make it. But it has to be worth fighting for."

"And your love with Krista wasn't?"

He meets my eyes. "No."

He says it so sure that I almost feel sorry for her. "Why?" I cringe as soon as I ask that. "You don't have to answer."

"She became someone I didn't recognize. Vindictive, spiteful, angry. All the parts that I fell in love with had disappeared. The manipulative games she played were the worst, and I was done."

"What do you think changed her?"

"Honestly, I think she always had a lot of that in her." He picks at the label on the water bottle. "I can't prove it, and I wouldn't change anything because I love my son, but I'm pretty sure she got pregnant on purpose. We'd only been married around two years at that point and were going through a rough patch. I think she thought a baby would fix things. I suppose it did for a while, but you can't fix a broken house with lies."

The doorbell rings then and he heads to get the pizza.

"I'll pay you back for this," I say, following after him. "I don't have any cash on me, but I'll give you some the next time I see you."

He pauses, hand on the doorknob. "Don't worry about it, Salem. I mean it."

There must be something wrong with me because that bossy tone of his makes my core clench with pleasure. I'm seriously fucked up.

He pays the delivery driver and closes the door. He carries the boxes into the living room and sets them on the coffee table.

"I'll get our drinks." I head back to the kitchen for them. I grab another Diet Coke from the fridge and turn to get his, but nearly smack into his chest. "Jesus Christ!" My hand flies to my chest. "Don't sneak up on me like that." He makes no move to back up. "Thayer?" His brown eyes stare at me intently. "W-What are you doing?" His tongue wets his lips, and I realize he's staring at my mouth. "Are you going to kiss me?" I blurt my thoughts out loud.

He towers above me, lowering his head so I'm cocooned with the mini-fridge behind my legs and his body blocking everything else. I know if I wanted to move, he'd let me pass. That's the kind of man he is. But the fact is, I don't want to.

His voice is deeper than normal when he asks, "Do you want me to?"

I swallow. *Do I*?

"Yes."

He doesn't hesitate.

His hand cups the back of my neck, his other at my waist. I'm pulled against his body. We're fitted together so tightly that you couldn't stick a piece of paper between us if you tried. His mouth meets mine, his lips warm and firm but somehow gentle at the same time. He begs my lips to part with the tip of his tongue, and I answer with a gasp, letting his tongue delve into my mouth.

Oh my God, I'm kissing Thayer!

It'd be a lie if I said I hadn't thought about this moment. What it would be like to kiss him. What his mouth would feel like. Would he be hard? Soft? Eager?

He's everything and more.

My ass bumps into the top of the fridge and he lifts me up, sitting me on top with him between my legs. He angles my head back, deepening the kiss. My hands are fisted in his hair. I don't want him to stop. If he suddenly changes his mind I'll be devastated.

He keeps one hand cupped to the back of my neck, but his other moves to my cheek. His thumb rubs my skin in slow, soothing circles.

He pulls away slowly, our noses touching. Long dark lashes touch the tops of his cheeks every time he blinks.

"Hi," I say stupidly.

"Hi."

"You kissed me." I bite my lip to hide my giddy smile.

"I did."

"Did you like it?"

He tries not to smile. "I did. Did you?"

"Mhmm." I nod eagerly, perhaps too eager. "I think we should do it again."

His eyes narrow on my swollen lips. "I shouldn't have done it."

I frown, panic surging in my veins. "But you said you liked it."

"And I did," he assures, leaning close enough that his lips brush over mine. "But it doesn't change the facts."

"What facts?" I'm pretty sure his kiss killed ninety percent of my brain cells.

"You're eighteen, Salem."

I duck my head, gripping onto his t-shirt. "Please, don't ... don't use that as an excuse. Not when this feels ... like *this*."

"I don't want to take advantage of you."

"You're not!" I rush to say. "God, Thayer." I shake my head roughly. "You would never."

"You're young." I flinch, hating that he's so focused on my age. I know, believe me, I know what it looks like with him so much older, but this attraction has to be worth battling what others might think. "Hey." He tips my head up with his finger. "I'm not saying that to be mean. It's just a fact. You're at a different part of your life than I am mine."

"So, what?" I retort. "That automatically means I don't know what I want?"

He shakes his head, his hair tickling my forehead. "Fuck, that's not what I meant." He presses his lips into a thin line, thinking. "It's just ... you have a life to live and—"

"What? When you turn thirty suddenly, you're old and don't have a life to live?"

He presses a hand over my mouth. "Don't sass me."

My gaze thins. "What are you going to do about it? Spank me?" I challenge.

His eyes flare with lust. "You're playing a dangerous game."

"So. Are. You."

He growls low in his throat, and I gasp when his mouth is on mine again. He's rough, like he's trying to scare me away, but it only awakens something inside me. I claw at him, trying to get his shirt off. He obliges, quickly tearing it over his head before he's kissing me again.

"Salem," he murmurs my name between kisses.

I wind my legs around his waist, gasping when I feel the hardness of his erection.

We are chaos. Unrestrained passion igniting with a single spark.

I moan, grinding myself against him.

Thayer. Thayer. Thayer.

His name is a chant in my mind. He fills all my senses. My thoughts, too. He's everywhere and I don't want him to ever leave. His warm, calloused hands skate beneath my shirt, and I shiver at the feel of them against my bare skin.

"Are you cold?"

"No," I pant. I don't tell him, but I feel like I'm on fire.

I'm hot. Achy. Fucking needy.

"We should stop," he says, but he keeps kissing me.

"No." I take my shirt off since it's bunched under my bra.

His eyes take me in, filled with lust and desire and something more, something infinitely tender.

"I'm not sure I can," he murmurs before he dives back in.

We're a clash of lips, teeth, and roaming hands. I moan when he cups my breasts, rubbing my hardened nipples through my bra. I curse myself for putting on one of my more plain ones instead of one of the sexier lace ones I own, but it wasn't like I expected this to happen when I came over here tonight.

Thayer picks me up, and I wrap my arms and legs around him. He carries me to the living room, sitting down with me on his lap. His hardness presses against my core, eliciting a moan from me. My fingers tangle in his hair, yanking his head back away from my mouth so I can look at him.

His brown eyes are heavy with lust, but concern begins to fill them. "Salem—"

I silence him with a kiss. Whatever is happening right now, I don't want it to stop.

Grinding against him, his fingers dig into my hips. My fingers go to his leather belt, his hand shooting out to grab mine. I look at him questioningly. "Are you going to let me take your pants off?"

His tongue wets his lips. He counters with, "Are we doing this right now?"

I grin wickedly, running my hand over his length, hard and ready for me. "It feels like you want to."

He drops his head back against the couch cushion. "I won't take advantage of you."

"You're not." I press a kiss to his neck. God, I want this. Want *him*.

"Your age—"

I press my hand over his mouth, shutting him up. I don't want to rehash the conversation we had in the kitchen before mauling each other.

"I'm young, I know, but that doesn't mean I don't know what I want." I know I have more growing up to do. More maturing. But right now, I know myself. I know how I feel about Thayer. I know I want this. And I know I won't regret it. "I want you," I tell him. "Right now, that's what I want. I'm not asking you to put a ring on my finger. Just to fuck me."

With a growl I find myself flat on my back on the couch with him fitted between my legs. He wraps his hands around my wrists, trapping them above my head.

"You want me to fuck you, Sunshine?"

Sunshine. He's never called me that before. It's officially the best nickname I've ever heard.

"Y-Yes." Normally I would be embarrassed over how

breathless and needy I sound, but I can't bring myself to care.

He holds my hands in just one of his, using his free one to gently glide his fingers over my cheek. "I shouldn't want you." His chocolate-colored eyes move to mine. "But I do."

"I shouldn't want you," I echo, biting my lip so I won't move my hips. "But I do."

With those words, his resolve crumbles. He kisses over the swells of my breasts, his hand sliding around to undo the clasp of my bra. The sound of it unsnapping seems so loud in the otherwise quiet living room. Suddenly feeling shy, I squeeze my arms against my sides so he can't pull it off.

"I want to see you," he begs. "All of you."

Loosening my arms, I allow him to pull the bra away from my skin. His eyes take me in, my small but perky breasts, round pink nipples. He looks at me like I'm the most stunning thing he's ever laid his eyes on.

"I have a confession to make," he murmurs, dipping his head to suck on the skin of my neck.

"W-What?" I ask, desperate to hear what he has to say but also not wanting his mouth to part from my skin.

"That morning," he begins, moving his lips over my collarbone, "in the hotel. After you, got off on my leg..."

I *hate* that he's bringing this up right now, but luckily the way he's kissing my skin is easing my embarrassment. "I remember," I say breathily when it becomes obvious he wants me to say something.

He raises up, pecking a kiss on my lips. "I went to the bathroom and had to jack off." He kisses me again. "You have no idea how hot that was." I feel a blush flush my entire body. "You're fucking gorgeous." He squeezes my breast. "And right now," he swirls his tongue around one of my nipples, eyes never straying from mine, "you're mine."

"Yours," I echo on a whimper.

He presses tender kisses down my stomach, swirling his tongue around my navel. His eyes never leave mine, his breath hot against my bare skin when he pops the button on my jeans. I wiggle impatiently, my pussy clenching relentlessly, desperate to be filled by him.

"Patience," he murmurs, unzipping and then wiggling the material past my hips.

My heart beats so fast that I fear I might pass out. My fingers tangle in his hair, yanking at the strands. "I need you."

"Tell me where you need me." He places a soft, barely there kiss on my pubic bone above the band of my panties.

"Your mouth," I pant, my hips rising up on their own. "I want it on my pussy."

His eyes flash hot and molten. "Fuck, say it again."

"I want," I enunciate each word, "your mouth," I lick my lips, "on my pussy."

His chest rumbles with pleasure at my declaration. He moves my panties to the side, exposing the most intimate part of me that's aching with want for him.

"Is this okay?" he asks.

"Yes," I cry out, ready to beg him to touch me.

His fingers skim lightly over my skin. "You're soaked," he groans.

I wiggle, worried he's going to delay this even longer, but then he lowers his head, tasting me with one long sweep of his tongue. I cry out, my hips rising off the couch and my hands splaying out to grab something, anything.

He licks and sucks at me like he's starving and I'm his last meal. He's an expert with his tongue. It's never felt this good before.

I whimper and cry as he works me to an orgasm and when I fall over the edge, faster than I ever have before, I scream his name over and over like a prayer.

He rises over my body and kisses me. I taste myself on his tongue, but surprisingly I don't mind it. His erection presses against me and I reach down, cupping him over his jeans.

"Need to be in you." He sounds like he's aching with the same need I am.

He shoves his jeans down and his boxer-briefs with them.

Thayer Holmes is naked in front of me.

I don't look away.

I take in every inch of him.

Every. Long. Perfect. Inch.

A part of me wonders how he'll fit. He's the most well-endowed man I've ever seen, but I know it'll be fine. My body is ready, desperate to be filled by him.

I touch the smattering of chest hair on his pectoral muscles that grows heavier beneath his belly button, framing his thick cock.

I wrap my hand around him and he bucks his hips forward, eyes falling closed. "Fuck, Salem. You're going to make me come too fast like a teenage boy."

I lick my lips, rubbing my thumb around the head of his cock and wiping the bead of precum into his tip.

"I like that."

"What?" He pants, clearly struggling for control. "That I can't control myself?"

"No." I shake my head, biting my lip. His eyes zero in on my breasts, watching the way they move when I do. "That you want me so bad."

"I've wanted you for way longer than I should've."

"Since when?"

"Since you brought the asshole next door cupcakes and tried to be his friend. You were all long tan legs and blond hair and gorgeous green eyes. I couldn't get enough but I knew it was wrong."

"And now we're here." I continue to stroke him, his hips rocking forward to meet my hand.

"So we are." He curses and it's not the good kind of curse. "I don't have condoms."

"I'm on birth control and ... and Caleb always wears a condom."

His eyes darken at the mention of my boyfriend.

God, I'm an awful person. Thoughts of my boyfriend should make me stop, to cover myself and flee, but I do no such thing. My need for Thayer is so acute that I'm afraid stopping might kill me.

"I'm clean," he promises me. "I got tested after my divorce. Are you sure about this?"

"God, *yes*. Please, just get inside me, Thayer." I grab his ass, my fingers digging into his skin and pulling him forward.

He doesn't hesitate. Grabbing the base of his cock, he plunges into me. I cry out, my back arching. He's so big and I'm so full.

"Fucking hell, Salem," he curses, exhaling heavily.

"Am I too tight?" I squeak, because my God, he's stretching me.

He shakes his head, brown hair falling over his forehead. I reach up, brushing it away so I can see his eyes. I need to see them. He can't hide from me that way.

"No," he rocks slowly out and back in, "it's just..." His

fingers tighten around my hips, angling me up to meet his thrusts. "You feel like mine."

I press my hand to his stubbled cheek. I don't say it, not with words, but it's felt between the movement of our bodies.

Because I am.

We've never said that one special word to each other.

Love.

But that's what he does.

He doesn't fuck me like I asked.

Thayer makes love to me.

Mind.

Body.

Soul.

I'm filled with him in more ways than one.

And I know, in this moment, in this space between us, I've been irrevocably changed.

I am his. He is mine.

Nothing, not time, distance, nor the complete obliteration of our world can change that.

CHAPTER THIRTY-ONE

Post sex pizza and Hocus Pocus playing on the TV might officially be one of my favorite things ever. I'm only wearing Thayer's t-shirt, completely naked beneath it. Every so often he lifts it to knead my breasts, suck my nipples, or simply to smack my ass.

Post sex Thayer is also now one of my favorite things. He's in a good mood, a weight that's normally on his shoulders gone for the moment. He smiles, laughing and joking with me. He seems younger somehow.

"I can't believe this is your favorite movie." He points a slice of pizza at the TV. He had to heat it back up in the oven but neither of us complained.

"This is amazing," I scoff. "I watch it all the time."

"Does this mean Halloween is your favorite holiday?"

"Yes, of course. It should be everyone's favorite."

He tries not to smile. "And why is that?"

"Because it's awesome." I bite into my pepperoni pizza.

"Has anyone ever told you that's a weak argument?"

I point to my face. "Do I look like I care?"

"No." This time he does smile. "But come on, you really think it's better than Christmas?"

"Yes, abso-fucking-lutely. I take it that's *your* favorite?"

"Yeah." He nods, reaching for another slice. "My mom would go all out for my brother and me growing up. I'm talking going as far as to make it look like reindeer had been in the yard.

It was..." He pauses, searching for the right word. "Magical. I've tried to keep that alive for Forrest. Kids deserve to believe in the unthinkable. Reality can be a slap in the face. Let them dream with their eyes open while they have the chance."

I take in his words, nodding. "That's a really beautiful way to look at things." With a shrug, I add, "I just like the spooky stuff."

He chuckles. "Do you carve pumpkins?"

"You know it." I tuck a piece of hair behind my ear, feeling suddenly shy with his gaze on me. "The town always puts on a pumpkin carving contest every year. There's a snowman building one too."

"That's kind of..."

"Over the top?"

"No. I think it's neat that this town is so tight knit."

"It's a community, not just a town, that's for sure."

He reaches over, wrapping his big hand around my thigh.

"What are you—"

He pulls me against his side and presses a kiss to my lips. "I wanted you closer." He skims his nose along my cheek to the shell of my ear. "I'm not finished with you yet."

A shiver runs down my spine at the thought of more delicious pleasure at Thayer's capable hands. "Well, you might not be finished with me, but I'm not finished with this pizza. Someone made me burn a lot of calories."

He chuckles. "Have your fill."

"And then?"

"And then I'll have my fill of you."

***

It's late when I walk back next door to my house. We finished Hocus Pocus and then he made love to me again, on the floor this time. It was sexy, intense, everything I didn't know sex could be.

The door creaks open when I step inside, and I silently curse the old house for being so loud. It's not that I'm worried about sneaking in. I don't have a curfew and my mom trusts me, but if she's asleep I don't want to wake her.

She's in the living room and sits up from the couch at the sound of the door.

"Sorry, Mom." I lock the door behind me. "I didn't mean to wake you."

"Where were you?" She yawns, stretching her arms. "I didn't mean to doze off down here."

HGTV plays softly on the screen, the only light in the room.

"I was with a friend."

"Oh." She looks a tad puzzled, probably because she knows other than Caleb and Lauren I don't talk to anyone else.

Caleb.

God, what am I going to do?

The guilt begins to settle into a pit in my stomach and I worry I'm going to be sick. This isn't like me—doing something like this.

She starts to rise from the couch, but sways. A hand shoots to her forehead as she sits back down.

"Mom." I rush to her side. "Are you okay?"

Her eyes are squeezed shut and she looks like she's in pain. "Fine. It's okay. Just dizzy. Lack of sleep, I think," she rambles.

I frown, concerned. I know she can have restless nights like I do, but this seems different and I can't help but be worried.

"Mom," I probe, gripping her hand to help her up. "What aren't you telling me?"

She pales. "Nothing." Once she's standing, she heads for the stairs, her hand shaking.

"I know when you're lying," I tell her retreating figure.

She pauses, her hand on the railing. She doesn't look at me when she says, "And you think I don't know the same about you? We all have our secrets, Salem, and we're allowed to keep them."

With those parting words, she disappears upstairs for bed, but I'm suddenly frozen.

Ice all over.

I look out the window at Thayer's house and then back upstairs.

There's no way she knows.

I have to believe that.

CHAPTER THIRTY-TWO

I'm solemn on the train ride to Boston. It's an unexpected trip but a necessary one. I'm revolted over my betrayal of Caleb. It's not right what I did, even if it felt so good. I can't let this continue.

When the train arrives, I hop off and head toward the campus and the address for his dorm that he gave me.

I'm nervous.

I love Caleb. He's my friend, my lover. He's been a rock in my life, a constant I could rely on, and I'm about to sever that. I know when I end things more than likely I'll never hear from him again. It sucks, because I don't want to lose him, I really don't, but I have to.

It's rainy and chilly, the sky a murky gray color. I tug the hood of my jacket over my head, tucking my hands into my pockets as I walk down the street.

I'm not good at this. I've never had to break someone's heart before, and it makes it even worse because I love Caleb. But what I feel for Thayer is all consuming, intense. It's a magnetism I can't deny.

Before Thayer came along, I thought what I have with Caleb was normal, how relationships are, how love feels. But I couldn't have been more wrong. Caleb has never made my heart race the way Thayer does. I should've ended things sooner with him, but I was confused over my feelings and didn't understand.

Now, I do, and I have to do the right thing.

I shoot Caleb a text and he gives me the information to come straight to his room.

I was hoping he'd meet me outside.

But I follow his instructions and suddenly I'm outside a door with a white board hanging on it. I knock on the door and there's some shuffling inside.

Then Caleb is there, opening the door with a beaming grin and yanking me into his arms.

He squeezes me tight, burying his face into my neck, and despite myself I sigh in relief at the contact. I *have* missed him.

I wrap my arms around him.

Are you really going to break his heart?

I already did. The moment things started swaying from platonic with Thayer, I hurt him even if he doesn't know it.

He sets me down and turns to someone in his room. "Matt, this is Salem."

Matt inclines on a raised bed playing some handheld gaming device. He has dark, almost black curly hair. "'Sup."

"Let's go." Caleb takes my hand. "Let me show you the campus."

He's so excited, his eyes lit up with happiness, so I can't say no.

We head out of the room holding hands. By the time we leave the building I've managed to extricate my hand from his. The guilt ... I just can't hold his hand right now.

Caleb leads me around the Harvard campus, pointing out various buildings and giving me information about when they were built and who paid for them and a bunch of other details that go right over my head.

After walking around for an hour, we grab coffee from a stand and find a bench to sit on. He wipes it dry with the sleeve of his jacket.

"It's beautiful here," I say, letting the pumpkin spice latte hit my tongue. "I can see why you like it."

"I wish you were here."

"I could never get into Harvard."

"I'm sure you could, babe. But there are other schools or you could live and work in Boston. Next year we could get an apartment together—"

"Caleb," I cut him off. *Don't cry. Don't cry.* "There's something we need to talk about."

"Sure, what's up? Is it my mom? Look, I know she was a hard ass this summer, but—"

"It's not your mom." *I. Will. Not. Cry.*

His brows knit together. "Then what is it?"

I wrap my fingers tightly around the coffee cup. "Caleb, be honest, can you say that things have been good with us since we graduated?"

"I ... Salem, it's normal for couples to go through rough patches from time to time. We've had some growing pains with me going to college, but it's nothing serious." He gives a rough laugh. When I don't join him, he sobers, his voice dropping. "Right?"

"Caleb," I choke on his name.

I don't want to break, but it feels inevitable.

"You're breaking up with me, aren't you?" He sounds shocked. Hurt. Broken-hearted.

I nod, chin wobbling. "This isn't working."

"Not for you, apparently. I ... I thought it was." He rubs a hand over his jaw. Normally it's clean shaven, but there's the barest hint of blond stubble.

"We're growing apart—"

"Really? Are we? Because I hadn't noticed."

I hadn't expected him to seem so blindsided. Is it possible I'm the only one who's felt the distance between us?

"Yes," I say softly. I don't want to turn this into an all-out screaming fight. "You spent most of the summer playing football and at the gym or doing whatever it was your mom wanted. You didn't even go to the concert with me—"

"I said I was sorry for that," he points out, eyes sad.

"And I forgave you, and I meant it. But you're here now," I gesture to the campus, "and this is where you belong. Not me. I think we need to break up. We need to grow and we can't do that together."

"Wow." He exhales heavily, rubbing a hand on his jean clad thigh. "You're really doing this, huh?"

I nod. "You're amazing, Caleb, but I need this. I need to see who I am on my own."

He shakes his head, looking up at the dreary sky. "It's not you, it's me? That's what this is?"

"I don't want to hurt you."

"Then why are you?" My face contorts with pain, tears burning my eyes. "It's someone else, isn't it? You have feelings for another guy."

"No!" I say too quickly. "Yes," I admit begrudgingly.

He laughs humorlessly. "Who is he?"

"It's not important."

Hurt flashes in his eyes. "Fine, don't tell me." He stands. "I hope you're happy with him, Salem. I know that sounds sarcastic right now, and maybe it is, but I really do just want you to be happy."

He walks away, head ducked low. I wait five minutes, letting myself have a moment before I get up and walk back to the train station.

When I get home, I climb in bed and cry.

CHAPTER THIRTY-THREE

"What about this one?" Forrest runs ahead of us in the field, picking up a pumpkin, tiny muscles straining as he tries to give it a shake. He gives it a knock on the side. "No, this one is a bad nut." He runs to the next.

Thayer gives me a speculative look at the bad nut comment. "We watched *Charlie and the Chocolate Factory* last week."

He shakes his head, trying not to smile. I wonder why he holds his smiles so close. He doesn't let them loose often. "Don't you mean *Willy Wonka and the Chocolate Factory*?"

"No." I scoop up a pumpkin, but find the bottom rotted. I frown. It was the perfect shape for carving. We're supposed to be picking out pumpkins to carve with my mom tonight. "I hate the first one. It gave me nightmares as a kid." I shudder. "Nope. Never again."

He throws his head back and laughs. God, I love that sound. "You're an interesting woman, Salem."

Woman. Not girl. I love that.

Up ahead Forrest groans, trying to pick up a massive pumpkin that not even Thayer could lift.

"Forrest," he scolds, jogging over to his son and squatting down. He's dressed today in a pair of khaki colored work pants, a plaid button-down shirt, and a vest. I didn't know vests could be so hot, but mountain man Thayer has changed my mind.

"I want this one, Daddy. It's huuuuge." Forrest spreads his arms as wide as they'll go.

"It's not ideal for carving," Thayer tells him.

"Don't care."

Thayer sighs but chooses not to argue. "Here, help me out."

And then Thayer picks up the huge pumpkin with Forrest attempting to help. Huh. Here I thought he couldn't do it and he proved me wrong.

I pull the cart behind me, and Thayer deposits the pumpkin onto it with a wink. "We'll conveniently lose that before we leave." Forrest is already oblivious, running ahead through all the pumpkins. "He'll be exhausted by the time we finish with this and a hayride."

"Don't forget the maze," I point out.

"And the maze," he adds. Arching a brow, he says, "Are you trying to get lost with me in a field of corn, Matthews?"

"Maybe, Holmes."

He walks beside me and picks good pumpkins for all of us, then ditches the massive no good one when Forrest is distracted by the goats.

"I'll tell him they wanted to keep that one but thanked him for picking such a good one."

"Good idea."

He nods, his smile a little broken. I know he's sad he won't be spending Halloween with his son this year. Apparently, Krista didn't even offer for him to tagalong with them and I know without a doubt Thayer would've extended an invite to her if he was supposed to have him. It makes me sad for Thayer. He just wants to be there for his son, but it's harder for dads.

"Dad," Forrest runs up to us as we're heading to the booth they have set up on the farm to purchase goods, "can I feed the goats? They said there are babies you can give bottles to!"

"Sure, bud. I gotta pay for it first." He points to the line we're in. "Go play and I'll get everything taken care of."

There's a huge area with well-built wooden play equipment off to the right.

"Okay." Forrest takes off running.

Thayer pays for the bottle for the goats and all the pumpkins, despite my protests to let me buy the ones for my mom and myself. I should know by now that arguing with Thayer is pointless. He's stubborn to a fault.

Thayer loads up the pumpkins while I grab Forrest and take him to feed the goats. Thayer joins us, watching the way I interact with his son.

It's funny. I never grew up with that innate desire to be a mom. I didn't dislike kids but didn't particularly think about what it would be like to be a mother. Perhaps it's my childhood that stole that from me. Regardless, kids have always liked me, and I find them to be pretty cool, fascinating little creatures. They say whatever is on their minds and their love is pure. But interacting with Forrest, hanging around him, it makes me think about the future. One where maybe I am a mother. I could see myself with a couple of kids, maybe more than a couple if I'm being completely honest with myself.

The goats empty the bottle Forrest was given and he begs for another. Thayer obliges once more before the three of us make the trek over to the corn maze.

"You know," Thayer starts, Forrest running out ahead of us, "it makes me fucking sad that I didn't appreciate these moments with him as much before." I wait, letting him say more if he wants. "When I was married it was all just *right there* and even though things weren't great, I guess I took for granted the idea that it would always be there. But it's not. And now I don't see him every day, sometimes not even every week, and so now every moment is that much more special."

"You're a good dad, Thayer." I feel like he needs to hear that.

"Thanks." I let out a small squeak when his hand snakes down to take mine. I love the feel of his large, rough hand encasing mine.

I look down at them and back up at him. "Is this okay?"

"Is it okay with you?"

I nod.

"Then it's okay."

We follow Forrest, who I'm pretty sure is oblivious to our hand holding because he's too busy running around trying to locate the exit and running into dead ends.

A squeal pulls from my throat when Thayer yanks me into one of the dead ends Forrest just darted out of. His eyes are heated and my pussy clenches at that look.

"Wha—"

He cuts off my question, pressing me into the corner of the maze, the dried corn stalks rough against my back, and then he kisses me. It's a rough, searing, soul-stealing sort of kiss.

Thayer Holmes has branded himself on me.

And I know, without a doubt, that whatever this is, whatever we become, if we grow and flourish like the wildflowers behind our houses, or crash and burn, it won't matter because when I'm old and gray, lying in bed thinking about my life, he'll be the best part.

***

"What are you carving, Salem?" Forrest asks, trying to figure out what I'm making. He's drawing on his pumpkin so

Thayer can carve it.

"A cat," I answer him, swiveling the pumpkin so he can see it better.

"You really like cats," he giggles, the sound light and sweet. In the background, *The Nightmare Before Christmas* plays on TV. My mom had Thayer bring in one of her folding yard sale tables and set it up in the living room on top of a sheet to collect the mess. Normally she would've done that herself, but she looks extra tired. I'm worried about her. I know I need to push her, because I have a feeling she's hiding something.

"I do. Cats are the best." Beneath us, Binx swirls between my legs and then Forrest's.

"Dad, am I old enough for a cat yet?"

"No," Thayer answers. He's extremely focused on his pumpkin. A dark curl of hair falls into his eyes and he flicks it away with a toss of his head. His tongue sticks out slightly between his lips, eyes zeroed in on his creation.

"When are you going to build my treehouse?"

"When I have time," he replies, not missing a beat. "But the weather is getting cold so it'll have to be spring."

"Fine," Forrest grumbles. He brightens almost immediately. "What about Christmas? Can I have a cat then? A puppy? What about a turtle?"

Thayer sighs. "You're not letting this go, are you?"

"No. Never."

My mom laughs at the little boy. I can tell having him here has lifted her spirits.

"In the meantime," I tell Forrest, searching for a way to appease him, "you can visit Binx anytime you want."

"Really?"

"Really, really."

Thayer chuckles, his eyes finally leaving his pumpkin to look across at me. "You're going to regret that."

I shrug. "I've extended the invite before. I think I'll be fine." I wink at Forrest.

The small boy tries to mimic the gesture but ends up blinking both eyes open and shut rapidly.

"Did I do it?"

"Not quite. We'll work on it." I pat his hand.

Beaming, he says, "I'm a quick learner."

"You sure are." I ruffle his hair.

Quiet settles between the four of us as we work diligently on our pumpkins. When mine is done I'm fairly pleased with my cat. It's not perfect, and pretty basic, but I like it and that's all that matters.

"You get a gold star sticker," Forrest tells me with a thumbs up. "That's what my teacher gives us when we do a good job."

"Thank you, Forrest," I tell him. "I'm going to check on dinner." We have a pot roast simmering in the crock pot since Thayer and Forrest are joining us.

In the kitchen, it looks like everything is coming along nicely. I grab a can of Diet Coke from the fridge and pop the top, listening to it fizz.

A hand presses against my lower waist and I gasp, spinning around to face Thayer.

"Sorry, I needed a drink." He acts innocent as his hand sweeps over my ass before opening the fridge. "You prefer the cans," he notes, nodding at the one clutched in my hand.

"Yeah, I think it tastes better."

"You should've said something. I would've bought those instead of bottles."

I lift my shoulders. "It's not that big of a deal."

"Still, I want to get you what you like." He pulls out one of the beers my mom keeps stashed in the back. She offered him one earlier and he turned her down. "Dinner smells amazing." He lowers his head, burying his face into my neck. "But *you* smell heavenly."

Cold hits my skin when he sweeps away and out of the kitchen like a figment of my imagination.

I take a moment, letting my heartrate settle before I return to the living room.

"What do you think?" My mom asks, turning her pumpkin my way and showing me the witchy face she carved into it.

"Whoa!" Forrest says before I can say anything. "That's so good, Mrs. Matthews."

"You can call me, Allie, sweetie."

Thayer's working on carving Forrest's. "What did you do?" I ask him.

"Hmm?" He's intent on his project.

"Your pumpkin. What is it?"

"Oh." He sets down the carving knife and leans over to pick up his pumpkin.

Stop staring at his biceps!

But I can't help it, not with the way they flex and strain beneath his shirt.

He turns the pumpkin around to show me the Sanderson Sisters and I know he only did this for me. I can't help but think of that night. In his arms. Him above me. Moving inside me.

God, I crave it again.

"I didn't know you were such an artist," I say, hoping the lust doesn't show too plainly on my face, not with my mom in the room. I told her I broke up with Caleb. She was confused but said she understood and even expected it with him leaving for college.

He shrugs. "I'm really not."

"That," my mom points at the pumpkin, "takes talent. *Hocus Pocus* is Salem's favorite movie. Is it one of yours too?"

He shrugs. "I saw it for the first time recently and enjoyed it. Seemed fitting."

"We'll put it on next." She points at the TV. "Play it while we have dinner."

"Yeah, I wanna watch it!" Forrest bounces in his seat.

"Careful," Thayer admonishes quietly when Forrest nearly bonks his head into his dad's elbow.

"Sorry." He stills, climbing off his chair. He goes over to where Binx sits in the window and pets his head.

"Do you want to set ours on the front porch?" My mom asks, indicating our finished pumpkins.

"Sure." I take mine out and then hers, not wanting to risk dropping one by taking both.

I set them both on the chairs on the stairs, making sure they're angled properly toward the street. When I head back inside, Thayer is laughing at something my mom said. It's so incredibly silly, but I flash back to what Georgia said over the summer, about our mom maybe going out with Thayer. I know she's not interested in him, but that doesn't stop this fierce feeling of *he's mine* from overtaking me.

I scurry into the kitchen before I do something stupid, like go sit in his lap as if I'm marking my territory. The roast is done, so I start cutting up the meat. Everything else is already made—mashed potatoes, peas, and rolls.

I feel his warm, calming presence before he steps up behind me.

I find myself sinking into him, feeling grounded in his

presence.

How is it possible that one person, someone I've only known a few months, can make me feel this way?

"What's wrong?" He murmurs, ducking his head into my neck. He presses his lips to the skin there, his hands wrapped around my waist.

"Nothing."

"Are you sure?"

"Just being irrational. I'm fine."

"Irrational, huh?" He lets me go, taking over with cutting the meat.

"Yeah. I felt jealous."

His movements halt. "Of what?"

"My mom was talking to you and it reminded me that my sister said at one point she thought my mom should date you."

He wets his lips with a swipe of his tongue. "That so?"

"Mhmm."

He resumes slicing. "Lucky for you, there's only one Matthews woman on my mind."

"That so?" I echo his words.

"Mhmm."

I smile. I love this game we play sometimes, where we spin things around and say each other's words back.

He glances over his shoulder, making sure we're still alone, and then presses a quick kiss to my lips. "You have nothing to worry about. I'm all yours."

I love the sound of that—that Thayer Holmes is one-hundred percent mine.

CHAPTER THIRTY-FOUR

The grump next door is handing out candy. For some reason, I didn't expect him to. I mean, he has a kid so it makes sense that he'd partake in the tradition, but I figured with Forrest being with his mom tonight that Thayer wouldn't feel like giving candy.

But I was wrong.

I ring the doorbell, bucket clasped in my hand. It's past the appropriate hour for trick or treaters. I did that on purpose. My mom's out with her friends tonight—a much needed night out for her if you ask me—and I haven't seen much of Georgia since she moved in with Michael. That meant it was only me passing out candy at our house, and once that was done I couldn't resist coming over to Thayer's.

The door swings open, candy bowl in his hand.

He's not dressed up—why would he when he already has the wardrobe of a lumberjack?

His lips part, taking me in. I'm in a black, bodycon dress with slits up the sides. I don't usually wear a lot of makeup, but for tonight I did a smoky gray eye and red lip.

I flash him a sharp-toothed smile.

"Trick or treat?"

"Trick," he answers, eyes heating with lust.

I pout. "That's not how this works. You're supposed to give me treats." I hold up my empty pumpkin shaped bucket.

"I'll give you treats." He nods for me to come inside. "What are you two?" He points at Binx in my arms. "A vampire and...?"

"He's my bat." I flick his little bat wings. "See? Every vampire needs a pet bat."

He shakes his head, shutting the door. "Only you would dress up your cat for Halloween."

"He likes it," I argue, setting my cat down.

When I straighten back up, Thayer wraps a hand around my waist, yanking me into his body. My hands land on his solid, hard chest.

"This dress," his chest rumbles, hands roaming over my body and ending up on my ass, "is something."

"You like?"

He rubs his lips together. "Very much."

"I put it on for you," I admit, running a finger down his chest. "I thought you'd like it."

"Mmm," he hums, stepping back to rake his eyes over me again. "I really, really do."

Standing on my tiptoes, I whisper in his ear, "I think it'll look even better on your floor."

Those words break the last of his self-control. With a low growl, he picks me up and pins me against the wall in his foyer. The dress bunches around my hips with my legs around his waist. He kisses me passionately; in a way I never knew existed before.

I worried, after that night on his couch, that he'd back away and regret what we did. It was a fear that kept me up at night. It was terrifying to think that it might've meant more to me than him.

But instead, that night unlocked a part of Thayer I'm not sure even he knew existed.

His hips push into mine and I gasp at the feel of him hard

and ready.

"Thayer," I pant.

He wraps a hand around my neck. I moan, surprised at how much I like his hand there. "Do you want me to fuck you against the wall, Salem?"

God, yes.

"Yes."

"Good."

Reaching between us, I undo his belt and make quick work of the button and zipper. He uses his legs and body weight to hold me against the wall, wiggling his jeans and boxer-briefs down enough to free his cock. I stare down at it. I can't help it. I stroke him as best I can with him holding me, but he shakes his head.

I give him a puzzled look, worried maybe I did something wrong, but he shakes his head.

"Need to be in you."

He shoves my thong to the side. Normally I'm a boy shorts kind of girl, but this dress wouldn't allow that.

And then he's inside me, both of us sighing in relief.

I've been dreaming of this moment since our first time.

He stares into my eyes, his hands gripping my hips as he lifts me up and down onto his cock.

"Fuck." The veins in his neck strain, holding himself back. "You have no idea how good you feel."

"I know how good *you* feel." My head falls back against the wall, his fingers finding my clit. "Thayer," I pant, breathless, "right there. Don't stop."

I fall over the edge, my orgasm rattling me to the bone.

His lips press open-mouthed kisses to my neck. He pumps his hips harder, faster into me, and impossibly I feel my body building toward another high.

"Thayer!" I scream his name, my orgasm rippling through me.

He groans through his own release. Without pulling out of me, he carries me up the stairs and to his bedroom. I've never been in here before. The only part of the upstairs I've seen is a hall bath and Forrest's room. It's dark inside, so it's hard for me to take much in when he sets me on the bed.

"Hang tight," he tells me, flicking on the light in his attached bathroom.

It gives me enough glow to look around his room.

Black furniture, gray walls. A picture of him and Forrest on the dresser. Blinds, no curtains.

It's very basic, but somehow so perfectly Thayer. It smells like him too. I let my body sink into the mattress.

He returns with a washcloth and gently guides my legs apart, cleaning me up. I shiver when he places tender kisses on my inner thighs. "I didn't hurt you, did I?"

I shake my head. "No. I'd tell you."

He nods, rising up from the bed. He tosses the washcloth into a laundry basket in the corner. Turning to me with hands on his hips, he says, "I should've talked to you about this before, but..."

I sit up, a bit worried where he's going with this. "But?"

"Look, with your past, I don't know your triggers or anything like that, so you have to be open with me if I do something you don't like or if there's a position that bothers you or just fucking anything, Salem."

I nod. "Of course. I would tell you. I..." I look away, not meeting his gaze. "Therapy helped me a lot. I still go sometimes when I feel like I need it. Yeah, I get nightmares, but I've come a long way. You don't know how bad it was. I'm in a good place now."

"Okay." He nods, his Adam's apple bobbing with a swallow. "I just always want you to be honest with me. I never—"

I sit up and grab his wrist. His skin is warm, the hair on his arm rough against my palm. "You wouldn't hurt me, Thayer. Please, stop worrying."

He stares into my eyes, searching for any hint that I'm lying. "Okay," he finally agrees.

Undoing the buttons on his shirt, I look up at him. "Stop worrying and make love to me."

He cups my face in his hands, kissing me deeply. "That I can do."

CHAPTER THIRTY-FIVE

It's been too cold for a while now to run outside so I've been going to the gym with Thayer joining me. He's a grump, more than usual anyway, of the mornings but I think he doesn't like the idea of me going to the gym that early on my own, so he insists on tagging along.

Therefore, I'm not surprised when I trudge out into the cold—wind whipping my hair around my shoulders—to find him leaning against my car.

"How long have you been out here?" I ask, like always.

He shrugs, like always. "Not long. We're not going to the gym, though."

"We're not?"

He shakes his head. "Nope."

I narrow my eyes. "Listen, sex is great and all, but that's not the workout I'm looking for right now."

He huffs, his breath fogging the chilly air. "I should fuck you just for using that sassy tone with me, but sex wasn't what I was referring to, smart ass."

"If we're not going to the gym then what are we doing?"

I thought he understood how much I need to run when I'm like this, but maybe not?

"Come on, this way." He motions for me to follow him over to his house.

I narrow my eyes but fall into step beside him. "What are you up to?"

"You'll see soon enough."

He leads me inside, and down the basement stairs, flicking on another light to illuminate the area.

My hand flies up to my mouth. *"Thayer."*

The whole basement has been outfitted as a gym. The floor is an extra cushy mat-like material, and there's a treadmill, elliptical, rower, and weight machine. There's a TV mounted on the light blue walls as well as mirrors all along the back wall.

I spin around, taking it all in. There's a yoga mat rolled up in the corner with hand weights that I missed before.

"You did all this for—"

I almost say *for me*, but that's silly. This is his house. He wouldn't put in a home gym for me.

"For you."

My mouth falls open. "What?"

"I did this for you. I know you prefer running outside, but the gym has to do when the weather is bad, but I figured this was better than going to a real gym and it's free." He shoves his hands in the pockets of his athletic shorts, shoulders hunched like this is no big deal.

But Thayer Holmes put in a home gym in his basement *for me*.

I think I'm going to cry.

He notices the tears gathering in my eyes and gently tugs me into his body, wrapping his arms around me. "Baby, please don't cry. I didn't mean to make you sad."

"I'm not sad." I rest my chin on his chest, tilting my head back to look at him. He places his hands on my cheeks, their large size nearly swallowing my face whole. "These are happy tears, because you are the kindest, most thoughtful human being."

He kisses the tip of my nose and it's so surprisingly sweet and gentle coming from my lumberjack.

"I want you to be happy, Salem."

I wet my lips with a slide of my tongue. "You make me happy."

He rubs his thumbs in gentle circles around my cheeks. "You make me happy too." The words are a quiet confession on his lips, one that I savor.

Who would've thought that the grumpy neighbor who was so rude to me when I first came over would now look at me like this?

Like I'm the entire universe grasped gently between his palms.

"I don't know if anyone's ever told you this," I whisper up at him, "but you have one of the most beautiful souls."

He laughs. "I thought you were going to say cock."

I grin. "That too."

Pushing up on my tiptoes, I kiss him. He deepens it, sliding his tongue past the seam of my lips. He groans when I pull away, eyes heavy-lidded with lust.

I give his chest a pat. "Time for me to go run." I eye the brand-new treadmill. It's a beast, and I know from the brand name it's expensive too.

"I'll just be over here." He tosses his thumb at the weight machine. "Pretending not to check out your ass."

"You can if you want." I do a little booty pop. "I won't mind." He growls looking ready to pounce on me. I wiggle a finger. "Nuh-uh. I need my run."

Maybe it's because I use the word need, but he sobers and nods. "Take your time."

Pulling my earphones and phone out of my pocket, I pop

them in and start my music with my favorite playlist to get me through a workout. I don't always listen to music, but sometimes it helps. It takes me a minute to get the treadmill started up, I almost ask Thayer for help, but I figure it out on my own and he's left in the corner on the weight machine.

I can see him in the mirror as I run, but it doesn't take me long to fall into a rhythm and forget all about him. I just run and run, leaving all my problems behind me.

***

I'm sweaty and gross by the time I finish my run and even spend a little bit of time checking out everything else. But Thayer doesn't let it stop him from pulling me into a searing kiss. I could kiss this man for the rest of my life and never get tired of it. I might be young, but I know this truth; his lips were made for mine.

"Come on," he gives my ass a light smack, "let me make you breakfast."

I press my lips together, trying not to show my smile. I love playful Thayer a little too much.

Love.

That word suddenly invades my thoughts as I follow him upstairs.

Do I love Thayer?

I think I do. No, I *know* I do. But I'm scared to tell him that. For now, I keep those words bottled up close to my heart. I'll tell him eventually, but today isn't that day.

In his now fully completed kitchen Thayer starts setting out ingredients for breakfast.

"What are you making me?"

"My famous breakfast sandwich."

I pick up a bag of arugula. "I'm intrigued."

He arches a brow, setting out orange juice. "You should be." I go to pick up the orange juice to pour a glass, but he snaps his fingers together. "Water first."

Sighing, I grab a clean glass and fill it with ice and water from the refrigerator. "Happy now?" I take a big sip.

He watches me down the entire glass through narrowed eyes and then gives a gruff nod of approval when it's drained. "Thrilled."

I refill the glass, leaning a hip against the counter while he cracks eggs into a mug. "Is there anything I can do to help?"

"Rinse off the arugula."

"You got it, Captain."

"Captain," he mutters.

"Aye, aye."

He shakes his head. "You're in a good mood."

"Don't you know exercise releases endorphins?"

Those brown eyes stare at me, and I know what he's thinking before he says it. "You know what else releases endorphins?" He pours a little bit of Club Soda into the mug, then grabs a fork to scramble the eggs together. "Sex. And sex is way more fucking fun than a workout."

"I disagree." I open the fridge and grab the bowl of grapes, popping one in my mouth before bending to search for a strainer for the arugula. "I think both can be equally invigorating."

"Hmm," he hums. "Maybe I just need to fuck you better."

"Thayer!" I nearly hit my head on the side of the counter on my way back up. I give him a light swat on his arm, my cheeks twin flames.

"What?" He plays Mister Innocent.

"You know what."

His eyes heat, raking over me. My hair is a damp mess, falling half out of my ponytail. My shirt is over-sized and baggy, falling halfway down my thighs over my black running leggings. There's nothing sexy about what I have going on right now, but you wouldn't know that by the look in his eyes, and dammit if that doesn't make me feel like the hottest woman on the planet.

He pours the eggs into the hot pan, adding some sort of seasoning to them, and then drops two English muffins into the toaster while I make sure the arugula is thoroughly rinsed. I do an extra good job with it, because after getting food poisoning one time I'm never letting that happen again. I spent hours puking my guts up.

Opening the fridge, he grabs two slices of cheddar cheese and spicy mayo.

We work together seamlessly, and when the muffins pop up, I plop them onto plates and slather some mayo on.

"This smells amazing," I say when Thayer adds the eggs onto each of our muffins, cheddar cheese melting on top.

"Hopefully it tastes amazing too." He puts some arugula on top of each and then I top them with the other half of the English muffin.

We sit down at the breakfast table—a real handmade wooden table one of his friends crafted—and he waits for me to take the first bite.

"Oh my God, Thayer, this is amazing." I didn't know a simple egg sandwich could taste so good.

He chuckles, clearly pleased. "I'm glad you like it."

I go in for another bite, saying around a mouthful, "Like it? I love it." I put a hand over my mouth while I chew my too big bite.

His smile is amused. "You're saying I should cook for you more often?"

"Duh. I do bake you cupcakes."

"We should do something today."

His statement surprises me. "Do something? Like what?"

He shrugs. "I don't know. Just go out together. To the store or something."

I run my tongue over my lips. "Okay. That sounds fun. I have to work at the store this morning but I'm off at two."

"All right. I'll pick you up."

"You're going to pick me up?"

He shrugs. "Why wouldn't I?"

"I..." I lower my head. "Okay."

"You don't want me to pick you up." He frames it as a statement.

"No, it's not that." I tuck a loose blond hair behind my ear. "I assumed you wouldn't want people to see that. It's a small town. People talk."

He finishes his sandwich. "I'm not in the habit of giving a fuck what other people think."

I crack a smile. "Good."

CHAPTER THIRTY-SIX

Sure enough, Thayer's truck is waiting outside A Checkered Past Antiques. I told my mom he wanted my help getting things to decorate Forrest's room. A total lie since the little boy's room was done before probably anything else. But I had to give her some sort of reason as to why our neighbor was picking me up from work.

Sliding into his truck, the leather warm on my jean-clad bottom, I smile at him. He's too handsome in a navy sweatshirt, jeans, and baseball cap. It's really not fair to my heart for him to be so hot.

"How was work?" He pulls out of the spot he was parallel parked in.

"It was good. It always is."

"Is that what you want to do? Continue running the store?"

"I don't know," I muse, looking out the window. "Maybe. I'm not sure. I'm not sure about a lot of things."

"Hey," he says softly, like he's worried he's offended me, "it's okay to not know everything and have it all figured out. You'll get there."

I bite my lip. "You think?"

"Sometimes paths aren't always clear, but as time goes by and you experience life, things start to make more sense."

I nod along. His words mean a lot to me, because it seems like most people expect me to have it figured out by now.

Thayer drives out of town, relaxing as he does. He rests his hand on my leg, his fingers wrapped around my thigh. I try not to let on that it makes me ache in all the right places.

"Where are we going?"

"I need to run to the nursery for some plants I need for a project."

"That's fine."

"You don't mind?" He looks at me skeptically.

I just want to be with you. I don't say that out loud though.

"Nope."

"All right."

We ride mostly in silence, but it's comfortable. I never realized how important that is, to find comfort in silence with someone else's presence. It's nice.

It takes us about thirty minutes to get to the nursery and when we do I follow him out of the truck and inside the greenhouse.

Upon entering he grins when he runs into a guy he knows.

"Hey, Marcus." He claps hands with him and gives him a half-hug. "How have you been?"

"Good, I've got what you need pulled to the side so you can checkout and load up."

"Thanks, I appreciate it." Thayer looks over his shoulder at me lingering behind him. "Salem, come here." He reaches for my hand, tugging me forward to his side. "Matt, meet Salem. She's my new neighbor. Salem, meet Matt, a good friend of mine."

"Hi," I smile, extending a hand, "it's nice to meet you."

He takes my hand, giving Thayer an amused look. "It's nice to meet you, too."

With introductions over, Thayer says, "I'm going to take a look around and see if there's anything else I should grab before we go."

"Take your time," Matt says, already turning away. "I'll be around. Just yell when you need me."

Thayer and I walk down the rows and rows of plants.

"This nursery is huge," I tell him, noticing how it goes on for as far as I can see.

"Matt's family is a big supplier to a lot of places. They even ship plants around the states."

"Wow." I tug a flower near my nose and give it a sniff. "And I guess you know what most of these are?"

He points to the flower I just smelled. "Gladiolus italicus." I arch a brow. "Better known as just Gladiolus or Sword Lily."

"Interesting," I muse. I move to a shrub of peonies. "My favorite."

"Peonies? I wouldn't have guessed that."

I nod. "I love the pink shade and how intricate and delicate they look." I bend, giving it a sniff too. "If you wouldn't have chosen a peony, what did you think my favorite would be?"

"Sunflowers," he answers without hesitation. "I guess that's because you remind me of them. You're so bright and happy most of the time."

"I didn't used to be," I admit mournfully.

His finger is warm beneath my chin, lifting my head to look at him. "Who we used to be doesn't matter, it's who we are now. What's in our hearts matters most. You're sunshine, Salem, but even the sun doesn't always shine." His hand moves to cup my cheek. A sigh passes through my lips as I lean into his touch. "I'm not bright like you, but I promise, when your days are dark, I'll be your light."

Tears prick my eyes. It's the most beautiful thing anyone has ever said to me.

"Thank you."

He rubs his thumb over my cheek. He does that a lot. I wonder if it's as much to comfort me as it is him. "You don't have to thank me, baby."

Standing on my tiptoes, I wrap my arms around his neck and kiss him. His hands go to my waist, and I know he wants to touch my skin, but it's not possible with my coat.

Stepping back down, I can't help but look at him and wonder how it's possible to feel this much for someone. Especially someone I haven't realistically known that long. Perhaps sometimes it's not about how much you know someone's personal details and more about how you feel about them. There has to be some sort of faith put into gut instinct, right?

***

"Where are we going next?" I climb into the truck, the bed loaded up with shrubbery and small evergreens.

"I'm going to drop these off at the job site."

I look at him in surprise. "You're going to take me to your job site?"

"Yeah." He cranks up the truck, turning the heat up. "You don't want to go?"

"No, I do, but—"

"But nothing," he cuts me off, backing out. "No one's going to say anything if that's what you're worried about."

I take in the strong set of his jaw. His wide shoulders. "Okay, then."

"I'm going to swing by and pick up some donuts for the guys first," he says, turning onto the road and heading south.

"What job are these for?" I toss my thumb over my shoulder like he doesn't already know what I'm talking about.

"A new bank that's going in over in Huntsburg." It's a town about twenty minutes from ours.

"That's cool. I bet things slow down a lot this time of year."

"Yeah," he sighs. "It's why I have some trucks for snow plowing. That brings in good money once it gets too cold and the ground freezes."

"Oh. I didn't even think about something like that. If you weren't doing this, what do you think you'd do?"

His eyes drift briefly over to me. "Are you interviewing me?"

I shrug. "Just curious."

I'm curious about all things Thayer Holmes. I want to know every detail about him.

"I'd probably be a carpenter. Make furniture, cabinets. Something like that. I do some of it now, just for myself, but I'm not that good."

"What have you made in your house?" He makes a noncommittal noise. I poke his side and he twitches like it tickles. "Tell me."

"I did the crown molding and the stair banister."

"You did?" I don't know why I ask this, since obviously the answer is yes.

"Yeah." He gives a gruff laugh. "I like to work with my hands."

My eyes zero in on his hands gripping the steering wheel—thinking about how those strong, capable hands feel on my body.

Thayer pulls into the drive-thru line of Dunkin' and asks me if I want anything. "Ooh," I bounce a little in my seat, "a strawberry sprinkle donut *and—*" I draw out the word, tapping my lip as I think. "—a caramel latte."

He places the order, tacking on a hot chocolate for himself. "Their hot chocolate isn't as good as what I make, but I want something hot."

"You make hot chocolate?"

"Mhmm," he hums, sitting up to pull his wallet from his back jeans pocket. I don't know why that's so sexy, seeing his arm flex as he takes out the folded leather wallet, but it is. He passes a credit card over to the drive-thru worker when we reach the window. "Hold onto those." He hands me the two boxes of donuts for his crew, a small bag with my donut and his on top. He takes his card back and tucks it away, returning his wallet to his pocket. Our drinks get handed out and then he's driving away.

"Do you want your donut now?" I ask, already reaching in the bag for mine.

"Yeah."

I pass him the apple streusel donut and then take out mine. "I think I'm a sugar addict."

"Think?" He flashes an amused smile.

I roll my eyes. "Okay, I totally am. But I do drink Diet Coke."

"And it has enough artificial sweetener in it that you'd be better off with sugar."

I frown. "I know but ... it tastes better."

He looks at me like I'm insane. "People who love Diet Coke are crazy."

I stare blankly at him, mouth agape. "Take that back."

He shakes his head vehemently. "It's true."

"You keep it in your house!" I argue.

He comes to a stoplight and slows for the red, flicking on the blinker. He gives me a slow, lingering look. "Yeah, for you."

I mean, I knew this. Or I guess I assumed, but hearing him confirm it sends this weird bubbly feeling through me. "You like me," I say slowly with a smile.

He shakes his head, fingers over his mouth to hide a growing smile. "I put a gym in my house for you and it takes stocking Diet Coke for you to realize I like you?"

I press my lips together. "But do you like me? Like really like me, Thayer?" I reach over, rubbing his scruffy chin between my fingers.

The light changes and he turns left. "Yeah, Sunshine, I like, *really* like you."

My heart swells. Being liked by Thayer Holmes is a rare thing, that much is obvious. But he likes me. The girl who trespassed on his property—by accident of course—who brought him cupcakes and practically pestered him into being my friend.

But I wonder if that like has the potential to turn into something deeper, more meaningful, or if maybe after his divorce he's not ready to love again. Maybe he'll *never* be ready to love again.

Thayer pulls into the freshly paved parking lot of the new bank and parks his truck.

I hop out with the boxes in my hands, following him over to the crew of about ten guys.

"Paul, can you unload the truck?" He delegates to one of the men. "We brought donuts too."

The guy who must be Paul, older probably in his forties and wrinkled from time in the sun, passes us for the truck.

A few of the others stop what they're doing and give me a

once over. One's eyes linger longer than necessary on me and Thayer snaps his fingers.

"Donovan, watch where you're looking."

The guy, younger than the others, smirks. "Boss, you can't expect to bring a hot piece of ass like that around and me not to take a look."

I want to shove the boxes of donuts at the jerk. How fucking rude. I'm standing right here.

Thayer's eyes thin to slits and he takes the boxes from me, like he knows what I want to do with them and doesn't want me to ruin the treat for the other guys. "Watch your mouth."

"What?" Donovan's smile grows and he leans against the metal rake he's using. He's probably in his early twenties, and he'd be good looking if he wasn't running his mouth. "Maybe you'll be more tolerable now that you're getting laid again."

The other men still, the silence louder than anything. Thayer passes the boxes to one of the men, his hands going to his hips while his jaw works back and forth. "Drop the rake, grab your shit, and leave."

"What?" Donovan's smile falters. "I'm just joking, boss. You know me, I—" His eyes dart from me to Thayer, as if only just now realizing what kind of hole he's dug for himself.

"Do I need to spell it out for you?" The other men back away from Donovan, grabbing their donuts and pretending not to pay attention to what's going down. "You're fired, Donovan. Get off my site."

"Boss," Donovan's face falls this time, "I was just kidding around. She knows I was joking. I—"

Thayer holds up a hand. "She has a name. You didn't bother to ask, did you? Take your misogynistic ass to your car and *leave*. I mean it."

Donovan must know better than to argue. Head hanging, he sets the rake down gently despite the anger obviously radiating off of him. He walks away and gets into an old Ford Ranger.

Another of the men clears his throat. "Boss, we—uh— you're gonna need him. We can't afford to lose someone with Terry and Brooks leaving."

Thayer hangs his head, rubbing his jaw. "I know ... it doesn't matter. We'll be fine. I'll find replacements soon." Nodding at the guys, he tells them things that need to be done and then leads me back to his truck, the bed now empty. "I'm so fucking sorry about that."

"It's okay."

"Don't say that. Don't fucking say that. It's never okay for a man to talk about a woman like that, let alone when she's standing right there."

"They said you needed him—" Guilt settles inside me over the fact this guy got fired because of me. If Thayer had come without me, or I stayed in the car, he'd still have a job.

He shakes his head roughly. "Don't you feel fucking sorry for him or bad for me. He made his bed."

"He was just being a guy." I don't really believe that and from the look on his face he doesn't either.

"I'm raising a son," he says firmly, "and if I ever heard him say that shit about a woman, I would know I failed him. Just being a guy. Boys will be boys. It's a bullshit excuse, Salem. Don't ever let some loser make you think otherwise."

"Okay," I say quietly, staring at my lap.

"I'm not mad at you." He feels the need to say.

Looking out the truck window, I reply, "I know."

He reaches over, taking my hand so our fingers are

wrapped tightly together. It's hard to tell where his hand begins and mine ends.

"You're my girl," he says it so surely, like it's a fact already known, "and *no one* talks about my girl like that."

CHAPTER THIRTY-SEVEN

Thanksgiving approaches, and with it, comes a pile of snow. We've steadily been getting snow for weeks now, but this was the worst one yet. Thayer was worried his parents wouldn't be able to make it for the holiday after all, but I watch as an older couple gets out of a car and Thayer comes out to help with their bags. I'm not spying—not on purpose anyway. With the turkey cooking in the oven, and the sides ready, I'm watching for Georgia and Michael to arrive. My mom wanted me to alert her—saying she needed a moment to fix her face before they come in. And by fix her face she doesn't mean makeup or anything of the sort. No, she has to remove the perturbed look on her face because they just got engaged and she knows Georgia is going to be excited. Mom, bless her, doesn't want to rain on her parade despite her dislike of Michael.

I'm not the guy's biggest fan either. He's kind of ditzy, but honestly in a lot of ways he's a good fit for Georgia and at least it *seems* like he's maturing.

Thayer greets his parents with hugs and a kiss on the cheek for his mom.

His brother arrived yesterday, but I didn't see him when he got there and haven't met him yet. I'm sure I will at some point. Especially since Thayer told me that he let him know I might be coming over to use the gym some. He added that he'd leave the outside basement door unlocked. He knew the last thing I'd want to do is disturb his family so he made sure I knew I could still use it without that happening.

I didn't ask him specifically, but I don't think he's told his brother or his parents about us. Not that there's really an "us" to tell them about. We're just ... fooling around, I guess? That feels like the wrong label for it. I know it's more than that, but we're not dating.

My phone buzzes in my pocket, and I pull it out expecting a text from Georgia or maybe even Thayer. But it's from Caleb.

Caleb: I just wanted to say Happy Thanksgiving. We were friends before we were a couple. I miss that. I miss you.

I frown down at the message, my chest heavy with remorse for hurting him. I know I should've handled the whole thing better, but I didn't know how, and I hate that Caleb got caught in the crossfire of my actions.

Me: Happy Thanksgiving. Miss you too. Have a good holiday.

He replies right back.

Caleb: Thanks. You too.

When I put my phone away, I spot Georgia and Michael arriving.

"Mom!" I yell out. "They're here."

She pokes her head into the living room. Pointing to her face, she mimes a happy smile. "Does this look genuine? I need this to scream that I'm so thrilled my oldest daughter is engaged."

"It doesn't quite reach your eyes," I tell her honestly, moving away from my creeper perch by the window. Binx's green eyes watch me steadily from his spot on the back of the couch, black tail flicking lazily.

"How about now?" She tries again

I stifle a cringe. "You keep practicing in there," I wave her to the kitchen, "and I'll stall."

"Great. Good idea." She smooths her hands down her apron that's decorated with turkeys.

Opening the door, I let Georgia and Michael inside. They remove their coats, much too heavy to be wearing in the warm interior.

Georgia hugs me first, squeezing me tight. I won't lie, I've missed having her around even though I didn't see her much with her shifts at the hospital. Michael grabs me into a hug next, lifting me off the floor.

"Oh," I say in surprise. "Hi, Michael."

He sets me down, grinning from ear to ear. His brown hair is slicked back and his cheeks are freshly shaved. The clothes he wears, fitted jeans and preppy sweater, screams rich prick elitist. Which he's not. He just has expensive taste in clothes.

Beside him, my sister is wearing a light blue sweater dress that compliments the dark blue of his top. I bet she coordinated that.

"Let me see the ring," I tell my sister, shoving as much elation as I can into those five words. I *am* happy for her, this is what she wants, but sometimes I lack the enthusiasm I know she wants.

She extends her hand, showing off clean nails and the shiny diamond ring on her finger. It's pretty and feminine, exactly what I would picture for my sister. It's not what I would want at all. I prefer something more unique, an antique with character and history. Georgia and I are polar opposites, but I wouldn't ask for a different sister. She's the best.

"It's beautiful," I say sincerely, cradling her hand in mine.

"Isn't it?" She grins at Michael. "He did so good."

He lowers his head, giving her a kiss. "Thanks, babe."

"Where's Mom?" She fluffs her perfectly curled hair. "I want to show her my ring."

"The kitchen."

She flounces off that way, leaving me alone with Michael. He's been around long enough that I can't help but rib him. "Break her heart and I'll gut you like a fish."

He chuckles, rolling up his sleeves. "You've always been something, Salem."

I narrow my eyes on him. "Fear me."

He ruffles my hair, making me wrinkle my nose. I'm not five. I smooth it back down. "You're too funny."

We meet the others in the kitchen, and I find my mom doing a much better job at acting happy for Georgia. It can be hard to see someone you love, love someone who you know isn't good for them. But after a while you can only say so much before you have to sit back and let whatever happens happen.

The food's almost ready so Michael and I get tasked with setting the table—which means I do most of the setting while he drones on and on about his job as an *assistant* to a realtor.

I'd rather watch paint dry, but I do a good job of slathering on a syrupy sweet smile and nodding in all the right places.

We never eat in the dining room except for holidays and birthday celebrations. Sometimes it feels like this completely separate part of the house that only exists on these days.

With the table set, it's time to bring the food in which all four of us take part in.

My mom lets Michael carve the turkey and he does a surprisingly good job at it. I find my mind drifting to next door. Does Thayer carve the turkey or his dad? Maybe his brother?

I'm snapped from my thoughts when we start passing food around the four of us. No one sits at the head. It's Georgia and Michael on one side and my mom and I on the other.

All in all, the meal is delicious, and the conversation never dulls.

We send Georgia and Michael home with leftovers, stuffing the rest into the refrigerator. We're going to be eating turkey for a week.

I don't mind, though.

When everything is put away, my mom turns to me. There's a sadness in her eyes that I can't pinpoint. She looks around, almost like she's trying to take everything in. Savor the memories.

"Is everything okay?" I ask her.

She nods, eyes shimmery. "Of course, Salem. Everything is fine."

But when she excuses herself from the room, head down like she doesn't want me to see her face, I know she's lying.

Whatever it is, it'll come out eventually.

The truth always does.

CHAPTER THIRTY-EIGHT

I couldn't sleep, and not because I had a nightmare. No matter what I tried, I couldn't stop thinking about my mom. She's keeping a secret.

It's five in the morning when I finally trek over to Thayer's, letting myself into the backyard through the gate, then down a set of three concrete stairs, in through the door.

And there he is, almost like he was waiting for me.

I shuck off my long coat—meant to help keep your legs warm too—and drape it over the back of a chair.

He sits on a workout bench, dressed in athletic shorts and a long sleeve shirt that clings to his muscular form.

"Were you waiting for me?"

It seems strange that he'd get up early just to wait in case I'd show up. But I think about those days when we first got back from the trip to Boston. Every time I had a nightmare and got up early to run, he was outside waiting. Then when I started going to the gym, he was there too.

"No."

I walk over to him, sitting on the bench beside him. I retie my shoes, making sure they're tight enough. His thigh is plastered against the side of mine. "Are you lying to me? You've been waiting for me every time since Boston."

He sucks his cheeks together, blowing out a breath. "You shouldn't run alone," is his only response.

"I was fine and safe before you came along. Don't feel

obligated—"

"It's not about safety. Okay, that's some of it," he acquiesces, picking up his water bottle. "Mostly, I just don't like the idea of you by yourself after a nightmare like that. You deserve to know you're not alone, that someone's beside you to fight your battles with you."

I think I might cry.

"Thayer..."

"You don't have to say anything. That's why I didn't tell you what I was doing before." He shrugs, setting his water down and standing. He stretches his arms, and I know it's because he's nervous. Thayer is the kind of person who does good things just because they're the right things. He doesn't seek out praise. That's not the kind of person he is. "Do you want to talk about it? Your nightmare?"

"I ... no nightmare tonight. I just couldn't sleep."

His eyes are warm with concern. "Why not?"

Moving from the bench to the floor, I stretch my legs. "I can tell my mom's keeping a secret and I have this gut feeling it's bad."

He hesitates, cocking his head to the side. "Like what?"

"I don't know, that's the problem. I can tell she's not sleeping much, and she's not eating a lot either. She seems stressed and ... scared," I tack on the last part. "I've tried asking her about it, but she gets cagey and I just ... hate waiting for the shoe to drop, you know?"

"I know what you mean. I can't guess what she has going on, but I'm sure she'll share it when she can."

I lower my head, staring at my purple leggings. "I hope so." Wanting to change the topic, I ask, "How was your Thanksgiving?"

"It was good. Would've burned the house down if my mom wasn't here to cook."

"Liar." I know he can cook.

He smirks, grabbing some weights. "How was yours?

"It was good. Lowkey. Just my mom, me, Georgia, and her fiancé."

"Sounds nice."

"It was." I walk over to the treadmill, pausing before I step on. "You really don't have to do this." I want him to know I don't expect him to get up at the crack of dawn every morning in case I have a nightmare.

"I know," he says, reaching for the dumbbells. "But I want to. It's what you do when you care about someone."

"What exactly?"

Chocolate brown eyes flicker over my body. "You find a way to let them know they aren't alone."

His answer chokes me up, and I don't say anything more. Turning the treadmill on, I run.

But for the first time in ... maybe, ever, I'm not running away from something. I'm running toward it.

CHAPTER THIRTY-NINE

It's a few days after Thanksgiving when my mom asks my sister and I to meet her for lunch. It's Georgia's day off and I can tell she's a bit disgruntled over the request in the group text, probably because she wants to be wedding planning, but maybe like me she senses that this is important and accepts the invitation.

I asked about the store, but my mom said it would be okay to close it for an hour.

In the middle of the day.

During holiday season.

I've never seen a brighter, more glaring red flag in all my life.

Bundled up against the cold—and to think it'll only get colder in the coming months—I shuffle my way outside and to my car.

My car, my trusty reliable car, chooses today not to start.

"No, no, no," I chant, trying again but the engine never turns over. "You have to be kidding me." I bang my hand against the steering wheel. "Don't fail me now, baby." Maybe if I sweet talk it, it'll work. "Come on, come on." I'm completely aware I'm begging with an inanimate object, but I don't have it in me to care.

The car isn't listening to my pleas.

A knock on my window nearly has a scream flying out of my throat. My hand goes to my chest, and I look over at Thayer, bent down at my car window with furrowed brows.

Opening my car door, I tell him, "My car won't start and I need to meet my mom and sister for lunch."

"I can take a look. You might need a new battery, but I'm about to head into town with my brother." My shoulders fall. "We can give you a ride."

"I don't want to inconvenience you."

He opens my door further. "Get in the truck, Salem."

Stifling a smile, I get out and lock my car. Not that anyone would want to steal the hunk of junk anyway.

Thayer's truck is already running in the driveway, the exhaust pluming in the air.

"You'll have to ride in the backseat," he tells me, walking up behind me, "Laith isn't enough of a gentleman to offer you the front."

"That's fine. I didn't expect for you to give me a ride."

His fingers gently stroke mine as he passes me, reaching for the back door to open it.

"Your car isn't starting. I'm not enough of an asshole to leave you stranded here."

"I'm hardly stranded," I argue, climbing in the seat. "My car is parked outside my house."

"Doesn't matter," is his response, closing the door on me.

Up front, his brother turns around with a wry grin. "Hey," he says in a smooth, deep voice. It's buttery and smooth. A purr where Thayer's is gruff and abrasive. "I'm Laith." He extends a hand to me while Thayer joins us in the truck.

"Salem." I fit my hand in his. It's softer than his brother's.

"Nice to meet you." His smile grows and he's not shy about looking me over.

Thayer smacks the back of his head. "Stop checking her out. She's eighteen and too young for you."

Too young for you.

I know his brother is younger than him by a few years. If I'm too young for him, then does Thayer really think the same about us?

Buckling the seatbelt, I cross my arms over my chest as he backs out of the driveway.

I don't want to overthink his words. He's probably trying to keep his brother from hitting on me, but dammit if it doesn't sting.

Thayer glances at me in the rearview mirror. "Where is it you need me to drop you off?"

I rattle off the name of the restaurant. Laith swivels around to face me in the back. "So, what's it like being this asshole's neighbor?" He gives Thayer a good-natured rough pat on the shoulder.

"Um..." I rub my lips together. "It's ... uh..."

"Don't grill her," Thayer growls, "and turn your ass around."

Laith sighs, spinning back around. "Always gotta be the big brother."

"One of us has to be the responsible one."

Thayer turns his truck onto Main Street, pulling up outside the restaurant. "Thank you so much for the ride," I tell him sincerely.

"It's no problem, Salem."

I feel his eyes on me as I climb out of the car, heading inside. The door is starting to close behind me when I hear the truck pull away.

I spot my mom and sister. Georgia waving at me madly so I can't miss them. Weaving through the tables, I join them and find a stack of bridal magazines at Georgia's side. Sometimes I feel so un-girly because I've never given thought to a wedding while my sister has been planning hers in her head since she was probably in diapers.

Giving each of them a half-hug I settle into a seat beside Georgia since my mom has her bag on the one at her side. "Have you all ordered yet?"

Georgia brushes blond hair over her shoulders. "Just drinks."

I peruse the menu and set it aside. We've eaten here a lot, so it never takes me long to decide.

"It's so nice having just you two girls together." My mom smiles across at us, something wistful and thoughtful in her gaze. "We don't spend enough time together anymore."

"Life's busy," Georgia reasons, sipping at her glass of wine.

Wine. At lunch time. Huh.

Maybe it's because I've never been one much for alcohol that I can't imagine wine at lunch.

The waitress swings by the table, we place our orders, and I tack on my drink.

Diet Coke, of course.

The waitress has barely left our table when Georgia starts in. "I'm thinking a summer wedding, so that means I need to start pinning down the location soon. Photographer and caterer too," she rambles, ticking them off on her fingers. "And I need to start dress shopping. The sooner the better. You know how picky I can be. Oh, and Salem, I was going to do this more formally, but will you be my Maid of Honor?"

"Oh." I'm taken off guard. We're plenty close, but I figured she'd reserve that spot for one of her friends. "Of course, Georgia. I'd be honored."

Her smile is beaming. She wraps her arms around me in a

hug the best she can with us sitting side by side. "I'm so excited! And Mom," she lets me go, facing our mother, "I was hoping you'd walk me down the aisle?" She bites her lip nervously like she's afraid she might say no.

"Here's your soda," the waitress interrupts the moment, setting my glass down and breezing away.

"Georgia." My mom clasps her hands beneath her chin, tears swimming in her eyes. "I would be honored."

Chat revolves around the wedding as we eat our food. My plate is almost empty when my mom sighs, pushing her half-eaten one away from her like she can't stomach another bite let alone continue to look at the plate.

"There's a reason I asked you girls to meet me for lunch."

"Insisted," Georgia points at her with her fork. "You insisted we be here, Mom."

She inhales a shaky breath. "There's no right way to say this—"

"Are you dating someone?" Georgia interjects and I could kick her for interrupting. It's so rude.

"No." She shakes her head, a humorless laugh bubbling out of her throat. "I ... no, it's not that."

"Mom?" Somehow, already, just from the crushing agony on her face I know this is going to be bad.

"I ... uh..." She sits up straighter, taking her napkin off her lap and setting it on the table. Steeling her shoulders, she drops the bomb.

"I have cancer and ... it doesn't look promising."

You don't just feel your heart break.

You hear it.

It's in the echo of words battering around in your skull like a pinball in a machine.

I have cancer.

I have cancer.

I have cancer.

"Salem!" My mom yells after me.

I didn't even realize I'd gotten up from the table. I stumble outside, throwing up what I'd just eaten in a nearby frozen bush. Someone on the sidewalk curses and runs like I have the plague.

Cancer.

My mom has cancer.

I don't even know what kind.

Does it even matter?

She said it doesn't look promising.

I ... I might lose her.

I inhale a ragged breath, struggling to get enough oxygen into my lungs. It's so cold and the air burns my lungs. Staggering down the street, I wrap my arms around myself. I fled the restaurant without even grabbing my coat. At least I have on a heavy turtleneck sweater.

Reaching the end of the street, I have enough presence of mind to wait for the crosswalk to let me across.

I'm almost to the other side when I hear my name.

But it isn't my mom calling after me.

Not Georgia.

Or even Thayer.

CHAPTER FORTY

"Salem!" He yells my name from across the street, exiting the Chinese restaurant with a to-go bag in hand. I can tell from the way he says my name this isn't him trying to get my attention in a friendly way. He sounds worried, sensing my obvious distress. He's the last person I want to see me having this breakdown. Caleb throws his hand up at a car that waits for him and he runs across to meet me where I crossed on the other side. His eyes are filled with nothing but concern and worry for me.

Me.

The girl who broke his heart.

"You're crying," he says, his gaze roaming over me. "What's wrong?"

I wipe hastily at the tears. They're cold on my cheeks. "N-Nothing," I stutter, rubbing beneath my nose. *Ew.* "It's nothing, Caleb." I look down at the ground, away from his penetrating stare.

His finger gently tips my chin up. "I know you better than that."

"It's cold," I say, hoping that'll be enough to get him to leave.

"Is your car around?" He spins in a circle, searching for it.

I shake my head. "No, it died this morning."

Died.

Like my mom might.

My face crumbles, and I start crying all over again. "Salem," Caleb says softly, pulling me into the protective cushion of his body. "What's going on? I know you're not like this about your car."

"I..." I can't choke out the words between my tears.

"It's freezing and you're not wearing a coat. My car is down the block. I can drive you home." He sets the to-go bag down and starts taking his coat off. "Here, put this on."

"No," I sniffle, wiping beneath my nose. "I can't take your coat."

"You can and you will," he insists, giving it a shake for emphasis. "Come on now, babe, put it on." He winces at the endearment that slid so naturally off his tongue.

"T-Thank you," I stutter around my tears, slipping my arms inside. It's warm from his body heat.

He reaches for my hand but catches himself, nodding for me to follow him instead. Down the street sits his car and he unlocks it, opening the passenger door for me. Once I'm inside, he closes the door, puts the food in the back and climbs in himself, cranking up the engine. The heat is turned all the way up and it doesn't take long for the car to warm up.

"Do you want to go home or somewhere else?"

He's already driving toward my house, but I find myself saying, "Would you mind driving around for a little bit? I need to calm down."

He gives me a speculative look but doesn't ask. "Okay."

We've been riding around in silence, save for the soft sound of the radio in the background, for around twenty minutes when I find the strength to tell him.

"My mom asked Georgia and me to lunch." I look down at my lap, spreading my fingers wide and flexing them. Stalling.

"She has cancer." My chin wobbles. Fuck, I don't want to keep crying, but all I can see in my mind is another funeral, but this time different. So different. There are no feelings of relief. Just crippling fear at how I'd go forward without my mom.

"Fuck," he blurts with an exhale. "God. Fuck. I'm so fucking sorry. Did ... do you know what kind?"

"I don't know." I wipe at my damp face and Caleb reaches over, opening the glove compartment and revealing the stash of napkins there. I forgot that he always keeps the thing stuffed full or I would've grabbed one myself. He passes it to me, letting me get control of myself. "I ran out before she could say. She just said that it doesn't look promising, and I freaked out."

When my dad got diagnosed with cancer, I thanked the universe and then pleaded with it to take him out of this world.

But not my mom.

Not her.

Please, don't take her from me. I'm not ready. I might be an adult now but I still need my mom.

"Salem, I want you to know that no matter what I'm always here for you. You always have me. We might not be together," he swallows thickly like it still hurts him to say that, "but I'm not going anywhere."

"She's too young," I croak. "It's not fair."

People like to argue that life isn't fair, and I think that's a stupid way to brush off things like they're no big deal. I don't want to ever overlook things or not acknowledge my own feelings on something because of that mentality.

"Your mom is strong," Caleb says assuredly. "She's a fighter."

"She is," I agree, sniffling, "but it doesn't matter how strong someone is, there are some fights you can't win."

Pity fills his face and I hate that. I don't want him or anyone else to pity me.

"It is what it is," I say, steeling my shoulders. "We'll get through this."

"You will, Salem. And so will she. I believe it."

I press my lips together, holding back more tears. "Thank you."

He nods, tightening his hold on the steering wheel.

Caleb takes me home then and before I slip out of the car, I curse. "Oh, fuck, Caleb I forgot about your food. It's going to be cold now. I'm so sorry."

He smiles that same blinding boyish smile that first made my stomach explode with butterflies years ago. "It's no biggie. That's what microwaves are for."

"Well, thank you."

For the ride.

For driving me around.

For listening.

For just being there.

He gives me a sad, longing look. "Always."

Inside, I find my mom waiting for me at the kitchen table. Her fingers are wrapped around a hot cup of coffee and there are cupcakes baking in the oven.

Cookie dough.

A pink apron with purple polka dots is wrapped around her torso.

"Sit." She tips her head at the chair across from her.

I walk forward, my feet heavy, and slump into the chair. The tears come immediately when I look across at my mom.

My beautiful, vibrant, resilient mother who has faced so much and deserves her happy ending. Not ... this. Not a battle she might not win the fight of.

"Hi," she says, like that's the simplest, easiest greeting.

"Hi," I echo back, the word flat and choked sounding.

Her lips turn down in a frown as she reaches across the table, gripping my hand. Hers is cold, slightly clammy. "I'm so sorry."

"You're sorry?" I parrot. "Mom," I shake my head back and forth, trying my hardest to hold it together, "you have nothing to be sorry for. It's not like you asked for this to happen to you. It just did."

"I know, honey." She gives my hand a slight squeeze. "But that doesn't mean I'm not sorry that you have to go through this."

"Please," I beg brokenly, "stop apologizing for something you can't control. What kind is it?"

"Breast," she replies. "They said for me to have a fighting chance, a double mastectomy is the way to go." She clears her throat, obviously struggling for composure. "I hate that you girls have to see me go through this."

"Mom," I beg, tightening my hold on hers. "Don't say things like that. We're here for you. *I'm* here for you. Whatever you need." Her eyes pool with tears. "We're going to get through this. I promise."

Getting up from the table, I go around to hug her. We cry together, and I hope with everything I have in me that it's a promise I can keep.

CHAPTER FORTY-ONE

I wake up to an unfamiliar sound and glance at the clock. It's eight in the morning. That means I slept through the whole night. That rarely happens. Even without the nightmares I usually have trouble going to sleep. But apparently crying your eyes out exhausts the body. Who knew?

Remembering the noise, I climb out of bed, straightening my too-big shirt that's twisted around my torso.

Reaching the window, I peer outside to see the hood of my car up with Thayer bent under it.

He's ... what is he doing?

Throwing on a sweatshirt, stuffing my feet in boots, and then grabbing my coat on my way out the door I stomp my way up the snowy drive, arms bunched under my chest like as if he could even tell I'm not wearing a bra with all the layers.

"What do you think you're doing?"

He looks over his shoulder at me. A worn brown beanie sits on top of his head, sandy brown curls poking from beneath. The scruff on his cheeks is heavier than normal and a plaid flannel collar pokes out haphazardly from beneath his coat.

"Working on your car," he says in a 'duh' tone.

"But *why*?"

His eyes shift from under the hood to me. "Because your car wouldn't start. I'm trying to figure out if it's the battery, or the ignition, or—"

I hold up a hand. "Car speak is a foreign language to me.

Speak English."

He turns around, crossing his arms to face me fully. "I know a little about cars. I figured I might be able to save you some money."

"You ... I ... okay." I take a step back. "Wait," I pause, "didn't you have to get into my car to pop the hood?"

"Yeah, you really need to start locking your car. Anyone can get in it."

"Thayer." I can't help but start laughing. "All right. I'll leave you to it, then."

"Don't worry, I'm on my way to help." Laith saunters over to us, grinning crookedly with a thermos grasped in his hand. He claps Thayer on the shoulder. "Can't let big bro have all the fun. Goddamn, though, maybe I should. It's colder than a witch's tit out here."

Thayer shakes his head. "I don't need your help."

"Aw, bro, see—that's your problem. You never need anyone's help. That's why you're divorced and I'm not."

I have to admit it's fun seeing Thayer get ribbed by his younger brother.

Thayer snorts, shoving his brother. "Shut up, you've never even been married."

Laith snaps his fingers. "Exactly! That's why I'm the smart one."

Rolling his eyes, Thayer turns his attention back to underneath the hood of the car. "Trust me, that's not how it works."

With a laugh, I walk away from the brothers, kicking the snow off my boots before walking into the kitchen. I'll make Thayer some cupcakes today for taking the time to look at my car.

My mom has already left to open the store for the day, which means it's only Binx and me. Speaking of my beloved cat, he saunters into the kitchen and meows loudly, demanding me to fill up his bowl.

It's already full, but I make a show of adding a few crunchies on top. He sniffs, and, satisfied, he digs in.

So picky, that one.

Grabbing a bowl, I pour some cereal and add milk. Eating as I go, I look out the front window. Thayer is still hunched beneath my hood, Laith off to the side talking a mile a minute and gesticulating wildly with his hands. I'm sure Thayer loves that.

With a shake of my head I venture back to the kitchen and finish up my cereal, rinsing out the bowl in the sink.

A text comes through, so I check my phone, finding that it's from Caleb.

Caleb: How are you? I wanted to check on you.

Me: I'm okay. Had a talk with my mom last night. We're going to fight this battle. She's scheduling surgery soon. Her doctors said she needs a double mastectomy to have a fighting chance.

Caleb: Damn. I'm so fucking sorry.

Me: We'll get through this.

Caleb: I'm here for you and I mean that. Need to talk? I'm your guy. Need

a shoulder to cry on? I can be that too.

Me: Thanks. You're a good guy, Caleb. The best.

I put my phone away and start a fresh pot of coffee. I don't like coffee made at home as much, but with no car and the frigid temperatures it's not like I can take my bike to the coffee shop. This will have to do.

While that brews, I run upstairs to change and grab my laptop. I'm thinking about redesigning the labels for my candles. They've had the same logo for a few years now and it's time for an upgrade.

Setting up my laptop in the kitchen, I fix a cup of coffee dumping in a heaping pour of caramel flavored creamer and sugar.

Sitting down, I get to work. I take a break after about an hour to start the cupcakes and then I'm back at it. By the time the cupcakes are ready to come out of the oven I've completed a logo I'm proud of and excited to switch to. While they cool, I get to work on updating my website with the new logo. I'll have to print new labels later today as well to put on the batch I'm going to work on this week.

A knock on the side door nearly has me jumping out of my seat. Binx watches me with his glowing green eyes like I'm crazy.

Maybe I am.

Opening the door, I let Thayer inside. "Looks like it's only your battery."

I blurt out, "It took you that long to figure that out?"

His expression doesn't waver. Always so serious. "No. I

went and got you a new battery and installed it." He drops his gaze, noticing his dirty boots on the tiled floor. "Shit. Sorry about that."

I dismiss his concern. "It's okay. I need to clean the floors anyway." Cocking my head to the side, I add, "You didn't need to go through all that trouble."

"It wasn't any."

I highly doubt that, but I'm learning that arguing with Thayer is a pointless endeavor.

"I made you cupcakes." I point at the cupcakes sitting pretty on a cooling rack, waiting for frosting.

The hint of a smile. "Cookie dough?"

"No, I thought this time I'd give you something different. It's peaches n' cream."

He makes a grossed out expression before he can stop himself. Clearing his throat, he says, "Uh ... sounds delicious."

I roll my eyes and start adding the frosting I made to a bag. "They're cookie dough. Calm down, mister."

"Mister, huh?" There's a glimmer in his eyes.

"Don't get any ideas." I roll my eyes. "It won't take me long to frost these if you're willing to wait. But I get to keep three."

"Why three?"

I twist the bag securely closed. "One for now, one for later, and one for tomorrow. Duh."

He chuckles. "Ah, makes sense."

"How much do I owe you for the car battery?"

"Nothing."

"Thayer," my tone is stern, "I'm paying you back."

"No," he insists in an equally severe voice, "you're not."

"You're so stubborn," I argue.

He arches a brow. "And you're not?"

Frowning, I focus my attention on the cupcakes. "You admit you're stubborn then?"

He snorts humorlessly. "It'd be pointless to deny it." He pulls out a stool and sits down, still looking warily at the mess he brought in on his boots.

"It's not a big deal. You can't avoid dragging mud in this time of year."

"I should've taken them off outside. My mom would be all over me if she saw this."

I try not to laugh, but fail, making his lips rise in a smile. "You're thirty-one, Thayer."

"So? That doesn't mean my mom doesn't still scold me like I'm a teenager."

"We're always kids to them, huh?"

He swipes one of the cupcakes I've done. "Always."

"Hey," I try to smack his hand, "who said you could have that?"

"You did. You made them for me."

Rolling my eyes, I say, "Have you always been this full of yourself?"

"You're the one who said they were for me." He takes a big bite.

Dammit, he has me there.

I finish frosting them and set my three aside before boxing up the rest for Thayer. "There you go. Be nice and share with your family."

His eyes rake deviously over me, sending a shiver skating down my spine. "I don't like sharing."

"Where's your holiday giving spirit?"

He stands slowly, his gaze never leaving me as he comes around the counter. He stops when there's less than a foot of space between us. "Can I kiss you?"

I nod, perhaps too eagerly based on the smile that curves his lips. He closes the distance between us, clasping my face between his large hands. I love when he holds me like that. Like I'm the entire world. I've never felt so special. Safe. Protected.

He lowers his head slowly, hovering, waiting for me to close the last breath between us.

Grabbing the back of his head, I pull him down the last bit. His chuckle is silenced by my mouth. We melt into each other, our bodies are desperate for one another since it's been a while since we've been together like this.

Alone.

The taste of temptation on our tongues.

His fingers dig into my hips, trying to pull me closer even though we're already plastered together.

I love this wildness between us. How we can't get enough of each other.

He lifts me onto the opposite counter, away from the cupcakes, and my ass lands on the hard surface. His hands go to my thighs, spreading me wider so he can stand between my legs.

My heart is racing a mile a minute, and yet I feel so utterly calm when I'm around him. It's a strange juxtaposition, but I don't mind it.

"You smell like sugar," he murmurs against my ear. "Pure sweetness." He gently bites the lobe. His lips drift across my cheek, lightly brushing against my mouth. "You taste like it too." His voice is barely above a whisper, raspy.

"Can you shut up?"

I don't give him a chance to answer. With my hand on the back of his neck I press him closer. His body is hot around mine, he's always so warm, like my own personal space heater.

Our mouths move in sync, while my mind chants his name over and over in my head.

It feels like an hour has passed when he pulls away, resting his forehead to mine. Our breaths are shallow, and his heart beats rapidly beneath my palm.

I look up at him through my lashes and I know, all the way down to the depths of my soul, that I love this man. I'll never love someone else as much as I love him. In a short amount of time Thayer Holmes has stolen my heart, imprinted himself in my very DNA, until no one and nothing can ever take his place. He's the only one for me.

It scares me, feeling so much for someone so quickly, but then I think about how many people say when you know, you know, so maybe it isn't so crazy after all.

My fingers play with the hair that skims the back of his neck. He looks at me intently, searching.

"Why do I feel like there's something you want to tell me?"

I swallow thickly, chest shaking with an inhale as I think of my mom. "The lunch you dropped me off to yesterday." I bite my lip, not wanting to say the words out loud. "My mom has cancer."

"Fuck." His head drops. "You let me maul you and you have this shit going on? I'm so fucking sorry, Salem." He wraps his big arms around me, holding me, caring for me. I'm safe. Protected.

"I wanted to kiss you." I don't want him thinking he took advantage of me. "I've missed getting to see you."

He smooths my hair back from my forehead. "What kind is it?"

"Breast. She's going to need a double mastectomy." My

chin wobbles.

This is a lot. Unexpected too. I can't imagine what my mom has to be feeling. Her freedom from my father has been so short-lived to now be saddled with something like this.

But she's strong.

Resilient.

I have to believe she'll get through this.

"If there's anything I can do, please let me know."

And I know he would. This man put in an entire home gym in his basement for me. He fixed my car.

"Just be there for me."

It's all I'll ask for. It's all I need.

He kisses my forehead.

Gentle.

Warm.

Reverent.

"I can do that."

And I know he will.

CHAPTER FORTY-TWO

The short holiday break ends, Thayer's family leaves, and my mom has her surgery scheduled for just after the New Year. Apparently, she'd already been doing chemo for months and said nothing to us. I was mad at first when that admission came out, but then I thought about how she must've felt and that she was just being a mom, not wanting to worry us.

"Please come and visit," Lauren says on my phone screen through our FaceTime call. She's walking down the street in Brooklyn, her nose tinged red from the cold. "We can go to Rockefeller Center and see the tree together—remember, we always used to talk about that? We can do some Christmas shopping too. Come on," she pouts slightly, "I miss you."

"I know, and I miss you too. I want to, but it's just not a good time."

"I was afraid you'd say that, so that's why I already spoke with your mom, and she agreed with me that it's a great idea, and she's insisting you come."

I adjust my position on my bed, fluffing the pillow behind my head. Thayer is picking up Forrest from Krista and then he's swinging by to get me so we can pick out Christmas trees. One for his house, one for mine. We figured it would be easiest that way since he has a truck to haul them. "When?"

She grins evilly and I can't help but laugh. "Next weekend."

"Damn. The devil works hard but Lauren Rowe works harder."

"Absofuckinglutely." She sticks her tongue out at me. "I miss my best friend and I want to see you. Besides, with everything going on don't you think getting away for a little bit would be for the best? It's just a couple of days."

I sigh, knowing she's right. "Okay." I smile slowly. "I'm in."

Her squeal is so loud but the people passing her by on the street don't even pay attention like this is a normal everyday occurrence. I guess for them it is.

"We're going to have so much fun, just you wait!"

We say our goodbyes and hang up. Just in time too, since I get a text message from Thayer that he's five minutes away.

Sitting up from my bed, I give Binx a quick scratch around his ears. "See you later, bud."

I yank on my boots and my winter coat, watching out the window for Thayer's truck. When I see it pull into the driveway, I hurry out the door into the frigid cold. Snow is constantly on the ground this time of year, shoved into big nasty gray piles everywhere from the constant plowing.

Climbing into Thayer's warm truck, I smile at Forrest in the back seat. "Hey, Forrest. How have you been?"

"Good. School is exhausting, though. I need a longer break."

Beside me, Thayer tries not to laugh at his dramatic son. "And how are you?" I ask him.

His eyes are heated when he rakes them over me, putting the truck in reverse to back out of my driveway. Just this morning, after I came over for an early run on his treadmill, he pulled me down onto the weight bench, yanked off my pants, and showed me exactly why so many girls rave about oral. I'm still reeling from the intense climax I had.

"I'm ready to get a tree picked out," he says, glancing in

the rearview mirror at Forrest. "We're going to decorate it with superhero ornaments."

"It's going to look so cool, Salem, just you wait and see. Do you think you and Binx could come over and help us decorate?"

I look at Thayer, seeing if he's okay with that. I don't want to impede on his time with his son. He gives a gentle nod, so I say, "Yeah, that sounds like fun. Maybe we could make cupcakes, too?"

Thayer chuckles, rubbing his fingers over his jaw. "Only if they're cookie dough."

"Ew cookie dough? I don't want salmon yellow poisoning, Dad."

"It's salmonella, son. And you can make cookie dough without raw eggs so it's edible."

Behind us, in the backseat, Forrest keeps trying to sound out salmonella, but it just keeps coming out as salmon yellow.

"What kind of cupcakes would you want?"

"Oh." He scratches the side of his nose, thinking. "Um, my favorite's chocolate."

"Chocolate is always an excellent choice."

Christmas music plays softly on the speakers. My eyes drift closed, as I listen with a smile. Despite everything going on right now, I'm trying my hardest to find the joy in the holiday season. When my dad got sick, I vowed to never again let anyone or anything steal joy from me—that even if life was giving me hell, I'd find one good thing in every day to keep me going.

Today, it's Christmas music, the man beside me, and the boy in the backseat.

We arrive at the tree farm, and more music is playing from their speakers when we hop out. Since it's the weekend, it's pretty crowded. There's a line of people at the snack stand and another line for people leaving with their trees.

Forrest runs over to my side and grips my hand, looking up at me with big eyes. "My dad said I either have to hold his hands or yours, so I picked yours."

I smile down at the boy, my heart melting. I give his hand a squeeze. "I hope you're ready to pick the best tree for my house too."

Thayer smiles, walking past us to get a saw.

"You want my help?" He points a gloved finger at his chest.

"Of course, I do. You're really smart."

His chest puffs up. "I really am. I got an A on my spelling test and everything."

Thayer returns and the three of us head down the rows and rows of trees, looking for the perfect one to cut. My boots crunch in the snow, my breath fogging the chilly air. But despite the frigid temperature there's no place I'd rather be.

"What about that one, Dad?" Forrest points out a behemoth of a tree.

Thayer shakes his head immediately. "Too big."

"Too big? That's tiny, Dad."

Thayer tries not to chuckle, a huff escaping between his lips instead. "It only looks small because we're outside. Trust me, it's too big. I think we need to head this way for the ones we need." He points to our left. "Watch your step." He holds out a hand to help me and Forrest across a particularly muddy path.

We make it to the more normal sized trees and Forrest pulls free from my hand, running. "What about this one, Dad?"

"Little dude, what have I told you about running ahead like that?"

Forrest drops his head. "Not to."

"Exactly." Thayer ruffles his hair. "It's a great tree, though.

Good pick."

Forrest beams up at his father, like a flower blooming beneath the sun. "You think? It's a good one?"

"Yep. This is the one."

It's a tad crooked and a bit sparse in areas, but he's right, it's endearingly perfect.

With a groan, Thayer gets down to cut the tree while Forrest cheers him on. He jumps up and down and says, "You can do it, Daddy! You're so strong!" Turning to me, Forrest grins. "I'm going to be strong like my Dad when I grow up."

"I don't know, you already look pretty strong to me." I give his tiny bicep a squeeze—well, mostly I squish his puffy coat between my fingers but the way he beams I don't think he notices the difference.

"Did you hear that, Dad? Salem says I'm already strong."

"I heard, kid."

Once Thayer has the tree down, he takes it to the front to be wrapped and tagged while Forrest and I search for one for my mom and me.

"What kind of tree do you like?"

I give a shrug, tugging on the branch of one to see if any needles fall. "I'm not sure. I guess I kind of like one a little quirky."

He wrinkles his nose at the unfamiliar word. "Quirky?"

"Different, unique. It's something other people might overlook."

"Oh." He nods his head up and down a few times. "I'll keep an eye out for that."

His feet sink into the snow, causing him to almost trip. My grip on his hand tightens. "I've got you."

"Thanks, Salem."

I smile down at him, surprised at how much I've come to care for this boy in the past few months. "I've always got you."

"I've always got you, too." He wrinkles his nose in contemplation. "Unless you fall. You're too heavy for me to pick up."

I laugh. God, kids. I love the things that come out of their mouths.

"That's okay. You can just call for help."

"I can do that. Hey, what about that one?" He points to a tree that's full and voluptuous on the bottom, but the top is curved downwards. It's whimsical and definitely quirky.

"It's perfect."

"What's perfect?" Thayer walks up to us, saw in hand. His cheeks are red from the cold and his beanie is sitting a tad crooked on his head.

"This one," Forrest and I say simultaneously, pointing at it.

"You guys pick the weird ones," he mutters with a shake of his head, amused.

"They deserve love too," I argue, hands on my hips. "Get me my tree."

"I like it when you're bossy," he quips, poking my chilled cheek before he drops to the ground to cut the trunk.

"Can we get some hot chocolate before we leave, Dad? I saw them selling it."

"No," Thayer grunts with the effort of cutting down the tree. "I'm not paying five bucks for watered down overpriced bullshit. I'll make you some at home."

"Mom says bullshit is a bad word."

"It is," Thayer says, "and that's why only adults can say it. When you're an adult you can use them too."

Forrest looks up at me with wide, excited eyes. "Sweet.

Being a grown up is going to be so much fun."

If you only knew, kid.

Forty-five minutes later, we're back home with both trees. Forrest runs around the yards while I help Thayer carry the trees inside each house. My mom is still at the shop, so I have Thayer put the tree in the corner where we usually have one and hope she's okay with it.

"Are we still making cupcakes?" Forrest shucks off his coat and muddy boots by the front door. They fall in a pile and Thayer eyes the mess.

"There won't be any cupcakes if you don't clean up your mess."

Forrest looks at the discarded items. "They're fine there."

"Forrest," he warns, pinching the bridge of his nose. "Didn't we have a talk about respecting property? Pick your stuff up and put it where it goes." He groans in a dramatic fashion but picks his things up. "Thanks, kid."

"Whatever."

Thayer fights a smile. "I swear, sometimes I'm reminded he's only six and other times he acts like a teenager."

I rest my hands in the back pockets of my jeans. "I think that's typical."

Forrest comes back into the room. "Now can I make cupcakes? And what about hot chocolate?"

"Lead the way," I tell him, and he runs off to the kitchen.

"I'm going to finish setting the tree up and then I'll make the hot chocolate."

"Take your time. We'll be fine."

In the kitchen, Forrest has already pushed a chair over to the center island and climbed up on top, inspecting the ingredients I swiped from my house. "Can I have one of these?"

He holds up a bag of chocolate chips.

I pretend to look around for his dad, then whisper, "Go for it."

He takes the clip off the bag and hurriedly pulls out three mini chocolate chips, tossing them into his mouth. "I love chocolate."

I bop him on the nose. "Chocolate is very lovable and so are you."

He grins at my words.

Bending down, I rifle around in Thayer's cabinets for bowls and everything else I'll need. Despite the fact that he doesn't bake he has a fancy black Kitchen Aid mixer, which helps me out a lot.

I let Forrest help me measure out the ingredients, both of us laughing when he gets flour on his nose. I stick my finger in the flour and draw a smiley face on his cheek, so of course he wants to do the same to mine.

We're a laughing, giggling mess by the time Thayer comes into the kitchen. He eyes the mess we've made. There's flour and sugar all over my green sweatshirt. It's probably in my hair too. I rolled Forrest's sleeves up, but he has flour practically up to his elbows.

But life's boring if you never allow yourself to get a little messy.

"It looks like you two are having a little too much fun."

"Daddy," Forrest giggles, "look, I drew a heart on Salem's cheek. And a smiley face too."

Clasping my hands playfully under my chin, I turn each way so he can see his son's handiwork.

Brows furrowing, he bends down to Forrest's eye level on the counter. "Where's my heart and smiley face?"

"You have a beard on your cheeks. None for you. But what about..." He dips his hands into the flour and brings them to Thayer's cheeks, rubbing them all over Thayer's stubbled cheeks until the thick scruff is white. Giggling uncontrollably, Forrest says, "Now you look like Santa Claus."

Thayer strokes his chin, turning to me for appraisal. "How do I look?"

I look him over, heart somersaulting. "Distinguished."

"You like me with a little white in my beard?"

"It looks good."

His eyes crinkle at the corners with a smile. "Ho, ho, ho."

I squeal when he picks me up around the waist, tossing me over his shoulder and running around the counter. "Thayer!" I laugh, smacking his back. "Put me down!"

"Dad, what are you doing with her?" Forrest laughs. "You're being silly!"

Thayer sets me back down where he first scooped me up, pecking me on the lips. Both of us pause, realizing what he's done. Almost comically, we both turn to look at Forrest. His eyes are wide, surprised.

"Daddy, why did you kiss, Salem?" We're both quiet, floundering for an excuse. "Do you like her *like her*?"

Thayer's eyes drop to me, gauging whether or not I'm comfortable with this. I give a tiny nod, letting him know I'm okay with whatever he says to his son.

"Yes," he makes sure to look into Forrest's eyes, "I do like her. Very much."

Forrest looks at me and back at his dad. "Are you going to marry her?"

Thayer sighs, giving me an apologetic look at his son's prying questions. "Sometimes people like each other a lot but it doesn't mean they're getting married. They might, but they don't have to."

"Oh." He looks confused. "I thought only married people kissed. That's why I asked."

"No. Other people kiss, too. Kissing's nice—but not until you're older."

"You guys are like ... boyfriend and girlfriend, then?"

I hold my breath, waiting for his answer. The worst part is I don't know what I want him to say.

"We're..." He places his hands on his hips. "We're figuring things out, but no, we're not boyfriend and girlfriend. Not yet."

"All right. I like Salem." Forrest's eyes drift to me. "It's okay with me if you want to love each other."

And I think I might cry.

"Thanks, bud." Thayer ruffles his hair. "How about that hot chocolate now?"

***

With warm hot chocolate clasped in my hands, ornaments splayed out across the living room, cupcakes baking, and 'Rockin' Around the Christmas Tree' by Brenda Lee playing softly in the background, I can't help but think that I could get used to this.

Thayer picks up Forrest, lifting him up to add ornaments up at the top of the tree. Watching them makes me happy. Being a part of their little family fills me with a joy I didn't know I was missing in my life.

I had no idea when Thayer moved in that I'd fall so hard for him.

Not just him, but his son too.

I can't imagine my life without either of the Holmes boys. Somehow, along the way, they became mine. I just hope I'm theirs too.

CHAPTER FORTY-THREE

Lauren's waiting for me when I get off the train, exuding cool girl vibes I'm immediately envious of. Her dark hair hangs down well past her boobs in messy artful waves that look like she just rolled out of bed, but I'm sure took her a while to perfect. She wears a pair of light wash jeans, a thick gray turtleneck, black boots, and a black leather trench coat.

I feel severely underdressed in my jeans, sweatshirt, and puffer coat.

"Salem!" She runs to greet me, throwing her arms around my shoulders.

I hug her back, inhaling the scent of her floral perfume. "I missed you."

And God, have I. We talk on the phone as often as we can, but it's not the same as having my best friend in the same town.

"I missed you, too." She pulls back, holding me at arm's length like she expects me to have changed drastically since she left. It's not like she's seen me on FaceTime either. "I'm so happy you're here for the weekend. We have so much to see and do." She starts carting me out of the train station and to the busy, bustling streets. "Are you hungry? Let's get brunch."

"I could eat." My stomach chooses that moment to rumble, but with the noise of the city no one can hear it.

She leads me to the subway and eventually we get off, making our way to a little hole in the wall restaurant. It's narrow and long, but with an open and clean aesthetic that makes it seem much brighter.

We're seated after a thirty-minute wait—one which my stomach vehemently protests to—and I eagerly look over the menu. My mouth waters over the options. I'm pretty sure anything would taste good to me right now.

The protein bar I shoved in my mouth during the train ride has done little to abate my appetite.

Lauren sips her ice water that a waiter dropped off shortly after we sat down and slides her menu to the side of the table.

"I've let you avoid the topic for long enough."

"What topic?" I don't lift my eyes from the menu, but somehow I still know she's rolling hers.

"The breakup with Caleb, duh."

My brows furrow. "It's been a while. There's nothing to talk about."

"Of course, there is. Is there another guy in the picture?"

I swallow thickly. *Did it suddenly get hot in here?*

"Why would there be a guy?"

She snaps her fingers, pointing at me in the process. "You didn't deny it, missy! Spill."

I'm given a reprieve, for the moment at least, when the waiter comes by for our orders. As soon as he's gone though, she's back on it.

"You and Caleb were like the it couple. I honestly thought you guys were in it for the long haul and you know how cynical I can be. But at the same time, I can see why you'd end things. You need to grow on your own and not be tied down in the same relationship for all of eternity. Talk about boring." She finally pauses to inhale a breath. "That means you should be out there having fun. Dating other people." She waves her hand through the air lazily at the word people.

"Are you dating anyone?" I volley back.

"I'm dating," she supplies. "Having fun."

"Are you being safe?"

She grins, trying not to laugh at my question. "Yes, Mom. I'm being safe."

"Just checking. We don't need an accidental pregnancy here."

She mock gags. "Ew, crotch goblins. No thank you. Not anytime soon, at least."

"What about you? Are you being safe with this mystery man? And don't even try to deny it." Her eyes narrow upon me. "I've had the feeling for a while you're hiding something—or someone, I should say."

If there's anyone in this world I can trust, it's Lauren. I don't know why I've kept it a secret this long from her, but I've been safe and cozy in my little Thayer bubble and since we don't really venture out of that space, I've wanted to keep it to myself.

"You know the new neighbor—"

She gasps, slamming her hand down upon the table and earning us more than a few spare glances in the process. "You mean that hot sexy piece of man meat that mows his lawn shirtless but always looks like such a grump? The man you babysit for? The man who is a dad? Who's way older than you? That guy?"

"Yep." I nod slowly, reaching for my glass of water. "That's the one."

"Holy. Shit." She enunciates each word. "You're banging a *daddy*—and I mean that in both the literal and figurative sense."

"Lauren!" I throw a napkin at her, my cheeks flaming red.

"What?" She blinks with mock innocence.

"You know what," I counter, looking around to see if anyone heard her.

"I can't help it." She lowers her voice, leaning across the table. "When did this start?"

And there lies the big reason why I haven't told her.

"It was innocent at first," I explain, nervously picking at my fingers. "Just some harmless flirting. A *feeling*. But then, suddenly, it was more."

Her expression softens. "You were still with Caleb, weren't you? When this something became more?"

I gasp out a tiny, "Yes." Swallowing thickly, I add, "I'm a liar. A cheater. I hate those labels, but they're true."

"Oh, hun." Lauren looks at me sadly. "You're not a liar. And a cheater ... that's just a label, sure, but it's not who you are. I know you. You wouldn't do this on purpose. Be kind to yourself. We're young, Salem. We're going to make mistakes and do things we regret. But it doesn't mean we're horrible people." She stares into my eyes with so much sympathy that I feel tears spring to my eyes. "We're just human. Anyone who thinks they're perfect is delusional. We all make mistakes, do things we regret, just because those things don't all look the same doesn't make someone better over another."

"I hate that I hurt him."

"Did you tell him what happened?"

"No," I admit. "I knew I was already breaking his heart—why shatter it completely? Was that wrong of me?"

"No." She shakes her head steadily. "You were protecting him because you still love him."

"I do love, Caleb. I think a part of me will always love him. But Thayer is..." I flounder, trying to gather my thoughts. "What I feel for him is so much more. I can't explain it. From the beginning there's been a connection."

"Maybe he's your twin flame?"

"My what?"

"Your twin flame," she repeats. "Your soulmate. Other half. Whatever you want to call it."

"You think things like that exist?" I ask skeptically.

"Listen, in a world where the megalodon once existed, I'm not ruling out twin flames."

I hold my hands up like I'm weighing something. "Twin flames, megalodon. Seems comparable."

"Oh, shut up," she laughs, tossing the napkin back at me that I'd thrown at her previously. "So, you're boning your hot neighbor and I'm exploring New York's finest members. We're quite the pair."

I cover my face, trying to hide my laughter. "Lauren!"

"Hey," she presses a hand to her chest, "it's a tough job, but someone's gotta do it. I even keep a notebook. Names, numbers, and score them on performance. Seven and above and you'll get a second call from me."

"You're horrible."

"No, no," she chants as our food is brought to the table, "I'm organized and prepared, there's a difference. No point in wasting my time on a dude that doesn't know where the clit is or what to do with any of his other appendages."

Thank goodness the waiter has already left before the last part of her speech.

"Listen, no more of that talk. I want to be able to enjoy my meal without thinking about that."

She laughs, digging into her yogurt parfait. "Fine, fine. I'll be on my best behavior. Well, I'll try at least."

"That's all I ask for."

***

My weekend with Lauren is over too soon. I didn't want to take the time away from home to make this trip, but now I find myself not wanting to leave. Lauren was right, I needed this break.

She hugs me tight, like she's trying to squeeze the life out of me—or maybe break a bone so I have to stay longer.

"Please, come back as soon as you can. And give your mom all the love and luck from me."

"I will." I hug her back just as fiercely, knowing that once I let go and get on the train it's back to reality.

Christmas is almost here, and then New Year's, and that means my mom's surgery.

The weight of the world is bearing down on me, but I take one more second to hug my best friend and remind myself what it feels like to be young and carefree.

"I love you," I tell her. "You're like a sister to me."

Lauren's shoulders shake with tears. "Don't let Georgia hear you say that. She'll get jealous."

"There's enough of me to go around," I promise.

Pulling away, she wipes at her tear-streaked face. "Don't be a stranger."

"Never." I know I have to go. I can't prolong it any longer. "Be good."

She laughs through her sniffles. "Never."

"Good luck with the job." I toss my bag over my shoulder. Lauren's starting an internship at a media company working in marketing. Apparently, she gave them a pitch on what she'd change with their social media, and they liked what she said enough to give her a chance.

"Thanks." She takes a step back. "Have fun with MacDaddy

next door."

I shake my head at the nickname she's given Thayer. "You have to stop calling him that."

"Nope, not happening." She grins, clearly pleased with herself for coming up with the moniker.

"I'll see you soon," I promise.

"You better." She winks, but I can see how much she wants to break down. It's hard saying goodbye. Hellos are so much easier.

Turning, I walk away and don't look back.

CHAPTER FORTY-FOUR

"You're going to do great." I squeeze my mom's hand, fighting back tears. "The surgery is going to go fine, and we'll go home, and you'll heal. You're going to kick cancer's butt, Mom. I know you are. I believe in you."

She gives me a weak smile from the bed. She's in a purple hospital gown, IV in her arm. The nurse waits at the end of the bed, giving me a chance to say goodbye before she's wheeled back to surgery.

They said she'd be in surgery for at least four hours, and then there's the recovery time after but she'll be able to go home tonight. I know she's happy for that, not wanting to stay in the hospital any longer than she has to.

I brush her thinning hair back from her forehead and place a gentle kiss there.

"I'll be waiting."

"Honey, go home for a while, you don't need to stay here."

It's an argument we've been having. "No," I insist obstinately, "I'm staying right here."

She pats my hand. "Stubborn girl."

"I wonder where I get it from?"

The nurse clears her throat. "We really need to get her back and prepped."

"Right. Of course. I'm sorry."

I step away from the bed, holding back tears.

I refuse to cry in front of her. It's not fair if I do. She's the one going through this. Living it. I exit the room before she's wheeled out, because I know if I stay here, I won't be able to hold it together.

The waiting room is sleek and white, with a mix of chairs and couches. I walk out to the cafeteria around the corner and order a coffee before returning to the waiting room. I grab a chair parked in the far corner and sip my coffee, settling in for the long wait. I brought a book with me, one I said I'd read at the beginning of summer and now it's January and I haven't started it yet. Cracking open the book, I read the first three pages before setting it down. I'm too stressed to read. Shocker.

I pass the time watching other people in the waiting room and messing around on my phone. It's slow goings, but I don't want to leave. Not if anything happens. I'd never forgive myself.

Georgia couldn't be here since she wasn't able to get off of work. That leaves me and I won't shirk my responsibilities.

"Salem?"

I look up at the sound of my name, expecting a doctor or someone else, but it's Thayer.

It's.

Thayer.

He stands in front of me, bundled up from the winter cold. His wild hair tries to escape the brown beanie plastered to his head. And in his hands, he holds a bag of food from the Chick-Fil-A a mile or so from the hospital.

"Hi," I say stupidly. "W-What are you doing here?"

"I thought you might want some company, so I brought lunch."

He sits down beside me, opening the bag of food. "You came all this way to bring me food?" The hospital is around an hour from Hawthorne Mills.

"I was in the area."

I don't believe him. He pulls out a box and passes it to me. "I wasn't sure what you'd like so I figured I was safe with a chicken sandwich."

"Thanks."

I don't have much of an appetite, but since he went to this much trouble, I'm going to make the effort to try to eat it.

"Here's some Diet Coke." He reaches into his pocket and pulls out a bottle, handing it to me.

He got me food. My favorite drink. He came to comfort me during my mother's surgery.

I'm beginning to think there's nothing Thayer won't do for me. I don't even have to ask him, he just does it—and things I would never expect in the first place.

"Thank you," I say after a few too long seconds, outstretching my fingers to take the drink.

"You're welcome." Lowering his voice, he asks, "Do you know anything yet?"

"No. It's only been about three hours and they said four hours would be the soonest she'd be done."

"Is there anything I can do?" He pulls more food out of the bag, passing me my own box of fries.

"You being here is more than enough."

His lips form a contemplative line. "I'm finding it's easy to be there for the right people."

And I think I understand what he's saying without actually saying it.

That Krista became someone he avoided.

I don't know many details about his marriage to Krista. I try not to pry because I figure he'll share what he wants, when he wants.

Even though I'm selfishly glad that he's mine now, for this moment in time, I do feel bad in a way. Once upon a time he loved Krista and she loved him. They had a child together. But love can change, and theirs did, and in the end they weren't what the other needed.

Biting into my sandwich, I do my best to eat as much as I can, knowing it'll be better for me in the long run if I have something in my stomach.

Thayer stays with me until my mom's out of surgery and I'm allowed to go back to see her. I'm pretty sure he'd hang around even longer if I asked him too.

When I hug him goodbye those three, scary, beautiful words are on the tip of my tongue but I hold them back.

Now's not the time, but I'm not quite sure when will be.

CHAPTER FORTY-FIVE

After my mom takes a pain pill and goes to sleep for the night, I bundle up in my coat and boots before sneaking across next door. I ring the doorbell and wait.

Thayer swings the door open with a confused expression furrowing his brow. His tense features relax when he sees me standing on his doorstep. "How's your mom?" He opens the door wider, letting me inside.

I take off my coat and hang it on the coat rack, setting my boots gently on the rug.

"She's okay. Emotional and in a lot of pain." Biting my lip, I add, "I think it just hit her, the reality of everything." I motion to my chest. "I can't begin to imagine what she's going through."

He shakes his head, his shaggy brown hair falling over his forehead. "It has to be rough. But she has you, and that matters, Salem."

"I'll be by her side every step of the way." It's a vow I don't hesitate to make.

He tips his head, motioning for me to follow him to the kitchen. "I know you will. She's lucky to have you."

"Thank you again for stopping by the hospital today. It meant a lot to me."

I'm not sure he knows how hard that is for me to admit. I don't like depending on people. When you expect too much from someone, you're setting yourself up for disappointment.

Thayer opens the fridge and bends down to pick up a beer.

"You want anything?"

"Diet Coke." I grin, holding out a hand eagerly.

"You and your caffeine." He grabs a can and passes it to me. "I wanted to be there, Salem." He lowers his head, long fingers gliding through the chestnut brown strands of his hair. "I didn't like the idea of you sitting there, going through it alone." He twists off the top on his beer and takes a swig. Crossing his legs, he leans back against the counter, letting his eyes drift to the floor. "Everyone deserves to have someone who's there for them. I want to be your someone."

My heart stops beating.

He looks up at me slowly through long dark lashes.

"My ... someone?"

"Yeah," he shrugs, long-sleeve shirt pulling taut over his firm muscles. "I'm thirty-one. I'm too old to be someone's boyfriend. I figure being your someone sounds better anyway."

"I like it." I set my drink down and step up to him, putting my hands on his chest. His heart raps a steady beat against my palm. Guiding my hands up farther, I wrap them around his neck. "Does that mean I'm your someone?"

His brown eyes are warm, a swirl of so many things neither of us will say yet. "No, Salem." He shakes his head slowly. Before I can feel the sting of pain, he says, "You're my everything."

I can't stop the smile the blooms across my face. "I like that even more."

His smile matches mine. "I thought you might."

He sets his beer aside, picking me up. My legs wind around his waist a second before his lips crash to mine. I ache for him. To be held, cherished, loved by him. He carries me up the stairs like I weigh nothing. He shoulders his way into his room.

There's nothing rushed, or desperate, or chaotic about

either of our movements.

Not this time.

It's different.

He lowers my body to his bed and turns on the light beside his bed. My eyes flick over to it and he must sense that I want to beg him to turn it off.

With his thumb and forefinger, he gently tips my head up. "I want to see you. Let me love you, Salem. The way you deserve. The way only I can."

I nod, perhaps a bit too eagerly based on his small chuckle.

He kisses my jaw, gliding his lips over to my ear. I want to ask him if he does, love me that is, but I keep my mouth shut.

Love is so much more than words.

It's a feeling.

And feelings can't be denied.

He takes his time kissing over my face, like he wants me to know he worships every part of me. He peppers light kisses over the freckles on my cheeks, my nose, beneath my eyes.

"Scoot back," he commands, and I do as he says. "Arms up."

I lift them and he guides my sweatshirt over my head. Dropping it to the floor behind him, he goes for my shirt next. In one smooth move it's off my body, leaving me in my simple white bra. It's nothing special. I picked my comfiest one to wear today, but he stares at me like I have on the sexiest lingerie he's ever seen.

He runs his fingers down my sides and I shiver from his touch. He undoes the button on my jeans and I lift my hips, helping him tug them down my legs. They join the growing pile of my clothes on the floor. He reaches to unclasp my bra, but I shake my head, shoving him back with my foot to his chest.

"You've gotta give me something here. Take your shirt off."

His lips tilt in a wry grin. Grabbing the bottom of his shirt, he yanks it up and over his head. "Happy now?"

"Immensely," I giggle.

With a shake of his head, he's over my body, crowding me.

He pulls down the cups of my bra, his tongue laving at first one nipple and then the next. I moan, my fingers pulling at his hair. He grips my right breast, his touch possessive. With every touch, every lick of his tongue, he's reminding me that I'm his.

"Thayer," I pant his name, holding him against my breast. He sucks my nipple into his mouth, his other hand skimming down my stomach. His fingers breach the edge of my panties.

There's a moment, just a second—less than one really—when horrible memories come flooding back and I freeze. It passes so fast, and I'm back in the moment with him, but he notices.

"Salem?" He blinks down at me, looking over my features to gauge where I'm at. His fingers are on my stomach, no longer under my panties.

"I'm okay." He looks doubtful. "I mean it." I take his face, his beautiful, rugged face into my hands. "I'm here. With you."

He looks at me for a moment longer. "Are you sure? I'll stop."

"Please, don't stop," I practically beg. "I need you."

He kisses me long and deep and minutes pass before he starts exploring my body again. He slips my panties down my legs, his fingers finding my pussy.

"Fuck, you're so wet."

"I told you," I wiggle, begging silently for his fingers to push inside of me, "I want you."

He moves down my body, his shoulders pressing my legs

open further. "You're perfect, Salem." He rubs his fingers in my wetness.

Not tainted. Not ugly.

Thayer Holmes thinks I'm perfect.

His tongue connects with my pussy and sparks ignite inside me. He sucks and kisses, adding his fingers to bring me over the edge, and then again.

"Please," I beg, not even caring that I sound desperate. "I need you inside me."

Thayer moves off my body, standing beside the bed. He stares at me, right into my eyes, as he undoes his belt, pulling it through the loops on his jeans. The sound of it falling to the ground makes my heart beat faster and I lick my lips in anticipation. Next goes the button. Zipper. And then he pulls his jeans and boxers down in one tug, freeing his erection. He's hot and hard and so ready for me.

"Wait." I find myself climbing off the bed and kneeling in front of him. "I ... I want to try." I bite my lip, looking up at him. "I've never given a blow job before," I admit shyly. "I never wanted to."

He tilts my chin up. "You don't have to do anything you don't want to."

"But I do," I say quickly. "With you. I want to try with you."

He hesitates, then nods.

Wrapping my hand around the base of his cock, I stroke him up and down. I can feel him watching, but he says nothing, does nothing. He's giving me all the power, the control, letting me explore him safely, in my own way, in my own time.

Sliding my tongue out, I lick the head of his dick. He groans, his head falling back.

"Is that okay?"

"Yes, God yes." I do it again, growing bolder. Pumping my hand up and down his cock I add more pressure and take more of him into my mouth. "Holy fuck." He looks down at me with heat in his brown eyes. Gently, reverently, he pulls my hair back away from my face. There's something about that, that I find so sexy.

He gives me little guidance, letting me find my rhythm.

"No more. I don't want to come in your mouth. Not tonight." I let him go, his dick bobbing in front of my face and slick with my saliva. His eyes flare with heat as he looks down at me. Grabbing my face between his fingers, his touch is firm but not bruising. "Open your mouth," he commands.

I don't hesitate and do as he says.

He bends down, slow, steady, his eyes never leaving mine. It takes me by surprise when he spits in my mouth, then covers my lips with his, kissing me long and deep as he pulls me up from the floor with his hand still on my face. Picking me up, he lays me down on the bed. His body is over mine in an instant. Gripping the base of his cock, he slides inside me and both of us moan in relief. Rocking his hips steadily against mine, he clasps our fingers together, resting them beside my head.

"You feel so good," he murmurs into the skin of my neck. "Fucking made for me, Salem."

"God, yes." I squeeze my legs around him. He rests his forehead against mine, our noses brushing, breath to breath.

He makes love to me and I soak in every bit of that, letting it fill me up.

This is what it means to be cared for. Cherished.

Anything less is second best.

CHAPTER FORTY-SIX

"Are you sure about this?" Georgia asks our mom for the millionth time.

Mom sits on a stool in the bathroom, a towel draped around her shoulders. Her hair is thin and stringy, bald patches beginning to show.

"Yes." She nods determinedly. "I want it off. All of it. Get rid of it."

Georgia and I exchange a look. We know how hard this is for her. I've never thought of myself as a vain person before, but I can't imagine what it must feel like seeing your hair fall out like this. I've been vacuuming the house like crazy to get it all up so she doesn't see it.

With an inhale, Georgia starts the hair clippers up.

She cries.

I cry.

My mom cries.

And when it's all done, we huddle together and hold on tightly to one another, the hair pooled on the ground around our feet.

"Battles are better fought together than alone," my mom cries steadily. "Thank you, girls, for fighting this with me."

And then we all cry harder.

***

"You look like you've been crying," Forrest points out, rolling up a ball of snow for our snowman. Thayer has him this weekend but needed to take care of some work things, so that means I get to spend time with his son.

"That's because I was."

"Why?"

"My mom has cancer. My sister came over this morning and we shaved her hair off."

I don't believe in lying or sugarcoating things to kids. They're far more intelligent than most give them credit for.

"Oh." He adjusts his hat, his nose red from the cold. "Is she going to die?"

Out of the mouth of babes.

"I don't know," I answer truthfully. "I hope not, but we don't know."

"I hope she doesn't. I don't know what I'd do if my mommy or daddy died." He wrinkles his nose. "You're a grown up but even grownups still need their mommy."

"You're pretty smart, kid." I tell him, the two of us lifting the middle section onto our puny little snowman in Thayer's front yard. I couldn't turn the boy down when he asked to make one.

"Thanks." He pauses, glancing toward the backyard in thought. I expect him to ask more about my mom, but he's already moved on to another topic of conversation. "When my dad finally builds my treehouse do you think you'll hang out in it with me?"

"You bet. I always wanted a treehouse growing up."

"You didn't get one?"

"No. I didn't ask for one," I add.

"Why not?"

"My dad wasn't as cool as yours."

"Oh." He picks up a ball of snow and packs it together. "He is pretty cool."

"I have to agree."

"You like him, don't you?" He stacks the ball on top for the head and it immediately falls off. He picks it up, frowning at the snow for betraying him.

"I do. Very much."

A car pulls up then, one I recognize, but it's not Thayer.

Krista gets out of her SUV with Forrest's teddy bear in hand, barreling toward us. I can tell she's pissed to see me with her son.

"Where's my husband?" She demands, cheeks flushed with anger.

"He had to run errands, so I'm babysitting Forrest for a little bit. And don't you mean ex-husband?" I can't help but jab.

"This is his time with Forrest. He should be here. If he thinks I won't bring this to the court's attention, he's wrong." She shoves the bear at Forrest who takes it, giving her a funny look. "And who are you to point out that he's my ex? Are you one of his whores?" She looks me up and down like I'm muck stuck beneath her shoe. "Does he make you feel special? Like you matter?" Her eyes are narrow, evil slits. "He cheated on me, bet he didn't tell you that, did he? He'll do the same thing to you. Once a cheater, always a cheater."

I look down at Forrest, horrified she's saying all this in front of her son. She can be angry at Thayer, but he's still her son's dad.

"Have a good day," I say in dismissal, refusing to stoop to her level.

She flips her hair over her shoulder. "You'll get what's

coming for you."

She bends down and hugs Forrest goodbye, leaving without a second glance.

Forrest runs over to put his bear on the porch. When he scurries back, he says, "I'm sorry she was mean to you."

"It's okay." I bend down, helping him make the head of the snowman bigger.

"It wasn't very nice. She tells me to be nice to people, but she was mean to you."

"Sometimes adults make mistakes."

"What did she mean about my dad cheating on her? Were they playing a game and he cheated?"

"I don't know," I tell him honestly. "Don't worry about it."

Before I forget, I send a text to Thayer letting him know she stopped by and what she said about court, feeling like he should know. He replies back almost instantly that he'll be home soon.

***

I'm chilled from being outside so long with Forrest, but I don't think he's a bit cold. I stir a pot of Kraft Mac n' Cheese for his lunch. I offered him better, healthier choices but he insisted this was the only thing he'd eat. He sits at the kitchen counter with a Marvel coloring book.

The front door opens and Thayer's boots are heavy on the floor. He greets Forrest first, pulling him into a hug and kissing the top of his head.

"Did you ask for Mac n' Cheese, again?"

"It's good, Dad!" Forrest cries, setting his crayon down.

Thayer shakes his head in amusement. With the cheese fully mixed, I ladle some into a bowl and add a fork, sliding it over to Forrest.

"You should have some, Salem. It's really good, trust me."

I don't bother telling him I practically lived off the stuff in elementary school and just do as he says, making myself a bowl before sitting down beside him. Thayer opens the fridge, searching for something. With his back to us, he says, "Your mom stopped by, huh?"

"Yeah, she was in a mood."

I stifle a laugh.

"What did she say?" he asks, pulling out a plastic container of leftovers. Popping off the lid he sticks it in the microwave.

"She said you were a cheater, Daddy. Did you cheat at a game or something? You told me cheating is bad."

Thayer's shoulders stiffen and he flips around from the microwave. "She said that?" he asks me.

I nod, stirring my bowl of macaroni. "Yes."

"You didn't believe her, did you?"

I don't say anything. It's not that I do believe her, but anything is possible.

"I swear to you, I would never ever do that. That's not who I am as a person."

"That's what I said, Dad." Forrest throws up his hand, almost throwing his fork in the process. "Oops."

"Salem," he stares deep into my eyes, leaning his body across the counter so he's on the same level I am, "I swear to you, I didn't cheat on my wife."

"I believe you." Maybe it's naïve, but I really don't think Thayer would lie about it. He doesn't have anything to lose by being honest.

Lowering his voice so Forrest can't hear, he adds, "You're the first woman I've been with since my wife."

And that ... it shouldn't make me happy, but it does.

Straightening, he turns around and grabs his reheated food from the microwave.

"Dad," Forrest speaks up around a mouthful, "will you build my treehouse for my birthday? I really want it."

Thayer sighs. I know Forrest has asked innocently since he moved in about it. "I can't right now, son. It's too cold. I'll build it this summer, I promise."

"You mean it, don't you?"

"I'm going to build it," he vows. "Don't worry about it."

"When's your birthday?" I ask Forrest curiously.

"It's March twelve?" He looks to Thayer for confirmation.

"Twelfth," he corrects.

Forrest looks at me with big eyes. "What he said. When's your birthday?"

"Oh, it was November twenty-eighth."

Thayer's head whips in my direction so fast, I'm surprised he doesn't get whiplash. "You didn't tell me."

I push the noodles around some more. It doesn't escape my notice that it's a statement, not a question. "No."

"Why not?"

"I hate my birthday," I answer simply. "It's not something I celebrate."

"You don't celebrate it." He rubs his jaw. "Why?" He demands, fists clenching. It's like he knows already.

Sliding from the stool, I grab his wrist and drag him from the kitchen away from Forrest's prying ears.

When we're safely far enough away, I drop his arm. "Because," I stare up at him, "it was my birthday. The first night he touched me, it was my birthday." Anger radiates off of him. "I thought he forgot to give me a present. I was so excited when the door opened." I start to cry. Even after all this time I can't help but get emotional for that little girl who endured so much. I told my therapist once that it felt like all of it had happened to someone else. "I was never happy when the door opened after that."

Pain spears his face, but he doesn't say anything to try to make it better. Thayer understands that there's nothing that can. He gently cups the back of my head and pulls me into the protective curve of his chest.

In the warm, safe cocoon of his arms, I quietly weep for the girl who stopped wishing on birthday candles.

CHAPTER FORTY-SEVEN

Time is a scary thing. How quickly it passes. In a blink it's March and Forrest's birthday—well, it's technically a few days after, but it's when Thayer has him to celebrate.

My mom and I are setting up decorations in Thayer's kitchen while he's gone to pick up Forrest. He knows we're here. He asked us the other day if we'd mind setting up and celebrating with them since Forrest loves us so much. Ever since we all carved pumpkins, he's become close to my mom. It's been nice for her to have a kid around. I think his enthusiasm for life has kept her mind off of this round of chemo. She's finishing her last round in another week and then we'll see what happens.

"Does this look okay?" I ask her, climbing off the step ladder to assess the blue streamers I hung across the archway into the kitchen.

She sits at the table taking a break. It's already decorated with a tablecloth, the cake my mom made, balloons, and some presents. Thayer told us not to get anything, that it wasn't necessary, but he's crazy if he thinks neither of us wouldn't do something.

I might've gone a tad overboard on presents, but he's my favorite kid so I'm allowed to spoil him.

"Looks great, sweetie," she says, sipping the glass of water in front of her.

She looks tired. Wary. I wish I could make it all better for her. But there's nothing I can do or say. Georgia has been scrambling to get her wedding planned for June. She might've wanted a summer wedding to begin with, but we all know she's making sure it happens early enough that Mom can walk her down the aisle.

I try not to think about the fact that I might not have the same opportunity.

"They should be back any minute. Is there anything else I should do?" Hands on my hips, I look around the kitchen for anything I might've missed. I sort of blacked out at the party supply store and went overboard. That's what Thayer gets for slipping me his credit card.

"It's perfect honey. Sit down and take a breather before they get here."

Grabbing a Diet Coke from the fridge, I sit down beside my mom. I think Forrest will be happy and that's all that matters.

My mom looks around at the freshly painted walls and renovated kitchen. "Thayer's done a good job with this place. He's doing all the work himself?"

"Most of it."

She sips her water. "You're close with him."

"I babysit for him some, that's it, Mom." I play nervously with the ends of my hair. Her eyes immediately zero in on the gesture. I let my fingers drop. "We're friends."

"Hmm." She hums. "Just friends?"

"Mom!" I blush, looking down at the blue plastic tablecloth covered with dinosaurs. "He's in his thirties. I'm nineteen. It ... that would be crazy."

"Huh." She looks puzzled. "All right."

"What?" I prompt.

She waves a dismissive hand. "Just mom stuff. I thought I sensed something between you two." She smiles, squeezing my hand. "Must've been my imagination."

I clear my throat. God, I hate lying to her. "Must have."

She adjusts the bright green floral scarf she has wrapped around her head. She picked it because it matches the apron she wears today. "Do I look okay?"

My heart softens. "You look beautiful. You always do." She pats the top of my hand. There are tears in her eyes she won't let fall. It happens often these days. "Please, don't cry," I beg. It's not that I'm afraid of her tears, I just don't want her to be sad. I try not to let it show, but I'm so angry this happened to her. If there's anyone in this world who deserves happiness, it's my mom.

"I'm sorry." She dabs at her eyes. "I can't help it. Ugh."

She goes to rise up for a tissue, but I beat her to it. Returning to the table, I pass it to her.

"Thanks, sweetie." She dries her eyes and exhales a weighted breath. "I need to pull myself together. This is a happy day." She motions to the presents and cake waiting for the birthday boy.

"It is," I agree, crouching in front of her and taking her hands. "But you're sad right now and that's okay."

She wipes fresh tears away. "I just started thinking about how one day it might be your kid's birthday, or Georgia's, and I might not be there."

"Mom," I beg, squeezing her hands tight, "please don't say that."

"I have to be realistic."

I lower my head. I know she's right. I know it's a possible reality I have to face. But dammit if I don't want to. I want my mom to always be there, and thinking about a world in which she's not is heartbreaking.

"You're strong," I tell her. "A fighter. If anyone can beat this, it's you."

"I'm trying." She pulls one of her hands from mine and tenderly strokes my cheek. "For you, for your sister, I'm fighting every day."

"I know."

And I do. If she loses this battle, I know she'll go out giving it everything she's got. That's just who she is. Because of my father some might view her as weak, but all I see is a survivor. I'll never judge her for that.

***

By the time Thayer arrives home with Forrest we've both managed to get our emotions under control and plaster smiles on our faces for the belated birthday boy. He runs into the kitchen, stopping in his tracks when he sees everything. His eyes go wide, mouth falling open in wonder.

"Wow! You guys did all this for me?"

"We did." My mom smiles at him, and I can tell she's put everything else out of her mind for the moment. "Happy birthday, Forrest."

"It was my birthday a few days ago but thank you."

Behind him, Thayer shakes his head in amusement.

"I know, but we get to celebrate with you now, so it's like your birthday all over again." She tweaks his nose, and he wraps his arms around her in a hug.

"Did you guys get me all these presents? There are a lot here."

"Those are all for you," I tell him. "From me, your dad, and my mom."

He laughs in excitement, eyeing a particularly large box. "You guys must really like me."

"You have no idea." He hugs me next, and I squeeze him tight. It's not just Thayer that took a piece of my heart when he moved in next door. "Can I open my presents now?" he asks his dad.

Thayer chuckles, pulling out a chair. "Go for it, kid. How about pizza after? Are you guys good with that?" He directs the next question to us.

"I'll never say no to pizza." Seriously, who doesn't like pizza? I blush, remembering what happened the last time we got pizza.

Thayer must think of it too because he shoots a smirk my way.

"Pizza would be lovely." My mom picks up her water and I notice she needs a refill. Grabbing the glass from her, I go to fill it up. When I return, she's saying something to Thayer in a hushed tone and he glances at me. His lips quirk up into a smile. There's no worry there, or anything, so I'm assuming she didn't ask him if there's more between us. A small part of me wonders what he'd say if she did question him.

Forrest tears through his presents, oohing and ahhing over the giant remote-controlled T-Rex I got him for his obsession with dinosaurs.

Thayer slips quietly out of the room and down to the basement to get Forrest's final present. Forrest doesn't even notice that his dad has disappeared from the room since he's so enamored with everything he got.

I try to hide my smile when Thayer comes into the kitchen with the Corgi-mix pup. I found her a week ago, abandoned across the street from my mom's shop and when I spotted her, it seemed like fate, considering I found Binx in such a similar manner. I called Thayer and told him, hinting that Forrest would absolutely love to have a puppy and he grumpily agreed to take a look. As soon as he took the puppy from my arms I knew he was a goner for her.

"A girl?" He'd said, holding her out at arm's length. "I don't know how to be a girl dad."

I slapped his arm playfully, and said, "You're going to learn."

Then the next thing I knew he was shopping and buying her all kinds of things—more cushions and toys than any one puppy needs, fitting her into a pink collar, and frankly spoiling her silly.

Forrest gasps when he spots the puppy in Thayer's arms. "Is that a puppy?" He screams loudly. "For me?"

Thayer chuckles and bends down, passing the puppy over to his son. "Yeah. Isn't she cute?"

"So cute." Forrest buries his face in her fur. "I love her so much."

Thayer chuckles. "You just met her."

"Doesn't matter. I love her. What's her name?"

Thayer pets the top of her head. "What do you want it to be?"

"I don't know." He shrugs his little shoulders, looking at the dog with awe. "Salem?" He turns to me. "What's a good name?"

"Oh." I hate being put on the spot. "Name her after something you love. I named Binx after a character in my favorite movie."

Thayer smirks at the mention of the movie. Cocking his head to the side, he says to me, "Do you have a suggestion from that, then?"

"Yeah," Forrest prods, "she needs a good name."

I bite my lip, thinking. "What about Winnie? Short for Winifred."

"Winnie," Forrest repeats. "I like it." He exaggerates the word like, making me chuckle.

Thayer nods along, still petting her head. "Winnie it is. It's perfect."

Over my shoulder, I glance at my mom who's watching us carefully. She doesn't look perturbed, just curious, and I know that despite what I said she still suspects something is happening with Thayer and me. Mother's intuition is a strong force.

Forrest sets Winnie down and laughs as she runs around on her stubby legs.

Thayer orders the pizza, and we settle in for the afternoon spent with the two Holmes boys, and I know that today has just become one of my favorites.

CHAPTER FORTY-EIGHT

Sitting straight up in bed, I throw the covers off my body. It's been a while since I had a nightmare this detailed, this vivid. It felt so real. Stumbling out of my bed and down the hall to the bathroom, I sink to my knees and throw up. My body heaves, emptying itself of everything in my stomach.

When I'm finished, I flush the toilet and brush my teeth, getting rid of the acidic taste burning my mouth. Sweat still clings to my skin. Grabbing a washcloth, I dampen it with water and pat it over my skin.

Binx meows from the doorway. "I'm okay," I tell him.

He stares at me with bright green eyes like he knows I'm a liar. Pulling off my sweat soaked clothes, I step into the shower and let cool water beat on my skin.

When I don't feel gross anymore, I shut off the shower, and pad across the hall into my bedroom. I quickly pull on my workout clothes and tie my shoes. "I'll be back soon."

Binx looks at me doubtfully.

Slipping out of the house, I head next door to Thayer's basement.

It's been a while since I've had a nightmare, so the last thing I expect is to find him waiting. Well, he's starting back up the stairs when I slip inside but he quickly pauses. He walks back down the stairs, giving me a sad look.

"I had a feeling," is all he says. I give him a weak smile. "What do you need from me?"

I don't hesitate. "Hold me."

His long-legged stride crosses the distance between us, and he gathers me in his arms.

I wrap mine around his strong body.

Safe. Protected. Loved.

His lips press tenderly to the top of my head. "I've got you."

I fist the back of his shirt, holding on as tight as I can. He lets me hug him for as long as I need to, and when I finally pull away, he takes my cheeks in his hands.

"Better?"

"Yeah."

"Do you still need to run?"

I press my lips together, looking down at my tennis shoes. I want to be stronger than always needing to try to outrun my demons.

"I don't know," I answer him honestly. "I want to try not running."

He gives me a small smile, his eyes warm in the muted light of the basement. "Come upstairs. I'll make you some food and you can help me with something."

"With what?" I ask, letting him lead me to the stairs.

"So nosy," he jests. "I'll show you." In the living room, he takes me to the card table he uses when he works puzzles. "It's not running, but it is a distraction."

I will not cry. Not over a puzzle. Not because of his kindness.

The puzzle is an ombre of colors from a light yellow, to green, to blue. I pick up a piece, rubbing my fingers against it. "You're going to let me help you with the puzzle?"

"Only if you want." He tucks a stray piece of blond hair behind my ear.

"Okay." I set the piece back down. "But feed me first."

"I can do that."

Despite the early hour, he makes me fresh waffles with eggs. When he sits down beside me to eat, I can't help but think about how much I love this—just existing with him, making breakfast and eating together. These are things we so easily take for granted, but it's the things that matter most.

Winnie nudges her head between us, begging for scraps. Thayer scolds her for begging, but then gives her little nibbles.

When we're finished eating, he rinses off the dishes and I load them into the dishwasher.

So simple. So easy.

He makes us each a cup of coffee before we sit down to work on the puzzle together. We've each added a few pieces to it when I look at him. I take in the slope of his nose, his full lips, the scruff coating his jaw.

Thayer Holmes shouldn't be the right guy for me. He's older than me, he's a father, he's running a business and has his whole life figured out. He's perfectly wrong in all the right ways.

He sets a puzzle piece down. "Why are you looking at me like that?"

And then, because I can't help it, because I'm tired of keeping it locked inside, I say, "I love you."

His warm brown eyes stare deeply into mine and I see the promise of a future there. One I think subconsciously I always thought I didn't deserve.

Picking up my hand, he laces our fingers together, kissing the top of my knuckles.

"I love you, too."

CHAPTER FORTY-NINE

The outside world begins to show signs of spring. The snow melts, trees begin to bud, and the birds chirp excitedly.

But most importantly, the ushering of the spring season brings with it the news we've been waiting for.

My mom is cancer free.

The look of relief on her face when she got the news is something I'll never forget.

"Do you think this is enough cupcakes?" I jokingly ask, loading them into her car.

The flea market in the center of town is opening this weekend and she'll be selling her cupcakes. I have a booth for my candles, debuting some new scents.

"I sure hope so," she replies with a smile, her eyes crinkling at the corners.

I tried to snag a cookie dough cupcake earlier, but she wouldn't let me.

Closing the trunk of her car, we hop in and head off together. Our booths are on opposite ends since they set it up in categories. I hang up my sign and decorate my little tent, trying to make it inviting to draw people in. I brought some of my leftover fall and winter scents, marking the prices down to hopefully get rid of them. I always try not to have too many leftovers carrying over into the next season.

Settling behind the table, I paste on a smile and chat with everyone who stops by. I'm surprised in the first hour how many candles I'm able to sell, but it makes me feel good that my little hobby is making me money. Not that a hobby must be profitable to have merit.

It's near the end of the second hour when I spot Thayer strolling the booths with Winnie on a leash. A pink bandana with polka dots is tied around her neck, her tongue lolling out of the side of her mouth. She's too cute for words.

Thayer approaches my booth and I struggle not to smile when he ignores me at first, pretending to only be interested in the candles.

"You make these yourself?" He plays dumb.

"All done with these little hands." I hold up my hands and wiggle my fingers.

His stoic expression cracks the tiniest bit. "Peony, huh?" He picks up one of the spring candles.

"It's my favorite flower."

His eyes meet mine, the intensity sending a shiver racing down my spine. "I remember." He unscrews the lid and sniffs. "I'll take this one."

"Is it for your mom again? I have gift wrapping." I go to grab a box and tissue paper.

"No." I stop swiveling around. "This one is mine."

"Oh?" I arch a brow, biting my lip to hide my growing smile.

He passes me a twenty, refusing change, so I tell him to grab two of them.

"It's a tip, Salem."

"And I want you to take two. You can pick a different scent if you want."

He grabs a cookie dough one. "Happy now?"

I grin. "Immensely." I put the candles in a little bag and

pass them to him.

"You're a stubborn little thing."

"Someone's gotta give you a run for your money." Wetting my lips with my tongue, I ask, "Why the peony?"

I have much more masculine scents he could've chosen from, not that a scent should be categorized by gender, but men can be such sensitive little creatures.

He pauses before leaving my booth, cocking his head to the side. "Because," he looks me up and down and it feels like he's undressing me with his eyes, but not in a gross way, no he's reminding me that he knows me in ways others don't, and more than just the physical sense, "it smells like you."

A tiny gasps flies past my lips. "It smells like me?"

"Yeah." He scoops Winnie into his arms, so she'll stop tugging at his pants with her teeth. "That makes it my favorite." My smile blooms and he answers with a grin. "There's my Sunshine." Tipping his head at me like some old timey southern gentleman, he says, "Now I'm going to go get me some of your mom's cookie dough cupcakes."

"Save some for me," I demand, pointing a warning finger at him.

He scratches under Winnie's chin, her head leaning into his chest with contentment. "No promises. They're my favorite."

It's cheesy, but the words blurt out of my mouth before I can stop them. "You're my favorite."

He sets Winnie down and she scuttles around on the ground excitedly. "You're my favorite," he starts, smiling wickedly, "after cookie dough cupcakes."

I burst into laughter. Second to a cupcake. I guess there are worse things I could be second place to.

"Oh." He shoves his hand in his pocket. "This is for you."

He pulls something small out of his pocket, enclosing it in his palm. He holds it out, indicating I should open my hand.

When I do, he drops a ring into it.

It's silver with suns stamped onto the surface.

I look at him in surprise. "What's this for?"

"Because, you're my sunshine."

I smile, slipping it onto my thumb. "Thank you."

He dips head. "You're welcome."

I watch him walk away, rubbing my finger against the ring he so thoughtfully picked out for me.

I make a few more sales before I put Thelma of all people in charge of my booth and run across the street to use the bathroom in one of the local restaurants. When I get back to my booth there's a single cookie dough cupcake waiting for me.

"That handsome neighbor of yours left that," she says in a reprimanding tone. "Cynthia," she continues, referring to the elderly neighbor across the street from where I live, "was telling me all about you sneaking over to that man's house early in the morning. She has a weak bladder , so she's up all hours of the night peeing." Information I didn't need to know. "She sees you going over there a lot. He's a good bit older than you, you know."

"I wasn't aware," I reply sarcastically, peeling off the cupcake wrapper.

"Mhmm," she hums, undeterred and still firmly seated in my chair. "He sure is nice to look at. Rugged. I can see the appeal. He looks like the kind of man who can throw you over his shoulder and ravage you."

I spit out little pieces of cupcake, choking on the bite I had half-swallowed.

"Virile," she goes on, not at all concerned about me choking and dying. "That's the kind of man in my heyday I would've let knock me up."

"Thelma!" I cry, still clearing my throat. My eyes water and I'm pretty sure there are crumbs lodged in my throat.

"Can you blame me?" She bats her eyes at me innocently. "What is it you do over there so early in the morning? Play Parcheesi?" She winks.

I blush. "I run. He has a home gym I use."

"Is that what we're calling it these days? A run?" She mulls it over. "I guess if I saw a man with an ass like that I'd run after him too." I can't help but laugh. She stands up slowly from the chair and pats my hand. "Have fun with that one. You're only young once." She sighs dramatically. "Oh, the stories I could tell you. We'll save that for another day, dear."

I watch her waddle off to another booth and immediately she starts critiquing the price list, insisting they're way too expensive and she'll offer them three dollars for whatever it is that's caught her eye.

Sitting back down, I finish my cupcake and manage not to choke this time.

I'm happy today, happier than I've been in a long time, but the paranoid part of me can't help but think this can't last forever. My mom being declared cancer free, Thayer and I being in a good relationship—something has to give, right? My life is never this perfect. I know my therapist would tell me not to think like this, that I'm just inviting negativity into my life, but I can't help the feeling of dread that sinks into my stomach.

Nothing this good can last. This I know.

CHAPTER FIFTY

The warm weather brings with it my ability to run outside again.

As grateful as I am for the gym Thayer built, nothing beats running outdoors. No nightmare sends me running out the door this morning, just my own eagerness to feel my feet against the pavement.

And there's Thayer, leaning against the lamp post waiting.

He looks me over and I know what he's searching for. "No nightmare. I want to go for a run. That's all."

"Good." He rubs his toned stomach, hidden behind the cotton of his shirt. "You're keeping me in shape with all this running."

"And you're even starting to keep up, old man." With a laugh, I take off, forgoing my normal stretching.

Behind him, I hear his echoing laughter. "Old man, I'll show you."

***

After our run, we return to his house, sitting on the back porch to eat a breakfast of pancakes made by Thayer and my contribution of a yogurt parfait. The pool cover is off, the water murky and in need of chemicals. It'll still be a few weeks before it's warm enough to swim.

"The greenhouse is going to be thriving once you finish it." He was able to get most of the work done last summer and fall, but there are a few things he still needs to do to complete it.

"I'm looking forward to it. Are you planning on spending time with me in it?"

I bite my lip, thinking about things that definitely don't involve plants and instead consist of me on the table inside and Thayer between my legs.

"I love plants," I say, instead of the thoughts running through my mind. "I'd love to help you with it."

He gives a small, almost boyishly shy smile. "Good." He leans over and pecks me on the lips. It's so easy, the two of us, like it was always meant to be. I hold the back of his neck, deepening it momentarily and smile against his lips.

"I was thinking," I start, ducking my head with sudden worry, "if you're okay with it, I want to tell my mom. About us."

He thinks it over and I expect him to shut down the idea. I don't know exactly why I feel that way. "Okay."

"Yeah?" Excitement almost bursts out of me.

"Sure. We can tell her whenever you want." He glides a finger gently down the side of my cheek.

"Have you told anyone about us?" I ask him, curious.

He chews a bite of pancake. "My brother. You?"

"I told Lauren." He nods like he assumed as much. "Oh, and Thelma knows."

He chokes on his food, spitting out a bite. "Nosy, busybody Thelma knows?"

"Yeah. Apparently, Cynthia told her."

"I knew I shouldn't trust that little old lady," he jokes, wadding up the food he spat out in a paper napkin.

"We're going to do this? For real?" Suddenly I feel nervous about my mom knowing. On Forrest's birthday, two months ago, she suspected, and I lied to her. Now I have to admit that. I might be nineteen now, but I hate lying to my mom.

He arches a brow. "I thought you were ready."

I nod steadily, centering myself. "I am."

"I have to pick up Forrest in about an hour. We can tell her tonight if you want? I can pick up steaks while I'm out and grill."

His thoughtfulness nearly brings tears to my eyes. "That would be nice."

"Good." He swipes a bit of yogurt off my lip, licking his thumb clean. His gaze intensifies, voice lowering. "I didn't think I'd find it."

I give him a funny look. "Find what?"

He traces the shape of my lips with his finger. "Something real. Before, I didn't know what real, true love felt like. Just a weak imitation of it. You've given me this."

My heart takes flight and soars right out of my chest. Grabbing him by the shirt I pull him in for a kiss. I don't think I could possibly be happier.

***

Sitting out on my roof, I gather my legs to my chest and wrap my arms around my legs. I've missed being able to do this. There's something about sitting on the roof, feeling the heat of the sun that will always make me feel good.

Pulling my hair back into a ponytail, I smile when Thayer's truck pulls into the driveway next door. Forrest gets out of the backseat, stomping away from the truck as Thayer calls after him.

"You're so mean, Dad! You promised! You said you were going to build my treehouse!"

"I am," Thayer insists. "But I can't do it overnight. We're going to work on it. I promise.

Forrest turns, putting his small hands on his hips. "All you do is say you promise but you don't actually do it. I hate you. You're the worst dad ever." He runs to the back of the house, sulking.

Thayer looks crushed. "Love you, too, kid." Lowering his head, he grabs the grocery bags. He must sense my eyes on him because he looks up and spots me on the roof giving me a disapproving but amused look.

I stick my tongue out at him.

With a shake of his head, he walks up the porch and calls for Forrest to come inside but I hear him yell something back about not wanting to.

Lying back on the roof, I close my eyes and let the heat of the sun lull me into a nap. I'm sure most people wouldn't want to fall asleep like this, but it doesn't scare me.

I'm not sure how long I've been dozing when I hear yelling next door.

"Forrest? Forrest? Where are you? This isn't funny!" Sounds Thayer's angry voice. "Don't hide from me!" I sit up, rubbing sleep from my eyes. "Forrest?" Thayer sounds scared, which raises my alarm and I shake off the last vestiges of sleep clinging to my cloudy mind. Thayer storms through the front gate and sees me still on the roof. "Did you see Forrest go inside? I didn't hear him, but he might've snuck in."

I shake my head. "No, I fell asleep."

He looks like he wants to murder me over that tidbit of information and I'm sure I'll get a lecture on almost killing myself by sleeping on the roof, but there are more pressing issues at hand.

"He's not answering me and even if he's pissed at me that's not like him. Forrest isn't a grudge holder." Thayer runs a hand through his hair, the lines on his face stressed.

"Did you check inside yet?"

"A little but I would've heard the alarm say a door opened and it didn't."

Sudden, horrifying clarity washes over me. "Thayer." Ice slides down my spine. It's thick, sticky dread. The kind of feeling you get when you know, know deep in your soul that something very bad has happened. Thayer's eyes meet mine and I think he realizes in the same second I do. "The pool."

CHAPTER FIFTY-ONE

I forgo trying to scramble back into my room, and instead try to reach the ground as fast as I can.

Breath whooshes out of my lungs when I hit the ground, something in my ankle twisting, but it doesn't break.

I watch as Thayer throws open the gate to the backyard. I chase after him as fast I can with my injured leg.

He doesn't hesitate when he arcs his body and dives straight into the murky pool over the fence built solely around the pool itself.

Running to the edge I look down, my hand pressed to my mouth in horror.

Please, let me be wrong. Oh, God. Oh, God. Oh, God.

"Forrest!" I scream for the little boy, panic clawing at my throat.

Please, let him run out from behind a tree. To have snuck into the field of wildflowers. Not this, anything but this.

Thayer comes up for air, flicking his wet hair roughly out of his eyes.

In his hand is a kid's tennis shoe.

I drop to my knees, sobbing.

I can't breathe. I can't breathe. I can't breathe!

He's gone again, under the water, and this time when he emerges he has Forrest's limp body clasped to his chest. He swims to the edge of the pool, heaving the body out before climbing out himself.

Blue.

Forrest is *blue.*

His lips.

His eyelids.

His fingers.

I hate the color blue.

Thayer tilts Forrest's head back and starts CPR.

"Stop," I shove at his soaked shirt. "You're doing it wrong. Call 911."

My phone was in my room, or I would've done it already.

Thayer pulls his phone out of his pocket, cursing and throwing the useless device to the ground.

"Mom!" I scream at the top of my lungs, my fists pumping against Forrest's tiny chest.

He's cold.

Oh, God, he's so cold.

The water was like ice.

And he was ... oh my God.

"MOM!"

Thayer's screaming too. I don't even know what he's saying. My mind can't seem to focus. I just keep screaming and doing CPR and screaming again.

But he's gone.

There's no life left in the boy beneath my palms. It's a shell. An empty one.

A corpse.

My mom runs over, and I hear her scream too.

We're all just fucking *screaming* and it's pointless because Forrest can't hear us. He's not here. Not anymore.

Sitting back on my legs, I look up at Thayer. His hands are behind his head as he paces. When he sees that I've stopped he drops to the ground beside me.

"What are you doing? You can't stop. He needs—"

"Thayer," I choke out through my sobs, "he's gone."

"No," he shoves me away, trying to resume CPR. "No. He's not gone. He's going to be fine. We just have to get the water out of his lungs."

I put my hand on his arm, the sound of my mom crying on the phone in the background. "He's gone, Thayer. I'm so sorry."

When his eyes meet mine, I've never seen pain like this. Heartbreaking, soul crushing pain—the kind of emotional anguish someone never overcomes.

He shakes his head back and forth. "No, no. He can't be gone. We were just ... we were going to..." His head falls back, and he screams at the heavens.

I crumble, crying so hard my ribs ache with every inhalation.

Forrest's body lies in front of us.

Empty.

God, it's so empty—so blue.

Wrapping my arms around Thayer's soaked body, I hold him together as best I can, but it's hard to keep someone from breaking when you're shattered yourself.

Death should never happen like this.

Not so suddenly.

Not to a kid.

Not ... just *not.*

"Mom," I say softly, my voice cracking. "Go inside and there's a list of contacts on the fridge. Call Krista."

I can barely function, but I know Thayer is in worse shape than I am, and Krista ... God, she needs to know.

She walks off and I bury my head into the crook of Thayer's

neck.

Sirens sound in the distance and then everything happens in a flurry as the paramedics' hurry into the backyard. I know from the looks on their faces they're never going to get over this either.

Death is inevitable—the great equalizer, but it should never happen to a child who has so much to live for.

Thayer doesn't stop crying, and screaming, demanding they do more, try harder.

He doesn't look when they move his body to a bed and cover him with a sheet.

We follow robotically behind them.

Krista's SUV flies down the road, the brakes shrieking when she slams it to a stop and runs out of the car.

If I thought Thayer's screams of anguish were bad, they have nothing on Krista's.

The cry of a mother realizing she's lost her child is the most heartbreaking sound in the world.

"My baby! That's my baby!"

An officer on the scene wraps his arms around her when she tries to yank the sheet off of Forrest's body before they put him into the back.

"My baby," she sobs, falling to the ground out of his arms. "Not my baby!"

I close my eyes. I think I'm going to be sick.

It's like everything is happening in a slowed down speed, but somehow incredibly fast at the same time.

I've never heard anything quite like the painful sounds leaving her body.

It's the sound of a mother's soul being ripped in two—half of it forever with her son.

Gathering herself up from the ground she storms toward Thayer and he lets me go, facing her.

"You did this!" She yells, beating his chest with her fists.

Thump.

Thump.

Thump.

Over and over again her fists connect with his chest, like maybe if she beats his heart enough it'll revive Forrest's.

"Our baby!" She sobs. "You let our baby die!"

Thayer sinks to his knees on the ground and she goes with him. He keeps saying he's sorry over and over again as her screams grow louder. Soon her words turn incoherent and only sobs leave her.

Thayer and Krista end up riding in the ambulance. I don't know what the point is. It's not like the answer's going to change once they reach the hospital. But I guess I wouldn't want to leave my child either.

My mom wraps an arm around my body, pulling me away and back toward our house.

Everyone that lives on the street that's home at this hour has been outside watching the entire scene unfold—all of our lives now entwined by this one horrific event.

In my room, I sit on the edge of my bed, numbness spreading through my veins.

This isn't right.

It can't be true.

Wake up.

I slap my cheek.

Wake up.

But this isn't a nightmare I can throw on my tennis shoes and jog away from.

It's real fucking life and you just deal with it.

CHAPTER FIFTY-TWO

I'm not sure what makes me get in my car and drive.

I drive and drive until I find myself in Boston on the Harvard campus.

I didn't text him. Didn't call him to say I was coming.

I just show up.

It's wrong of me after we broke up—after all the sins I've committed that he doesn't even know.

It's getting late when I stroll through the dorm and straight to his door.

I hesitate a moment before I knock. He could be in there with a girl for all I know. Not that it matters. We broke up, after all, and it's what I wanted. But right now, I need my friend.

I knock on the door, and my head falls back as the tears come again.

He opens the door with a funny look that turns to concern when he finds me of all people outside his door crying.

"Salem?" He blurts in surprise. "Are you okay? Fuck," he curses, "stupid question. Is it your mom?" I shake my head, my face wet with tears.

"Come here." He pulls me into his familiar arms. His shoulders are narrower than Thayer's but he's well-built from years of playing football. He rests his chin on my head, rocking me back and forth before carefully guiding me into his room. His roommate's bed is rumpled but empty, and I'm so grateful a strange guy isn't there to witness my breakdown. It's not really that I'd be mortified, it's that I don't want to share *this* with a stranger.

"Talk to me." He cups my cheeks in his palms, staring down at me with those caring blue eyes that were always so comforting to me.

My lip quivers and I place my hands on his sides, needing the support to stay upright so I don't crumble apart more than I already have. "Next door," I sob, finding it impossible to get control of myself.

His eyes darken. "Did that bastard do something to you?"

"No, no," I shake my head vehemently. "His son ... Oh God, Caleb, it's so awful."

"Shh," he hushes. "It's okay. *Breathe*, babe." The endearment rolls naturally off his tongue.

"The little boy. Forrest. You know, I watched him some." I gag from my tears, and hope I don't throw up on Caleb.

"What happened?" He brushes hair off my forehead, staring into my eyes. He looks like he's on the verge of tears too and he doesn't even know.

"He ... uh ... he died." I choke on that word. It's my least favorite word in the English language. The worst combination of four letters. "He drowned. He was there, alive, and then he just wasn't. In the blink of an eye." I snap a finger for emphasis. "Like a candle being blown out. Life's so fragile and I just..."

I couldn't go to Thayer, so I went to the next best thing.

Caleb guides me over to his bed and pulls my body down with his. He wraps me in his arms, pulling the blankets over us.

And he just holds me.

It's exactly what I needed, why my subconscious mind brought me here.

He holds me for hours, letting me cry, talk, whatever I

need.

And I tell him everything.

About my dad.

About Thayer.

I lay it all out, every truth, every sin staining my soul.

I expect him to shove me out of the bed, to tell me I'm a horrible person. Because I am. I cheated on him after all.

But that's not Caleb.

He holds me tighter, pressing kisses to the top of my head.

"I wondered," he admits, in the quiet of his dorm room, "if you'd met someone else. I didn't think it would be *him*."

"I'm sorry I did this to you."

"It hurts." I like that he doesn't sugar coat it with me. "But I know I played a part in this. With college, and football, my parents breathing down my neck..." He curls his body tighter around mine. "I took you for granted. I thought you'd always be there, so I didn't put in as much effort to make you a priority. That was my failure. What you did was wrong, but it'd be a lie to say that I wasn't a factor in why you did it." Silence falls between us again, and I've almost drifted off to sleep when he asks, "Do you love him?"

"Yes."

"How much?" His body tightens like he's bracing himself for my answer.

I whisper like a confession, "So much."

"More than me?"

"I ... it's different, Caleb."

"So, yes, then?"

I rub my lips together. "I don't know."

"It's okay." He clears his throat and reaches up to turn the light off. "It's not him you're with tonight."

***

Caleb takes me to breakfast before dropping me off at my car and sending me home. He offers to drive me back himself, but he only has a few days of classes left and he needs to be here.

When I arrive back in Hawthorne Mills the whole town has a somber feel.

It makes sense. It's a small place and a tragedy like this has the whole town mourning together.

I pull into our driveway, noting the fact that Thayer's truck is missing. I don't know where he is and I don't want to pester him. The poor man just lost his son.

Looking at the fence separating our homes, I start to cry all over again. I don't know how any tears are left in my body. Forrest was just there yesterday. Alive and well. He got out of the truck, breathing, moving, running, and now he's not.

Pulling myself back together as best I can, I head inside to find my mom sitting at the kitchen table with a cup of tea in front of her.

"You went to Caleb," she says before I even close the door. I sent her a text last night letting her know where I ended up and that I was staying the night.

"I-I did," I stutter, turning toward the fridge. I grab a Diet Coke, but I'm not sure I even want it. I just need to busy my hands.

"Huh." She picks up her tea, emptying out the half-drank liquid. "Isn't that interesting?"

"We were friends, Mom. Before we dated, he was my best friend next to Lauren."

She sighs, looking at the spot where she wishes there was a dishwasher. "But you didn't go to Lauren, now did you?"

She has a point.

"Caleb's closer," I grumble out.

Taking the soda from my hand she sets it on the table and pulls me into a hug. "How are you coping?"

"I think I'm still in shock," I admit, holding onto my mom.

I wish she could make this better, but she can't. "I called your therapist," she says and I freeze in her arms. "I made you an appointment for later in the week if you want it. I thought you might need it."

I swallow past the lump in my throat. "Thank you."

"I know nothing can make this okay, but you have me. You can talk to me anytime you want."

I kiss her cheek. "I know, Mom. I love you."

She touches my cheek reverently, like she's trying to memorize how I look. "You girls are the best thing I ever created. I wish I could've been a stronger mother for you both."

"Please," I beg her, "never doubt, that you were as strong as you could be."

Her lip wobbles with the threat of tears and this time I'm the one pulling her into a hug. And we stay like that for a long time. Sometimes, you have to hold another person and seek comfort and that's okay. It doesn't make you weak to need human touch.

CHAPTER FIFTY-THREE

I hate funeral homes.

You'd think they'd do a better job trying to look a little cheerier. This place has old maroon colored carpet and smells like moth balls.

My mom and I sit in the back. Up front, the small casket is closed.

I haven't seen Thayer all week, but now he stands beside the casket looking despondent. I've never seen someone look so lost, like he's in his body but not. His parents are beside him, his brother speaking to Krista who cries at the casket.

There are two large blown-up pictures of Forrest beside the casket. In one he's holding a baseball bat from little league.

I didn't even know he played.

In the other he's dressed in a blue suit at someone's wedding.

I.

Fucking.

Hate.

Blue.

Blue is lifeless.

It's cold lips and stiff limbs.

It's the color of his death.

I'll never like the color again.

Thayer greets people robotically, going through the motions but not really here, while Krista breaks down in front of the casket. An older couple picks her up and guides her away, out to a side room. I assume they're her parents.

Beside me, my mom puts her hand on my knee. "How are you doing?"

Struggling to hold myself together, I say to her, "I'm doing the best I can." I rub my finger against the ring Thayer gave me, trying to seek comfort in the cool metal band.

She nods woodenly. "It doesn't seem right. Does it?"

"No."

Someone slides onto the pew beside me, and I look over, surprised to find Caleb in a light gray suit with a green shirt underneath. His dirty-blond hair is brushed away from his face, the slightest hint of stubble on his jaw.

Confusion mars my brow. "You're here. Why are you here?"

His cheeks flush with a hint of pink. "Because I thought you might need me."

The lump in my throat grows heavier and I grip his hand in mine. "I do. I really do." I reach for my mom's hand with my free one. "Both of you."

I look between the two of them.

Somehow, someway, I'll get through this. I have to. And what I feel is nothing compared to what Thayer and Krista are experiencing.

***

Only immediate family attends the graveside service, but the three of us do go to the wake held at the community center. I'm pretty sure the entire town is in attendance. At a table front and center so they can watch all the happenings is Thelma and Cynthia.

The side of the room is lined with buffet style dishes. People serve themselves, conversations soft and subdued.

There's a table with a handful of boys. I didn't notice them at the funeral, but they must've been friends of Forrest's. I can't imagine being that age and faced with the tragedy of such a death and the knowledge of how vulnerable life really is.

"You need to eat," Caleb tells me, pulling me toward the food.

"I'm not hungry."

"Fine, you sit, and I'll bring you a plate. Eat what you can. I'll get you something too," he tells my mom.

I open my mouth to protest, but he's already walking away.

My mom gives me a significant look. "He's a good one."

I nod, looking down at the table. "He is."

But he's not the one my heart beats for.

Caleb returns and sets down plates in front of each of us before returning to get one for himself.

I look around, trying to see if Thayer's arrived but I don't spot him or Krista. I do see his brother.

"I'll be right back," I mumble to my mom, pushing back from the table.

I don't hear what she says, because I'm already making my way to Laith.

"Hi." I grip his arm. He turns around to face me. "I don't know if you remember me—"

"Of course, I remember you." His smile is subdued as he pulls me into a hug.

"How is he?" I ask when he releases me.

The small smile he had disappears entirely. "Not good. I've never seen my brother..." He shakes his head, eyes on the ground. "I can't imagine what he's going through right now."

"I can't either. It's awful." My voice cracks and I worry I'm going to fall apart all over again. My mom was right to schedule me to see my therapist again. I can't stop thinking about how Forrest looked when his body was pulled from the water. His limp form when I placed my hands on his chest.

"I know you were there," he continues. "My brother told me. How are you coping?"

I roll my tongue in my mouth, searching for the right words. "It doesn't feel real. I keep waiting to wake up from this bad dream."

His hands flex nervously at his sides. "Me too." He shakes his head back and forth. "This isn't something any parent should have to go through. To outlive their child."

"It's heartbreaking."

"I told my brother he should sell the house."

My heart freezes. "What did he say?"

"That he couldn't. It's the last place Forrest was alive, and he won't leave. He keeps mumbling something about a treehouse too, but there's no treehouse."

A tear leaks from the corner of my eye. "Forrest wanted him to build a treehouse. He kept saying he would and now..."

"And now it's too late."

I drop my head, staring at the plain pair of black wedges on my feet. "I just want you to know I'm thinking of all of you right now."

"We appreciate it." He pats me on the shoulder.

Heading back to the table, I scan the room again for Thayer and find him at a table with his parents. He looks exhausted, like he hasn't slept at all since the accident. I want to run to him, wrap my arms around him, tell him I love him. But something holds me back.

Rejoining my mom and Caleb, I pick up a fork, forcing myself to make an effort to get something in my stomach.

"Thank you for getting the food for me."

"No problem." Caleb watches me carefully, probably looking for signs of imminent break down.

"You're..." I take a deep breath. "I don't deserve you."

"Just let me be here for you."

My mom's eyes flit back and forth between us.

"Thank you."

Caleb Thorne is so much more than I deserve, and I know for as long as I live, I'll never be good enough for him.

CHAPTER FIFTY-FOUR

It's been a week since Forrest was laid to rest, and I still find the idea that he's really and truly gone to feel so wrong. Like some cruel, twisted joke.

Next door, the incessant banging of a hammer is like a drumbeat.

Thayer's working on the treehouse.

With cookie dough cupcakes in hand, I make my way over to the backyard.

"Hey," I say softly, worried about disturbing his workflow. "I thought you might want some cupcakes."

When he looks up at me from his knelt position on the ground it's like I'm a stranger meeting him for the first time all over again. His angry, sullen expression is so much like the first one he ever graced me with.

"I don't want cupcakes."

I shrug, refusing to let his rough words bother me. "I'll set them inside then. You might want them later."

"I won't."

I don't argue with him, knowing it's pointless.

"Do you want some help?"

"No."

"Well, is there anything—"

He drops the hammer down and sits back on his heels. His brows are heavy over his eyes, anger radiating off of him. "Do I look like I want your help, Salem?" I try to say something but he plows on. "All he wanted was this stupid treehouse and I kept putting it off and now...and now..." He breaks down, sobs shaking his entire body. "I-I'm going to make sure he gets it, even if it's too late."

"It's not too late," I whisper, itching to reach out and put a hand on his shoulder but something holds me back.

He surges up, crowding my space. "Not too late? My son is *dead*. If that's not too late I don't know what is. But I'm going to do it anyway. Maybe wherever he is he'll know that I'm sorry, that I love him, and that I'm building him the treehouse he deserves."

"Thayer—" I reach for him but he jerks away from me before I can touch him.

"No." He throws his hands up like he's blocking me. "*No*."

He kneels on the ground, his back to me, and I know I've been dismissed.

The man I love is slipping through my fingers like sand and I'm helpless to do anything but watch it happen.

***

It's four in the morning a few days later and I haven't been able to sleep at all tonight.

Slipping from my bed, I throw some clothes on and quietly let myself out of the house and over to Thayer's.

The basement is pitch black when I slip inside and for some reason that stings. I know I shouldn't take it personally, but I can feel Thayer pulling away from me.

Taking the stairs up, I'm shocked at what I discover.

His family left only three days ago, and I have a feeling there's no way his parents would've left things in the state of disarray they're in now. It's a *mess*. The rug in the foyer is ruffled, a total tripping hazard, and as I make my way into the kitchen the sink is full, the trash can is overflowing, and Thayer...

Thayer is slumped on the floor, an empty bottle of liquor at his side. There's an ashtray on the kitchen table filled with cigarettes and it *reeks*. It smells like a bar way past closing time.

Thayer groans from his position on the floor, his back leaning against the cabinets.

"Hey." I crouch down beside him, gently pushing his hair back from his forehead. "It's me, Salem. Let's get you up."

He groans again in reply.

Taking his heavy arm, I wrap it around my shoulder and use my arms around his torso to try to pull him up. There's no way I could do it on my own, but by some miracle he manages to get his legs under him and push with me.

Stumbling from the kitchen, he nearly careens into the wall in the foyer.

"How much did you drink?"

I don't get an answer.

Getting up the stairs with a drunk Thayer should earn me an Olympic medal. The man is seriously heavy.

I manage to get him to the bathroom and turn the shower on. I put the water on the cold side, hoping that'll help sober him up.

"You wanna get me naked?" His drunkenness slurs the question as I pull his shirt off.

"Not like this," I mumble.

"You're so fucking pretty." He strokes my cheek with the tip of his index finger. "Too pretty for me. Too young. Too good."

"Shh," I croon, tossing his shirt into the hamper. "I need to get you in the shower."

"I'm a bastard," he continues. "I wasn't a good father. I'm not a good man. You deserve someone better."

I drop my head. "That's not true."

"It is."

He starts crying and I feel my heart breaking all over again.

I don't know how a heart can continue to break like mine does. It would seem after a while it wouldn't be able to sustain more damage, but mine keeps taking beating after beating.

I manage to get his shorts down to his ankles, deciding to leave his boxer-briefs on. Sure, I've seen everything, but might as well leave the man with a little dignity since I'm about to shower him.

"In you go." I give him a push to the shower and strip down to my bra and panties.

He doesn't get in the shower, instead watching me undress with a broken but hungry expression.

"I love you so much," he mumbles, "but I'm not good enough for you."

"Don't say things like that."

I give him another little shove toward the shower and when he sees that I'm joining him, he goes more easily. The icy water pelts his back, dampening his hair. If he notices the cold temperature, he doesn't show it. His hands settle on my hips, fingers dipping beneath the top of my panties to settle on the curves of my ass.

"I have to let you go."

I shake my head, shutting out the words he spoke.

"I want you." I curl a hand behind his neck. "I *choose* you."

His brown eyes swim with tears. "Why?"

"Something inside me knows you're mine."

He looks away. "You're too young to know that."

I shake my head. "Don't say that. It's such a bullshit argument, that someone's age determines their knowledge. What I feel in my heart matters, no matter how old I am."

He presses his forehead to mine, holding my cheeks in his hands. I shiver and he reaches over, adjusting the temperature on the water.

"I need to let you go."

"No." I keep my voice steady, not wanting to show the pain I actually feel at his words. I place my hands on his chest, feeling the pounding of his heart beneath my palm. "Why are you pushing me away?"

"Because," the tendons in his neck stand out, "you deserve more than this." He repeats what he basically already said a moment ago.

"More than you?" I arch a brow, doing my best to stay calm.

His chest deflates, shoulders curling inward, cocooning our bodies. "Yes." It's a hesitant, guilty whisper. "I'm a broken man now." His eyes look more coherent, the haze of booze clearing. "You don't need me to hold you back from living your life. Going to college, traveling the world, exploring who you are as a person."

I want to beat and punch his bare, wet chest. I don't. One of us has to remain logical in this situation.

"That's very egotistical of you."

"Huh?"

He looks so genuinely confused it's almost comical, but of course that took him by surprise. *Men.*

"I said, that's egotistical of you. You think you're the reason I'm not at college? Not out there traveling? Exploring, as you put it?" He cocks his head to the side, listening. "I wasn't planning to do any of those things before you came along. College isn't for me. I'm happy here, in this small town, making my candles, working in my mom's shop, and if suddenly that's not okay, then I'll figure something else out." I take a deep breath. "But don't you dare," I grind out between my teeth, "think for one second that it has anything to do with you. You're my choice, just like staying here is one."

I'm not prepared for the crash of his lips to mine.

I taste liquor on his tongue, it's harsh and bitter like the two of us in this moment.

One of his arm winds around my back and he lifts me effortlessly, pressing my back to the shower wall. His erection presses into my core, my hips grinding against him on their own accord.

"Yes," he encourages, guiding my hips with his hands, "get yourself off on me."

He kisses me again, and it's rough, aching, so desperately needy.

My fingers grapple against his slick back.

I rock my hips harder, faster. It feels so good. He feels so right.

My orgasm shatters through me so fast with so much force that I scream.

Ripping his lips from mine, he groans. "Fuck, you're so hot when you come on my dick." He grips one of my breasts through my wet bra. "It hurts how much you look like mine."

"Is that a bad thing?" I pant, still trying to recover from the orgasm.

He looks at me, trying to memorize my features, every sun kissed freckle on my nose. "It is when I can't keep you."

Holding his cheeks in my hands, his stubble rubbing against my palms, I tell him, "You can if I say you can."

He kisses me again, achingly desperate, and turns the water off, carrying me from the bathroom. A trail of water follows his steps until he reaches the bed and lays me on top of it.

He strips my wet bra and panties off my body, kissing over my entire body.

"Thayer," I moan his name, my fingers entwining in his damp hair. I rock up into him, my body begging for more, for everything, for the love only he can give me even if he doubts himself.

He swirls his tongue around my clit, and I cry out, my hips rising off the mattress. He grips my hips tighter, holding me down.

His right hand disappears from my hip. Blinking my eyes open, I see his hand shoving his boxers out of his way so he can grip his cock in his hand. I moan at the sight. There's something so hot about seeing him stroke himself while he gets me off.

"Thayer, please," I beg as the high grows closer. "I'm almost there." And when I fall, he catches me, silencing my cries with his lips on mine.

In one sure movement he's inside me.

He holds my gaze, making love to me.

But he's also saying goodbye.

I feel it.

"Don't let me go." A tear leaks out of the corner of my eye and he kisses it away. "We're worth it, Thayer." *I'm worth it. Don't throw me away.*

He kisses and sucks on the skin of my neck, my arms wrapping tightly around his torso like if I hold him tight enough, love him hard enough, he won't leave me.

"I love you," he says, like a vow, a promise, but a curse too.

"I love you," I say back, crying fully now.

"I love you."

"I love you."

We say the words and then we say it with our lips against each other's, with our bodies, with our souls.

But deep down I know it's not enough.

CHAPTER FIFTY-FIVE

I sleep for a few hours in Thayer's arms, before I climb from his bed. My panties and bra are in a wet heap on the floor so I pull my clothes on without them. Downstairs, Winnie wags her tail excitedly when she sees me. I turn on the coffee pot to brew, then grab her leash for a walk. Her tongue lolls out of her mouth when I clip it on her collar. Since she has short legs and is still a puppy she tires quickly after a trip around the block.

When I get back to my street, I stop dead in my tracks when I see Thelma on Cynthia's front porch.

The two are kissing.

There aren't a lot of secrets in a small town—but Thelma and Cynthia have managed to keep the biggest one of all.

Thelma turns, catching my shocked expression before I can hide it.

"What? You've never seen two women kissing before, missy?"

"Love is love," I reply.

She smiles back. "That's right, girly. I knew I liked you."

She heads into Cynthia's house, the door closing behind her.

Scooping up a tired Winnie, I let myself into Thayer's house and unclip her leash. Filling her food and water bowl, I hear Thayer's feet on the stairs just as I'm pouring two cups of coffee.

He seems surprised to find me in his kitchen, and I'd be

lying if I said it didn't hurt.

He closes his eyes, inhaling a breath. Opening them, he says, "Last night shouldn't have happened."

"W-What?" I stutter, setting down the cup I poured for myself.

He lowers his head. "I shouldn't have fucked you when I know this has to end. We can't go anywhere, Salem. Surely you can see that as easily as I can."

"Nothing about what we did was *fucking*," I snap, angry and hurt. "You made love to me and you know it."

He looks at the ground. "You can think what you want."

"No, Thayer." Suddenly I'm in front of him, my irritation propelling me forward. I shove a finger in his chest. "Don't fucking gaslight me. You're better than that."

"No, I'm not." He grasps my wrists. "I'm an almost thirty-two-year-old man fucking a nineteen-year-old. There's nothing *good* about me. We can't be together. What would people think?"

"We were going to tell my mom!" I scream at him. "We were *happy* and you certainly didn't give a shit before, so what changed?"

"My son died!" He yells back and Winnie whimpers, running from the room. "My son died," he repeats, softer. "And that changes everything."

"I know this is devastating. I feel his loss too. But how does this have anything to do with us?"

A long moment passes between us, and I see it, the tether between us fraying. I'm struggling to hold onto it, to keep us together, while he's taking shears to it and ripping it apart.

"Every good, happy part of me died with him. There's nothing left for me to give you."

"I'll take whatever I can get." God, I sound desperate, but

I don't care. I might be young, but I know what we have is rare. It's rare and beautiful and too precious to give up so easily.

He tries a new tactic. "What will people think, Salem? You and me? Our ages? I'm a divorced man—that's practically a sentence straight to hell to some of these people."

"Don't give up on us. I don't care how complicated this gets, or what people say. I want you. In this big crazy world, I choose you. Isn't that enough?"

The pity he looks at me with breaks what's left of my mangled heart.

"No, it's not. You have your whole life ahead of you. You'll find someone else."

"Thayer," I grip his shirt in my hands, holding on to him, "you are my life."

He shakes his head sadly, sympathy in those brown eyes that once looked at me with so much love and passion. Taking my hands, he removes them from his shirt. Plucking my fingers off one by one.

It's symbolic in a tragic sort of way.

He's letting me go, letting *us* go, like nothing between us ever mattered at all.

It's then that I know that no matter what I do, what I say, I've lost him.

"Are you really okay with this?" I ask him, feeling the need to say more. I can't let us end as easily as he can. "You want me to leave you? To what? Fall in love with another man? Have his babies? While you what?" I wave a hand around at the mess, the bottles of liquor, the full sink and cigarettes. "Drown yourself in misery? It was a tragic accident, Thayer, one you'll never get over. I know that. I understand it. Do you think I'm not affected by it? But you still deserve to be happy." He stares back at me with a numb gaze. Shutting down. Blocking me out. There are no emotions in that once warm brown. Cold, unyielding. *Dead.*

My Thayer, the grumpy man who I fell so hard for, died that day with his son.

I see that, I know it, but I love him despite it.

But he won't give me false hope.

The man standing before me is a weak imitation of the one I first met.

Shaking my head, I turn and walk away.

CHAPTER FIFTY-SIX

It's mind-blowing how fast and slow time can go all at once.

A month passes and I give up trying to communicate with Thayer. He's shut down and there's no reaching him as he spirals into a dark place. He's a shell of the person I love. I keep trying, keep reaching out my hand, but it's not enough. I can't save him if he doesn't want to save himself.

I let myself into his house.

He won't talk to me, completely ignores my presence when I see him, so I've taken to coming over when he's gone just to keep the place tidied up. It doesn't sit right with me, letting him live in filth, and wallow away. So, I do what I can.

It helps me to feel close to him when I'm here and I always feel a little bit better when I leave.

I don't stay long today, I can't.

Georgia is getting married today.

When his house is cleaned up to the best of my abilities in the short time I have, I drive downtown to the local inn where Georgia and Michael are having their ceremony and reception. I'm running late, so I'm not surprised when those words are the first thing out of my sister's mouth.

"You're late," she accuses, pointing to a chair. "You need your hair and makeup."

My mom shoots a worried glance my way. Parking my butt in the chair, I let the makeup artist and hair stylist go to town on me and do whatever it is Georgia requested. When that's done I slip into my dress and everything happens in a flurry.

One of Michael's friend's walks me down the aisle and I find myself scanning the crowd of guests. I know Thayer's not here. He wasn't even invited. Why would he be? He would've been if we'd gotten the chance to tell my family about us, but we didn't, and now it seems like we never will.

The music changes and everyone rises for my sister to make her grand entrance.

Michael clears his throat, crying before she even emerges. Maybe I should give the guy more credit. He clearly loves my sister.

The French doors open and my sister steps into the room holding our mom's arm. Her hair is starting to grow back but it's short and fuzzy. She was going to wear a hat, worried her shorn scalp would embarrass Georgia, but my sister merely kissed her on top of the head and shot down the idea.

Watching them exchange vows fills me with a strange sort of melancholy. I stupidly thought I might marry Thayer one day and now ... now I know nothing.

It seems like the whole wedding happens in a blink but like I'm watching in slow motion.

It's how I've felt ever since that morning I left Thayer in his kitchen. Without him time ticks differently. I'm a witness, a bystander in my own life now as I watch everything take place around me.

I give my speech at the wedding robotically, but no one must notice how out of it I am, or at least Georgia doesn't. She cries, hugging me when I've finished.

Caleb's there and when he asks me to dance I say yes, because I see no point in turning him down. He spins me on the dance floor, and I end up laying my head on his shoulder.

"He hurt you." It's not a question, but an accusation.

"Yes."

"I should kill the bastard."

I smile, perhaps my first genuine one in weeks. "He'd probably thank you."

He sighs, holding me tighter. "It's horrible, what happened to his son." His hand on my waist tightens.

"I don't want to talk about him."

He clears his throat. "Okay. What do you need?"

I answer him honestly. "I don't know." We sway back and forth, only half-dancing at this point.

Clearing his throat, he asks, "When you figure it out will you let me know?"

On my tiptoes, I press a kiss to his cheek. "You'll be the first to know."

***

Caleb drives me home from the wedding. I insisted I could drive myself, but I think with as checked out as I am it really worried him, so I finally agreed. Plus, with the late hour I figured it might be safer anyway.

We pull up outside my house, and he puts the car in park. "Are you okay or do you want me to come in for a while?"

"I'll—"

I plan to tell him I'll be okay, but then I see Thayer getting out of his truck.

He's not alone.

A lump lodges in my throat when I watch a woman giggle and press her body all over him.

I climb out of Caleb's car before I know what I'm doing.

"Thayer!" I yell after him. I feel like my body is being painfully carved apart. "What are you doing?"

He turns, looking surprised to see me.

Bastard.

The woman giggles, swiping a finger down his chest. "Who is this? Your sister?"

Sister? Gag me.

"What are you doing?" I repeat.

Why is my face wet? I touch my cheek, realizing I'm crying.

Thayer doesn't respond. He seems frozen, stunned.

"Come on, Salem." Caleb wraps a hand around my arm to pull me away.

Thayer snaps to life. "Don't fucking touch her!"

Caleb steps in front of me, shoving me behind him in protection. "Who the fuck are you to tell me not to touch her? Huh? You're the one that fucked her when she was my girlfriend."

I don't know who throws the first punch, but suddenly both of them are on the ground, throwing fists and kicks.

"Stop!" I scream, hiccupping. The other woman watches in confusion.

"This is too much for me," she mutters. "I'm calling a cab." She walks down the street, phone pressed to her ear.

"Stop it!" They ignore me. "Oh, God." I slap a hand to my mouth and turn sharply, throwing up right in the bushes Thayer painstakingly planted and trimmed last summer. My body heaves as I get sick. Cool fingers touch my neck, pulling my hair back.

When I look, I stupidly expect it to be Thayer at my side, but it's Caleb.

"Hey." He rubs my back. "I'm sorry I snapped. Are you

okay?"

I ignore his question, searching for Thayer in the darkness. He's watching me, staring back.

Something in me just snaps, finally breaks.

I'm not perfect. I make mistakes. I hurt people. But I'm a strong girl, one who's been made weak by Thayer.

I wipe my mouth with the back of my hand and straighten up, holding onto Caleb while I let go of Thayer. I take the ring off my thumb finger, the one he gave me months ago at the flea market, and shove it against his chest. It falls to the sidewalk, and he looks down at it.

"Goodbye, Thayer." My voice cracks.

For the first time in weeks, his face shows some sort of emotion other than confusion.

He knows.

I'm closing the door on us.

Ending the chapter.

We're a period at the end of a sentence.

Full stop.

I thought our love story was written in the stars; destined, remarkable, once in a lifetime.

Turns out we're nothing but a memory gone up in flames, ashes scattered in the wind.

CHAPTER FIFTY-SEVEN

Lauren's squeals fill my ear drums when she opens her door. "I know you're going through it right now, girl, but I'm so happy you decided to move in with me."

I've never liked big cities. Hawthorne Mills has always been more my speed. But I needed a change of scenery, so the day after Georgia's wedding I called Lauren, and now two days after that here I am.

I can't be in that town with Thayer. It's only big enough for one of us and I know he'll never leave, not after what happened to Forrest, so that meant my leaving.

So here I am.

New York City will be an experiment of sorts, I guess. It'll certainly push my boundaries, that's for sure.

"Thank you for letting me come."

She locks up behind me as I look around her tiny space. It's hardly big enough for one person, let alone two, but that's New York City for you.

"I would've loved for you to move with me from the start."

I give her a wobbly smile. "This will certainly be an adventure."

She gives a small answering smile, leaning against the butcher block countertop of the small kitchen. "I'm sorry, you know. About you and—"

"Don't say his name," I beg, closing my eyes. "Please, don't."

She nods. "Can I hug you?"

I open my arms and let my best friend hug me. "There's something I need you to hold my hand through."

"Oh?" She gives me a puzzled look. "What?" I bend down and open my purse, pulling out the plastic bag. Passing it to her, she takes it and looks in the bag. "Salem." She gives me a worried look. "No."

"I think so."

"What are you going to do?"

"I don't know. That's what the test is for."

"Oh, Salem." Her eyes fill with tears. "It's his?"

"Are you serious?"

"I'm sorry, I didn't mean it like that. I just thought maybe you'd slept with someone else since then."

"I haven't." I take the box from her.

"You're doing this now?" She sounds so surprised.

"I have to know."

She nods. "I'd have to know too. All right," she claps her hands together, "let's do this."

She waits outside the bathroom while I go, and I lay the pregnancy test on the porcelain sink while I wash my hands.

I'm torn on what I want it to say.

I'm only nineteen—I'd be twenty when the baby's born if I am pregnant, but that's so young to become a mother. On the other hand, if I'm not... I know I'll be sad. It'll be like losing Thayer all over again.

"Are you done? Open the door," she pleads, so I crack it open.

"It said it would take five minutes for results."

"God, that's so long."

Closing the toilet lid, I sit down on top, chewing at my thumb nail. I miss my ring. I went out to get it from the sidewalk the morning after throwing it at him, but it was gone. It's for the best, I suppose.

"I want you to know, if you are pregnant, everything's going to be fine. We'll get a bigger apartment and I'll help you. We'll sister wives this shit. We've got this."

Laughter bubbles out of me and I'm shocked by its genuineness. "Thank you."

"That's what friends are for."

"How long has it been?"

She glances at the test. "Nothing yet."

I lean my head back, waiting.

Another minute passes, and I get up. Lauren watches me pick up the test and look at the results.

I close my eyes, tears leaking out of the corner of my eyes.

I said goodbye to him, and I meant it. I don't deserve to be half-loved by someone, shoved aside. He's grieving, I know that, but I would wait—I'd help him through this if he only let me.

The universe doesn't want us to have an end, but a new beginning, because I'm still a little bit his.

Thayer and Salem's story continues in
The Resurrection of Wildflowers.

Keep reading for an exclusive bonus scene from
Thayer's POV on page 355.

ACKNOWLEDGMENTS

Salem and Thayer's story hit me out of nowhere a few months ago and I knew I had to drop what I was doing and write it. When I sat down to plot this story, I quickly realized this was going to be way more emotional and angsty than I originally thought, but I knew this was going to be one of those stories that stays with me long after I finish writing it. Thayer and Salem still have a ways to go and I hope you'll enjoy the rest of their journey in book two.

Emily Wittig, not only do you continue to wow me with your creativity with cover design, I mean seriously this duet is stunning, but you're the realest friend I could ask for. Who would've thought this is where we'd be ten years after you sent me that first message? I'm so thankful to have a real, genuine friend like you. So many people aren't blessed enough to have someone as kind-hearted as you are in their life. You're always there to cheer me on, talk me off the ledge, or make me smile when I'm feeling down. Love you lots!

Kellen, thank you for your friendship and unwavering support. I'm so thankful to this book world that we met. You're one of the real ones.

To my doggies who are always by my side with every book I write; I love you, Ollie, I love you, Remy, I love you, Romeo, and yeah, I even love you too, Tucker, you moody smoosh face.

To my family, I know I suck and don't acknowledge you in every book, but I am so blessed to have your support. I know not everyone that strays from the traditional life path and decides to take a risk with writing has the kind of support I do, and for that I'm grateful.

The teams at Barnes and Noble in Ashburn, VA and Fairfax, VA I have no idea if you'll ever see this, but thank you for taking the risk and stocking Sweet Dandelion in your stores. I've been thrilled that it's selling, but more importantly you helped me realize my dream of seeing one of my books in your stores.

Thank you to the bloggers, bookstagrammers, booktokers, and every single one of you I've met along my journey since 2011. I'm inspired by your passion for books and the love you spread through the community. It's so appreciated.

And lastly, to you dear reader, whether it's your first time reading or your twentieth, or maybe even more than that, thank you. Thank you. Thank you. Thank you. Because of you I get to live my dream, write the worlds and characters in my head, and that's the greatest gift I could possibly ask for.

ABOUT THE AUTHOR

Micalea Smeltzer is an author from Northern Virginia. Her two dogs, Ollie and Remy, are her constant companions. As a kidney transplant recipient she's dedicated to raising awareness around the effects of kidney disease, dialysis, and transplant as well as educating people on living donation. When she's not writing you can catch her with her nose buried in a book.

BONUS SCENE

The Concert Night from Thayer's POV

One bed.

One fucking bed.

I've been fuming about it since we got to the hotel earlier and now that the concert is over and we're on our way back there I'm still mad about it.

Salem's words echo through my skull, giving me a migraine.

"Yes, Thayer, I planned on fucking my boyfriend tonight, but he bailed."

She didn't know it, but that one little sentence sent X-rated visions through my mind of her with me.

I keep reminding myself she's eighteen, but my boner doesn't give a fuck. My dick has a mind all his own.

Salem's attractive. Bright and bubbly. But mature in a way that sometimes I question what she's been through. I don't like the idea of anything bad happening to her, but there's something there. It's the something she tries to escape every time she runs early in the mornings.

We ride the elevator up to our floor, and I'm not sure Salem realizes it but she's humming one of the songs under her breath. Surprisingly, I liked the band. It was a little more rock and nowhere near the boyband sound I expected.

"Did you have fun tonight?"

Her bright, happy eyes turn to me.

A sense of pride fills me—I made her happy. Just by bringing her to the concert her boyfriend bailed on. I'm the one who put that sparkle in her eyes.

I'm such a fucking bastard for being pleased over it.

"So much. I still can't believe you got me all that merch. I'll babysit for free or something to pay you back."

"You're not paying me back."

The doors slide open, and we both step out, walking side by side down the long hallway.

"Thayer," she looks up at me and something inside me stirs, something that's been dead for *years*. I checked out of my marriage a long time ago—not even the marriage, it was just Krista. Our connection fizzled and it's not that she's not attractive, but *I* wasn't attracted to her anymore. It wasn't any fault of her own. We just grew apart and the things that drew me to her before just weren't enough. "You bought pit tickets on top of it since I'm such an idiot and left mine behind. I have to pay you back in some way."

"Trust me, you really don't." If she knew the explicit thoughts I had about her, she'd run far and fast. Sometimes, though, I catch her looking at me and I'm not stupid, so I know there is some attraction on her part. But she's young and it's probably the appeal of me being an older guy. Besides, she has a boyfriend.

"You're so stubborn."

I pull out the key to our room. "I've been told."

She pouts out her bottom lip and spins into the room when I open the door.

"Tonight, was amazing. Out of this world."

I put the locks in place. "Out of this world, huh?"

"Did I say that out loud?" Her cheeks are flushed a pretty pink and there's a light sheen of sweat on her skin.

"Yeah."

"Well, it's true." She falls onto the bed with a sigh. "Can you help me get these off?" She lifts one leg, wiggling her foot and the shoe attached.

I take hold of her foot and unzip the boot, giving it a pull. It doesn't budge. "Damn, that's really on there." I wiggle it around, pulling a little harder and it comes free. Then I get the other one off.

"My feet hurt." She gives a little whimper. "I'm never wearing shoes like that ever again."

"I don't blame you. These never fail me." And by these, I mean my trusty work boots. I'm pretty sure they're damn near indestructible.

She rolls off the bed, rifling through her bag. "I'm going to shower, if that's okay."

I sit down to take off my boots. "Take your time."

I definitely won't be sitting out here thinking about her in the shower. Naked. Wet.

Fuck me.

"Need any help with those?" She tries not to smile at her own joke.

I force a smile. "I've got it." I set one boot on the ground.

She winks. "If you're sure."

Her hair swishes around her shoulders and the bathroom door clicks shut behind her.

My cock strains against my pants, and I palm it over the fabric. I contemplate jacking off for all of about two seconds before I decide against it. Salem could have forgotten something and come out here any moment. Once I'm in the shower I can take care of business.

While she showers, I untuck the covers, muttering to myself that the night will be fine. I'm not an animal. It's not like I'm going to maul her. I can keep my hands to myself.

It's going to be just fine.

Salem takes a surprisingly quick shower. The door opens, steam billowing out. She's dressed in a big shirt and tiny shorts. It shouldn't be fucking turn on, but it is.

"Your turn," she tells me.

"Thanks." I fake a yawn, hoping to distract myself from my boner.

I take the fastest shower imaginable, taking care of business. When I leave the bathroom, I ask her if she wants me to leave the light on.

"It doesn't matter to me."

I leave it on, but almost completely close the door so there's only a tiny bit of light leaking through. I move across the room, feeling Salem's eyes on me. I take off my watch, laying it on the dresser. Then plug in my phone. I'm trying to delay the inevitable—sleeping in the same bed with her.

She yawns, her eyes continuing to dart back and forth from my body to a spot on the wall.

I don't know what makes me say it. I shouldn't say it, but it blurts out of me.

"See something you like?"

She sinks under the covers like she wants to disappear. "*No.*"

"Sure." I eye her skeptically. Only her pretty green eyes are left poking out. "Are you going to jump me if I sleep without a shirt?"

I can't help but fuck with her a bit.

"No shirt I can handle." She nods to herself like she's coming to terms with something.

I take my shirt off, because I really do hate sleeping in one, and toss it at the bottom of the bed. I climb into bed and there's a sea of space between our bodies. I don't know what I was so worried about. This will be fine.

"Thank you for tonight. You have no idea what it meant to me."

I grunt. She's really got to let this go. I didn't do anything special. "You don't have to keep thanking me."

"I know, but—"

"But nothing," I cut her off. "I was happy do it."

"Why?"

I can tell she's truly curious. Maybe no one's ever done something for her just because it was the right thing, the nice thing, to do.

"Because I wanted to." It's the simple answer. I look at her lying in the space beside us. "I don't do things I don't want to, Salem. I'm a selfish man."

And it's the truth, if I'd really been opposed to the idea I wouldn't have offered. But she looked so sad and broken, and I just wanted to make her smile.

Turning the light off, I say, "Night, Salem."

She whispers, "Goodnight."

***

"N-No! No! NO!"

Salem's body thrashes like she's being attacked. I come

awake with a start, worried someone has broken into our room, but there's no one there.

"Salem," I say her name, trying to wake her from her very obvious night terror. Maybe you're not supposed to wake people up when they're in this state—or is that only sleepwalkers? "*Salem.* I have you." I wonder if I sound as desperate as I feel. I grab onto her gently, touching her cheeks. "You're safe. Wake up, dammit!"

I lower my body over hers, trying to use my weight to stop her thrashing but it only makes things worse.

"Don't touch me! Stop!" Her hands fly through the air, her nails nearly scratching my cheek. "Get off of me! I'm your daughter." She sobs in her night terror, real tears leaking out of the corners of her eyes. My heart turns to ice. This isn't just a normal nightmare. This is ... so much fucking worse. "Stop, I'm your daughter," she begs.

I gasp, bile rising in my throat. "Wake up," I beg anew. "Please, wake up." I have to get her back here, to me, to *now*, and away from the nightmare she's trapped in.

Her eyes fly open so fast it actually scares me.

She cries brokenly and her eyes are sad, scared. You *know*, they seem to say. *You know now.*

This is why she runs so early. She's trying to outrun her memories.

"Hey." My hand hovers over her cheek, too scared to touch her. When she doesn't flinch, I brush her sweaty hair back and off her forehead. "You're okay. You're safe with me."

She continues to shake. She can't stop crying. I just want to make her feel better, for it all to go away.

"Is this okay?" I stroke her face. I'm still carefully holding my body above hers. She nods, her lower lip shaking. "Your nightmare ... " I pause, closing my eyes. I hate asking her this, but I need confirmation on what I suspect. "It was real, wasn't it? A memory?"

She nods.

"Fuck," I curse, wishing I could kill the bastard who did this to her. As a father myself, I can't ... I can't fucking imagine what kind of sick son of a bitch does that. "Salem," I say her name softly, desperately.

She shakes her head back and forth, more tears leaking from her eyes.

"What can I do?" I ask.

"Nothing."

"I'm sorry." I glide my fingers softly over her face. "I'm so sorry, Salem. That should've never happened to you." I clear my throat, getting choked up. I'm going to fucking cry myself. "Fuck, I'm just so sorry."

"Can you hold me?" She asks it softly, hesitantly like she's terrified not only to ask the question and show neediness, but that I might say no.

The stupid AC turns on, and she jumps beneath me from fright.

There's no way I can deny her request. "I'll hold you as long as you want me to."

I turn back onto my side of the bed, gently tugging her with me. She wraps her legs around me, her hand splaying on the bare skin of my stomach. She plays with my chest hair absentmindedly. I cup her arm, rubbing my thumb in circles. With my other hand I massage the back of her head, trying to relax her so maybe she can get more sleep.

"Breathe," I whisper softly when I notice her holding her breath.

"I'm trying."

"I'm right here. I'm not leaving. You're not alone." I feel like she needs the reminder. "I've got you." I press my lips gently to her forehead. I don't know what makes me do it, but it just seems like the right thing.

"I'm so sorry."

"For what?" I angle my head to look down at her. I'm perplexed at what she could possibly be sorry for.

"Waking you up."

"Salem." Her name rumbles through my chest. "Don't be fucking sorry. I can't fucking take you being sorry for this."

She stiffens in my arms, and I try to let her go, worried she doesn't want to be touched right now, but she latches back on not letting me release her.

"Please, don't look at me differently after this. *Please.*"

I hold her that much tighter. "Never."

I start humming. It's an old lullaby I used to sing to Forrest, and soon she drifts back to sleep in my arms.

***

Something is rubbing against my leg. I put my hand out, still half-asleep, and confused why something is wiggling.

"Oh my God!"

My eyes pop wide open at the cry of pleasure.

Holy fucking shit, Salem just orgasmed against my leg.

Blood rushes to my dick, because he has no logic—hearing a beautiful girl orgasm equals instant boner for him.

"Oh my God," Salem says again, only there is no pleasure this time, just complete and utter horror.

I don't move. I lie frozen. Especially after what she revealed last night, I don't know what to do or say in this moment to make it easier for her. She was sleeping, she didn't mean to, and I don't want to make this awkward for her. Well, more awkward than it probably already is.

Her pussy is still pressed against my thigh, and I can feel the wetness through her pajamas. I grit my teeth.

She slaps a hand over her mouth, tears in her eyes. "I didn't mean to."

"It's—"

It's on the tip of my tongue to tell her it's okay, that she doesn't need to be upset or worried, but she launches her body out of the bed. She falls on the floor, and I don't even have a chance to ask her if she's okay before she's grabbing her bag and locking herself in the bathroom.

I get up from the bed, pressing my ear to the door. I want to make sure she's not crying. She seems to be pacing inside the small space, muttering to herself.

I think she says something about me having nice hands which makes me grin.

Moving away from the door, my aching cock reminds me of how we were woken up.

I bite my lip, glancing toward the bathroom. Do I risk it?

Fuck. Make it quick.

I slide my hand underneath my boxer-briefs, squeezing my cock. I lean against the wall, closing my eyes. I don't mean to, but her sounds of pleasure come to mind.

Don't think about her.

Don't you fucking do it.

But I can't help it, because when I come it's her name on the edge of my lips.

Salem.

Salem Fucking Matthews.
I knew she was trouble from the very first cupcake.